Exile

A Historical Romance

Exile

A Historical Romance

G.G. Vandagriff

Cover design by Carol Fiorillo

The Orson Whitney Press

Other Books by G.G. Vandagriff

Historical Fiction

The Last Waltz—New Edition

Regency Romance

Lord Grenville's Choice

The Baron and The Bluestocking

Lord Trowbridge's Angel

Rescuing Rosalind

Miss Braithwaite's Secret

The Taming of Lady Kate

The Duke's Undoing

Women's Fiction

The Only Way to Paradise

Pieces of Paris

Suspense

The Arthurian Omen—New Edition

Foggy with a Chance of Murder

The Arthurian Omen

Alex and Briggie Mysteries

The Hidden Branch – New Edition

Tangled Roots—New Edition

Poisoned Pedigree—New Edition

Of Deadly Descent—New Edition

Cankered Roots—New Edition

Non-Fiction

Deliverance from Depression

Voices In Your Blood: Discovering Identity Through Family History

{ 1 }

March, 1938

Escaping in a limousine from Innsbruck to Zürich, Doctor Andrzej Zaleski studied the pink dawn as it crept over the Swiss Alps. He breathed deeply in gratitude. At last: They had lived to see a new day.

His gaze returned to the woman he had loved over half his life. He expected her to begin weeping at any moment, but Amalia was staring dry-eyed out the window. Her mahogany-colored hair was concealed under a knitted ski cap, her long, graceful limbs invisible under heavy ski clothes and the ski jacket she had worn for their aborted escape over the Austrian mountains.

Nineteen years ago, he had lost her through gross stupidity. Every day since, he had ached with that loss.

Now, by the early light, he could see that the landscape they were traversing was suitable for their grim purposes. "You should stop somewhere along here, I believe," he said to Max, their erstwhile chauffeur and longtime friend. "It would be awkward if we were to be observed."

Max grunted his agreement and turned off, bumping their automobile across a farmer's field, sticking to the hedge boundary for added protection from prying eyes. He reached a large fir.

"This will be as good a marker as any," he said.

Andrzej helped Amalia to alight. Her two sons, eighteen-year-old Rudi and sixteen-year-old Christian, followed. As his mother shivered in the bone-aching cold, her youngest son drew a plaid wool blanket around her shoulders and, with one arm, held her against his side. Rudi joined Andrzej and Max as they opened the trunk.

Six hours had passed since the brutal death of Rudolf, Baron von Schoenenburg, and what was left of him looked like a frozen gray effigy of himself. His chest, torn open by SS bullets, was still gory with blood that seemed scarcely dry. Andrzej, once again assaulted by the sight, hastily pulled off his overcoat and spread it over the baron's body before he, Rudi, and Max lifted him out.

Rudolf, Amalia's husband and Rudi and Chris's father, late Cabinet Minister to Austria's Chancellor, was tragically and incomprehensibly dead, leaving their entire party in shock and grief. Carrying him to a spot of ground beneath the towering fir, Andrzej set the body down with unusual reverence. During the Great War, he had buried many a friend, but never in the presence of his grieving family.

He and Max proceeded to dig a grave with picks and a shovel they had found in the stolen SS limousine's trunk. Fortunately, the spring thaw had begun. Amalia stood by shivering, and Andrzej felt her sorrow in every part of him. Though her marriage had begun as one of convenience, she had loved Rudolf more than Andrzej had ever realized.

When the time came for them to lay the baron to rest, she raised her voice over her tears, saying, "I'm sorry, Rudolf. I'm sorry you had to die. We're only leaving you here until Hitler himself is underground. When your home is free again, we'll return to take you back to the Schloss, where you should have been free to live out your life."

Throwing a handful of earth over the wounds on his chest, she murmured, "*Aufwiedersehen, Liebchen.*"

Rudi, the new Baron von Schoenenburg, followed suit, saying, "I'll fight your battle, Father."

Christian, holding his head rigid as he looked at the horizon, tossed his handful of earth blindly and said, "We'll put the bully underground, Father."

Andrzej knew that despite the family's despair, their resolution was real. Amalia's sons would follow her lead in this. For the third time in her life, she had lost everything, but he had no doubt she would recover. He only hoped that as time passed, she would allow him to help her.

When they finally arrived in Zürich later in the day, Amalia found the early spring weather blustery and bitter. She preceded Andrzej, Rudi, Max, and Christian into the wood-paneled, gleaming lobby of the Hotel Metropole. While the men saw to booking their rooms under suitable aliases, she was drawn to the fire burning in a massive grate. Sitting in an overstuffed leather chair by the hearth, Amalia stretched her hands out toward the warmth. In what seemed like another life, this was where she was to have met her husband following their escapes.

Through her numbness, she was aware of Turkish carpets in jeweled tones covering marble floors and well-polished brass fittings and lamps shining all about her. She might be a million miles from that cold and bloody deathscape on the mountain above Innsbruck, but she couldn't seem to get warm.

It was midday, and savory smells issued from the adjacent dining room. She remembered Rudolf saying she would enjoy the Swiss fondue. Now, it seemed days since she had eaten a proper meal.

Giving up on the prospect of ever feeling warm again, she rose and followed the delicious fragrance across the lobby to a set of wood and glass doors. Through them, she watched oblivious men and women dressed in woolens, eating and conversing as though it were any normal day.

Images of Hitler's fist crashing down upon her beloved Vienna and Rudolf's violent death were foreign thoughts, foreign events. They would never happen here. Switzerland was too careful, too neutral.

Suddenly, she wanted to smash the glass doors, the cozy picture. She wanted to hear the glass shatter, see the stunned faces of the diners, watch them cower from the glass fragments as they flew—beautiful but deadly.

"Don't be angry at them, darling," Andrzej said as he came up behind her. "If it weren't for Swiss impartiality, we wouldn't have this refuge."

"How did you know I was angry?" She turned her back on the diners.

He smiled and took one of her hands. "Your fists are clenched."

Rudi joined them. "I think it is time we had our luncheon," he said in an odd, flat voice.

Andrzej dropped her hand.

"The doctor was keeping me from smashing the glass," she said.

Her son's eyebrows rose.

Amalia continued, "The shock is wearing off. I am becoming angry."

"Would you really have smashed the glass?" Rudi asked, opening the door.

"It was a close thing," she said as they moved into the dining room and sat around a table.

Through her numbness, she felt the comforting warmth of Andrzej's presence snaking through her, bringing her much-needed solace. She bit down on her tongue. His green eyes were watching her across the table with the same tenderness he had shown long ago at the deaths of her beloved uncle and her mother.

She knew it didn't look right, traveling with her former fiancé, but even if she wanted to, she couldn't possibly leave him behind. Andrzej's help was needed for the vital mission to England. With Rudolf's death, Andrzej alone was her partner in this. Though a second son, he had been born into the Polish aristocracy and was at home in the type of society they would need to mingle with in London. She badly needed his English language skill. She spoke only French and German.

There was so much to discuss and plan, though her heart was barely functioning, it was so heavy.

Rudi asked Max, his father's occasional bodyguard and sometime butler, and Dr. Zaleski—whose relationship to his father and mother he didn't quite understand—to meet him and Chris in their rooms after luncheon. They needed to discuss their future plans. He was aware his father had confided in them. He also knew his father would have told his mother every detail of their plans, as well, but she needed rest and solitude for her grieving just now. He settled her in her own suite under a pile of feather quilts with a warm cup of chocolate at her side. Her eyelids were finally drooping.

The suite he and his brother shared was spacious, with an adequate sitting room for their conference. A welcoming fire burned in the grate. Rudi ordered hot spiced Glüwein for everyone and they settled around a walnut table.

He opened the discussion. "Herr Doktor, I have not thanked you."

"For what, Baron?"

"First of all, for rescuing my mother from the Gestapo in Salzburg. And secondly, for trying to save my father last night when you stepped forward on that mountain, claiming to be him."

"I am more sorry than I can say that the ruse didn't work."

"Why would you do such a thing?" Chris asked. "You didn't know Father well."

Zaleski took out his pipe and filled it from his tobacco pouch. As he was tamping it down, he said wearily, "You are wrong. I knew your father very well. But that is part of a long story I may tell you another day."

Rudi shifted uncomfortably in his chair, thinking of the doctor holding his mother's hand outside the dining room.

"Were you privy to my father's plans?" he asked.

"Yes," the doctor said. "The night I arrived from Warsaw, he and I and Max discussed what we would do in the event of an *Anschluss*. I know that he had his funds wired here. I followed his example. After a suitable interval while we must deceive the SS as to our intentions, we are to proceed to England."

Max handed the young baron a paperback book. Rudi looked at it. Mein Kampf, by Adolf Hitler.

"It is time for you to read this book, Baron," Max told him. "Hitler wrote out his entire strategy while he was in jail in the 1920s. His next target is Czechoslovakia."

Max opened his small, worn silver case and removed a cigarette. "Your father believed the world to be at a crossroads. If the Western democracies do not stop Hitler now, the cost to stop him later could be millions of lives."

Rudi's eyes narrowed. "War, then. Just what Mutti has always been afraid of."

"And what your father had been working to avoid. Your father met Hitler, remember," Max said. "The man is not completely mad, as many seem to think. He cannot be dismissed as such."

Max looked even more war-weary than usual, his eyes locked on the table, his battered visage quiet with the weight of his thoughts. Rudi watched as he hesitated, drawing on his cigarette. Finally, he raised his eyes. "Your father had firsthand knowledge that Hitler's aggression will never stop with Austria."

Rudi felt dread clamp his heart and understanding dawned. "That is why the SS were ordered to kill him."

"Yes, not just because he was an enemy. And that is why we are still in danger now."

Rudi leaned forward on his elbows toward Max. "Tell me about this evidence."

Dr. Zaleski warned, "The secret could cost you your life."

"It may be assumed that I know anyway," Rudi said.

Chris added, "We must know."

"Your mother will not be happy with me," Max said.

"She will get over it," said Rudi.

Max tapped his cigarette on the edge of the ashtray. "The Western democracies are being led to believe that Hitler only wants to consolidate the German-speaking peoples. Do you remember when I drove your father and Chancellor von Schusschnigg to Berchtesgaden to meet Hitler?"

"Yes," Chris said before Rudi could reply. "I remember worrying that he might not come back."

"If they had realized at the time what he heard, he might not have been allowed out of the fortress," Max said. "You see, he overheard von Ribbentrop, an intimate of Hitler's, speaking to Goering, the Reichsmarshal of the Air Force. Von Ribbentrop is an irresponsible braggart. He was denigrating the West for being weak and naïve, for believing Hitler's promises and for not foreseeing his 'inspired' goal of a German conquest of Europe."

Rudi's palms grew damp and his heart sped up. "Do they know he overheard?"

"I think they must have deduced it somehow," Zaleski said. "Nothing else explains why they didn't want him to leave the country. If it were just that he was anti-Fascist or anti-Hitler, one would think they would have been content to see your father flee."

"But he was only one man," Christian protested. "What did they think he could do?"

Max drew on his cigarette and for a moment, there was silence. After exhaling, he said, "The same thing your mother and Zaleski are going to do now. Go to Churchill and tell him he is right. Offer to help him convince the rest of the government before they allow Czechoslovakia and the rest of Europe to go the way of Austria."

"Churchill?" echoed Rudi and Chris together.

Zaleski said, "Winston Churchill. A prominent Member of Parliament who is not currently serving in the government but seems to have taken Hitler's measure. He is a 'voice crying in the wilderness,' much as your father was. People are dismissing him as a warmonger."

Rudi frowned. "What makes you think he would listen to us? Father, perhaps, but we have no credentials."

The doctor said, "You do not know this, but I fought beside the English in the Great War for Polish freedom. I learned the language and made friends." He drew on his pipe and for a moment said nothing. "Too many of them were killed, but the few who survived serve in the government."

The skin between Zaleski's eyes puckered in a frown. "They have been keeping me informed. Britain and France are weary to the bone of war. But my friends are just prescient enough to believe that the present blindness is going to lead to another one. They back Churchill. They know him. They will vouch for us."

"We must be very discreet," Max said, his voice stern. "I am certain the SS will follow us here. We must fool them. They must be made to think we intend to remain in Switzerland. Meanwhile, through my socialist contacts, I will arrange a secret passage to England. This is what your father would want."

Zaleski spoke up quietly, "Hitler's propaganda machine is busy burying the true facts of the *Anschluss.* No doubt the Swiss papers will be full of his justifications."

Placing his pipe carefully in an ashtray, he said, "Rudi and Chris, no one must know who you are. Switzerland is neutral, but Hitler has a long reach."

{ 2 }

Amalia woke bewildered as the sun was setting. Where was she? She felt at her side for Rudolf's bear-like presence. Emptiness. Pain slammed into her with the force of an avalanche.

There is an empty place in this bed. This time yesterday, Rudolf was alive. I am like my amputee patients in the hospital. I never understood how they could still feel their limbs when they weren't there.

Someone moved in the shadows beyond her bed. Andrzej was sitting there smoking his pipe, silently vigilant. For a moment, she remained still, barely able to breathe because it hurt too much. Then she cried out, "I can't believe that he's gone, Andrzej. How can someone just disappear from your life with such finality? He's not coming to join us. We left him in that farm field under all that dirt, and he's gone forever."

Rolling over on her side, she curled herself into a fetal position and wept.

Some time later, Andrzej's voice came out of the darkness. "I can't even begin to imagine what you are feeling, Amalia. He was a giant of a man."

It's all wrong. Rudolf should be standing here in this room. He should be with us, planning what to do next. This was his idea—going to Churchill.

Like a flash, another emotion overtook her. "Andrzej, how do I live with this hatred?" she demanded, sitting up. "That wicked, horrible man has murdered my husband. Do you have any idea how much I hate him and his swastika? It is a poisonous spider, a bloodsucker!" As she got out of bed and began to stride through the room, her fists clenched.

Bridging the space between them, Andrzej took one of her hands in his. She wanted his comfort, but pulled away. He said, "I know, darling. But we will give Britain some ammunition. They are a tough nation when their backs are against the wall." He cupped her cheek with his hand. She felt his thumb wiping her tears, and part of her core melted at the contact. But then misery came rushing back. It should have been Rudolf's thumb there. She jerked her face away.

Andrzej continued. "But like you, most of Britain is weary of war. We must be very convincing."

"Has no one bothered to read Mein Kampf?" she asked, her outrage building.

"If they have, they think it the ravings of a delusionary madman. But Churchill takes it seriously. He is the only one who understands the hold Hitler has on the Germans. He even compares him to Moloch."

"Who in the world is Moloch?"

"An ancient Phoenician god who required the sacrifice of young children."

She clenched her jaw and began to pace. "I do want to meet this Churchill. Rudolf should be here to tell his story himself."

"We both wish that, darling." Andrzej said this softly.

Amalia knew in part of her brain that Andrzej felt her pain. It hadn't always been the case. They had a complicated history, and she had to resist her childish need to find comfort in this man's arms now.

"Where are the boys?"

"Making a reconnaissance with Max. Trying to appear to be innocent tourists."

She was still dressed in her bulky ski clothes; they were all she had. She moved to the vanity table. Under the guise of finger combing her wavy coiffure, she studied Andrzej in the mirror. Somehow, despite the harrowing days they had spent dodging the Gestapo and the SS as they had tried to escape Austria, he looked as handsome and self-contained as ever. His black leather, wool-lined jacket sat perfectly on his broad shoulders. Except for the forelock over his forehead, his black hair was ordered and his square jaw was shaven as though he had just returned from the barber.

How can he be whole and unharmed and so wretchedly handsome when Rudolf is dead?

Andrzej met Amalia's tired eyes in the mirror and was stirred by their tragic look. Then he said the words that had to be said. "Amalia, I belong with you. I'm meant to help see you through this. I know it's awkward, but it is how things must be."

There was a lengthy pause. He threw more coal on the fire. Soft light from a gas lamp left most of the room in shadow. His eyes traced her features. She had the aristocratic bone structure of her grandmother, who had been the daughter of a count—high cheekbones, a delicate jawline, perfectly formed lips. Her best feature had always been her eyes, large and deep blue with feelings she could never disguise. Right now, she was refusing to look at him.

"My emotions are so confused, Andrzej. I was so numb in the car. I never cried until I saw him in the ground. Then all at once, there's this horrible pain. Then anger. And there's guilt. For a few moments, one feeling will be there, and then it gets replaced by another."

He restrained himself from pulling her off her vanity bench and gathering her in his arms. "First of all, I want you to know that Rudolf anticipated his death. He left you in my care. So there's no need for guilt."

"That sounds like him." Her eyes were soft for a moment. Then she clenched a fist and pounded it on her knee. "But you misunderstand me."

"Talk it out, Amalia. Tell me."

There was another pause. In the dim light, he watched her gather her thoughts.

"Rudolf wasn't a political man to begin with," she said finally, her voice coming from far away. "I don't think you ever knew, but I went to the university after the war. I studied history. I wanted to understand why and how the war had happened."

She stopped and fiddled with the waistband of her ski trousers.

"I'm curious. What did you learn?"

"The university was filled with three kinds of people—Communists, Monarchists, and Pan-Germans. I was alarmed. No one could see past the Treaty of Versailles. And no one had the least idea of how to run a democracy."

He was not surprised to hear this. "A Polish weakness, as well," he said.

"Rudolf wanted to marry me, but he knew my heart was dead where love was concerned."

She looked up at him and their eyes locked. For the millionth time, he cursed the misunderstanding that had misshapen their lives. "So he induced you to marry him by promising to take up your political cause for democracy."

"Yes. He worked very hard at it, but he never had the passion for it that I had. Hardly surprising, since he was born into the aristocracy. But he was always afraid of disappointing me." Her voice broke on the last sentence.

"Let me guess the rest. You blame yourself for his death."

"Yes. I always will, I'm afraid," she said, her voice now small and shattered. "I put him there. I put him in the ground."

He gripped his hands behind his back. "Rudolf was not your unwilling pawn. I knew him well enough to know he chose his own path. He saw what the Nazis were doing to his country. He loved Austria. He tried to do everything he could to save it. Don't turn your anger on yourself, Amalia. You were right the first time. His death is Hitler's doing."

He truly sympathized with her feelings, but there was a battle going on inside him. Every instinct bade him comfort and protect her, but he knew she had to work through this grief. The numbness and pain and anger and possibly the guilt were all part of it. The only thing he could allow himself to do at this moment was to show her the bigger picture. He began pacing.

He said, "I don't want to sound unfeeling, Amalia. I'm not, as I'm sure you know. But now we must set guilt aside. You must press forward in spite of your grief. We must focus on the situation we have before us. That is what Rudolf would want us to do." He stopped for a moment to let this sink in. "Most likely, we have been followed here by the SS. We stole one of their vehicles, after all. It would be easy for them to trace us if they want us dead. But are they willing to cause an incident?" He stopped pacing and faced her. "Our friends in Austria know what happened on that mountain. If the Baroness Von Schoenenburg is murdered in Zürich, it will be clear who is behind it."

He resumed his circuit of the room. "We have no idea how much sympathy the SS has in Zürich. Max is going to try to find out. They may even have a cult here who would carry out their orders. It is not outside the realm of possibility that if such a cult committed a murder, the Swiss might decline to capture the culprits in order to maintain neutrality. We cannot consider ourselves out of danger."

She shivered. "You are trying to scare me."

"I just want you to focus on the situation. We really do not have the luxury of indulging in feelings of guilt. We must look sharp. And until we have a better picture of what is going on, we dare not give anyone a hint of our plans to go to England. If Rudolf was killed to prevent him from getting to Churchill, they will not hesitate to kill us for the same reason."

He could see her posture stiffen and her eyes narrow. His words had had an effect.

"You do not need to lecture me, Andrzej. I understand the situation. Forgive me for muddying the picture with my emotions!"

"That's better," he said. "Be angry. Be angry with me all you like. You have every reason to grieve, but burdening yourself with guilt, as well, will paralyze you. We need your best here, Amalia."

"I think you had better go now, Andrzej." She stood.

She was angry with him. Perhaps he should have followed his inclinations to comfort her, after all.

"Forgive me if I have been overly harsh. I am trying to save your life."

"You have made yourself quite clear, but I need to be alone now."

He could no longer deny the needs of his heart. Walking across the room, he took her in his arms. She was stiff and unresponsive. "I truly believe Rudolf chose his lot in life willingly, perhaps because he loved you, but he chose it nevertheless." Little by little, she relaxed. Coaxing her to rest her head on his shoulder, he said, "Again, Rudolf's death must be laid at Hitler's door. And now we must do our bit to stop him."

It had been a very long time since he had held her in his arms. Her soft, yielding form stoked the fire inside him until it burned fiercely. He had imagined this for years—holding her heart to heart, soul to soul. How very easy it would be in this moment to forget Hitler, Rudolf, the boys . . . everything. Andrzej laid his cheek against hers. Then she stepped out of his arms.

"Andrzej . . ."

"Yes, I know." He shook his head. "We had better go down to dinner. Then you had better get some more rest, Amalia. And tomorrow, you must see about getting some clothes." He smiled at her with all the love that warmed him. "I will see you downstairs in—" he checked his watch, "one hour."

He expected she would mourn deeply that night. He had tried to give her a sense of purpose, but the fact was that Amalia never loved half-heartedly. Even after the death of that rotter, her first husband who had died in the Great War, she had nearly been carried off by grief.

Shutting himself in his room, he knew he needed something to do to keep his mind off of the feeling of Amalia in his arms. After a few minutes of pacing, he sat and began a letter to former Major Anthony Fotheringill, his commanding officer in the late war against Germany. He needed to inform him of their safe arrival in Zürich and their future plans.

&

Rudi glanced at his mother across the breakfast table. Even at the height of the danger in Austria, he had never seen her look so worn. There were purple shadows under her eyes. Her skin seemed as translucent as an onion's and he could see the tiny blue veins at her temples.

"Mother, you do not look as though you slept well," he said.

"Don't worry about me, Rudi. How was your sleep? And you, Chris?"

His brother was stirring a thick bowl of porridge without eating. "I slept all right," Christian said.

Rudi didn't answer. He did not wish to add to his mother's worries. Instead, he asked, "Has Herr Doktor Zaleski already gone out?" He hoped his question sounded sufficiently casual.

"I have no idea. Did you wish to ask him something?"

"Not really."

"Why don't you and Chris go out and look around the area some more? After all, you are new arrivals in town."

Rudi took heart. He had not wanted to remain in the hotel with nothing but memories of the bloody scene on the mountain. He had relived the horror over and over all through the night, unable to sleep. Today, the shining sun offered some hope.

What he needed was diversion from his morbid thoughts. He could not help his mother if he allowed himself to swim in his grief.

His reconnaissance with Max the afternoon before had been in the city proper. Now he wanted to explore the interesting area near the River Limmat. "If you think that would be of use. I am trying to think of what Father would have me do."

She cast him a warning glance and lowered her voice. "You father always was a great one for gathering facts. I think that is what he would do in this situation."

Rudi said, "Later, when you are feeling more recovered, we need to go to the bank where the money is and open an account you can draw from."

She reached across the table and covered his hand. "Max will take me. I need to buy some clothing. For today, you and Chris work on orienting us."

Christian, always ready for action, leapt up, his breakfast still uneaten. "I'm ready, Rudi. Let's go while the sun is still shining."

After picking up some stationery to make a map, he and Chris went out into a glorious morning. His brother marched ahead—always a great walker, always in a hurry. They descended the tiers of streets, Rudi labeling each one on his map until they reached the quay. Unlike the Danube, the Limmat River was blue and flowed swiftly under Zürich's bridges. A light breeze blew, sufficient for the sailboats already out tacking across the water. On the far side of the river were large, important-looking buildings, all somewhat alike, and what looked to be two graceful church towers. After the architectural feast of Vienna, it appeared uninspiring to Rudi, but he was the last person to consider himself an expert on the subject.

He noted the huge railway station that lay behind him, marking it on the map. Excellent in case they needed to get away.

Their potential danger lurked in the back of his mind, but he forced his limbs to relax and saunter. Was anyone watching him?

Looking at the river and the row of shops, hostelries, and restaurants along the quay, he thought about how for months, his family had prepared for the eventuality of escaping to Switzerland. Ever since 1933, when Hitler had become Chancellor of Germany favoring *Anschluss*, Rudi's father had been in danger. The first Austrian Chancellor he had served had been murdered in an attempted Nazi coup. Now the Baron von Schoenenburg, who had seemed larger than life, was gone, to be replaced by his eighteen-year-old self. He was virtually swimming in inadequacy.

Christian awaited him underneath an arched structure that abutted the quay. Across the water, an outdoor restaurant built on a dock was full of Swiss businessmen reading newspapers under a mustard-and-white-striped canopy.

When he reached his brother, Rudi asked the question that had been plaguing him hand in hand with his grief. "I know this is rather awkward, but do you think that Zaleski is in love with Mutti?" Rudi looked into Christian's light eyes. The boy shifted his gaze, looking down at his feet.

"I know they're close friends. Ever since I was knocked out by the Nazis at the bakery and he rescued me when I was ten."

He looked up, his eyes troubled. "Do you think there's more to it?"

Rudi pounded his right fist into his left palm. "I don't know." He took off walking at a faster pace. "She loved Father."

"Of course she did," Chris said. "She was devoted to him."

Rudi tried to dismiss the worry from his mind. "I suggest we keep an eye on him. We don't want him imposing himself on Mutti." Looking ahead, he said, "Let's get on with our exploration. What in creation is that ugly thing?"

An enormous twin-towered church rose on their left. At that moment, bells from the towers of all three churches in their view rang out, chiming the hour of nine o'clock.

Christian said, "It is supposed to be a cathedral, I think."

They crossed a large bridge and found that the river had suddenly become a lake. Dozens of sailboats were tied up by the quay, and a tree-lined promenade faced them.

Though he was still preoccupied, Rudi's eyes fell on a long-legged girl in a white skirt and sky blue pullover jumping to the pier from a small sailboat, line in hand. Her dark hair was worn unfashionably long and straight under a wide-brimmed sunhat. Suddenly, he was completely present to the moment as he found himself approaching her. She was looping the line over a cleat.

"*Guten Morgen*," he greeted her, wondering if she even spoke German. The doctor had told him that a German hybrid—Sweitzerdeutsch—was the local language.

She looked up and smiled at him—a glorious, bright smile. Never had a smile been so welcome or seemed so beautiful. His bruised heart turned over.

"'Morgen," she said, studying Rudi boldly for what seemed the longest moment of his life. He returned her look with frank interest.

At last, she bent down to finish tying up her boat. When she straightened, she came closer and he saw her eyes—the color of deep, dark chocolate. He closed the gap between them, holding out his hand. "Baron Rudolf von Schoenenburg. From Vienna. "

Putting her smaller hand in his, she said, "Fraülein Hannah Gluck. Also from Vienna!"

He gave her hand a single shake but continued to hold it. "Extraordinary. Of all the beautiful girls I have met this morning, you are the only Viennese. How long have you been in Zürich?"

"A few months," she said. "And you?"

"We just arrived. I am getting oriented. Perhaps you might be of help?"

She smiled again, repossessing her hand. "None of the other beautiful girls were available?"

"I wouldn't know. I didn't ask them."

Christian stepped forward and offered his hand. "I am Christian, the little brother. Don't take any notice of me."

Laughing, she said, "Pleased to meet you. I'm Hannah."

Putting her hands on her hips, she asked Rudi, "What would you like to know?"

"What is that big ugly church I just passed? The one with the towers?"

"Ah!" The girl laughed. "Ja, you are from Vienna. Don't let the Swiss overhear you! That is the Grossmünster. The heart of Swiss Protestantism. Zwingli himself preached there. There is a statue."

"And who might Zwingli be?" He looked into her merry eyes, crinkling in the morning sun.

"The Swiss equivalent of Martin Luther."

"A sober man, it would seem. You must have coffee with us and tell us all about him," Rudi said.

In an enchanting gesture, she gathered her dark hair in one hand and pulled it over her shoulder, where it hung halfway to her waist. "I would truly like to join you, but I have a class."

"Class? You are in school?"

"Yes, when I am not sailing the Freiheit, I study biochemistry at the University. I am studying for my Ph.D."

"A worthy ambition," Rudi said, realizing that she was most likely his intellectual superior. He hated school.

"Freiheit is your boat?" Christian asked.

"Yes."

Rudi sensed some tension take hold of her. "Were you thinking of freedom in the sense of sailing in the breeze, or does the word have some larger meaning?" he asked.

"No," she said, smiling again. "Just sailing in the breeze. Have you ever sailed?"

"I haven't," said Rudi.

"You must try it sometime. And now, I must be on my way."

He suddenly had no doubt that she was a refugee as well. He felt he couldn't ask her without revealing his own status. That would be unwise until he knew more of her. Suddenly, he realized he had already been grossly unwise. Without thought, he had given her his true name.

"Aufweidersehen, Fraülein," he said.

"It has been nice to meet some fellow Viennese. Maybe we will run into one another again," she said.

Rudi watched her as she ran to catch the streetcar, knowing that his life had taken another unexpected turn. Zürich no longer seemed like the hinterlands. He would find a way to see Fraülein Hannah Gluck again.

With a bit of discomfort, he realized he hadn't thought of the scene on the mountainside for the last ten minutes.

{ 3 }

Amalia was restless. The events of the past week had been so intense and harrowing that her body was spent, but she could not stop revisiting the bloody scene in the snowstorm. She was so raw with sorrow and regret that she felt stuck. She certainly could not go back in time. Austria, Rudolf, and her life of the last nineteen years were lost to her. And forward? What awaited her in a country where she was unknown, did not speak the language, and had no influence upon a people who wished to continue to be blind to the disaster that awaited them?

And then there was the verboten Andrzej.

Andrzej. In spite of this horrible mixture of anguish, those treacherous feelings for him had a life of their own and were rising in her again.

What kind of a person am I? My husband has just died! I am like two people—the grieving widow and the girl of nineteen who has danced a waltz with the man of her dreams. Or is that girl just trying to escape her grief?

Of course, that is it. The sudden loss of Rudolf has made me as needy as a child.

Against all these complex feelings, Andrzej's plan for her to go buy some clothes carried little appeal, though, of course, it was necessary. They had only escaped with what they stood up in.

Walking out of the hotel, she suddenly wondered if she was being watched. The idea jerked her fully into the present. Should she have sent the boys out on their own? What if they were picked up by the SS? With difficulty, she restrained herself from looking behind her. She needed something to do.

It was some time before she realized she was walking down streets filled with tiny shops displaying the latest fashions. However, she had no money. Perhaps she could try on a few things and have them put aside for her. Dressed in a royal blue ski ensemble, she bore little resemblance to a baroness. Amalia imagined that buying a new wardrobe would be the first order of business if she were planning to make her home in Zürich. It would undoubtedly throw dust in the eyes of the SS, if they were observing her.

She had never bought clothes off the rack. However, after a couple of hours, she had made some agreeable headway. She was in mourning, after all. She had a black dinner dress put by, along with a suit and hat, a nightgown, underthings, and three cheerless dresses. Perhaps Max would take her to the bank this afternoon.

When she left the shops behind, memories of Rudolf suddenly crashed through to her consciousness once more: Rudolf on horseback beside her as they rode out over his vast and lovely estate in the country. Rudolf worried and pacing his study as they tried to devise together a new strategy to ward off the increasing Nazi presence in his government. His pleading, hopeless look when he had to inform her that Chancellor Dolfuss had dissolved Parliament. And of course, that horrible last vision of him surrounded by swirling snow, giving himself up to the four SS soldiers who were trying to annihilate them. In spite of Andrzej's words of the night before, guilt returned, threading itself through her grief. There in the street, she began weeping.

If it hadn't been for me, Rudolf would have lived out his days on his estate. Hitler wouldn't even have known his identity.

Exhausted, she seated herself at a table in one of a string of outdoor cafés, wiped at her tears with her fingers, and absently noted her surroundings. Most of the patrons were student age, dressed colorfully and speaking with animation. Some of the girls wore Dirndls and some of the young men were dressed in Lederhosen. A youthful waiter came and took her order for hot chocolate with whipped cream.

Afraid of another burst of tears, she took up the copy of the Zürcher Zeitung someone had left behind. She sat up with interest as she noted a speech to the British Parliament by Winston Churchill quoted on the first page. It was clearly a response to the *Anschluss.*

The gravity of the event of March 12 cannot be exaggerated. Europe is confronted with a programme of aggression, nicely calculated and timed, unfolding stage by stage, and there is only one choice open, not only to us but to other countries, either to submit like Austria, or else take effective measures while time remains to ward off the danger, and if it cannot be warded off to cope with it . . . If we go on waiting upon events, how much shall we throw away of resources now available for our security and the maintenance of peace? How many friends will be alienated, how many potential allies shall we see go one by one down the grisly gulf? How many times will bluff succeed until behind bluff ever gathering forces have accumulated reality? . . . Where are we going to be two years hence, for instance, when the German Army will certainly be much larger than the French Army, and when all the small nations will have fled from Geneva to pay homage to the ever-waxing power of the Nazi system, and to make the best terms that they can for themselves?

It was the first time she had read anything penned by Mr. Churchill. It would seem that he had seen through Hitler, indeed. Andrzej and Rudolf were right. A feeling of purpose penetrated her gloom in a new way. They must make their way to this man and give him some ammunition that would be more deadly than his own sole vision and convictions about the situation. The paper also gave a full account of Parliament's negative reaction to the speech.

The waiter brought her chocolate and suddenly Andrzej was there, seating himself at her table.

"What are you doing here? How did you find me?"

"Just luck." He indicated the street in a vague manner. "How are you today?"

His green eyes were far too penetrating. She didn't want to discuss her feelings with him again. "Well enough. You must read this speech by Mr. Churchill to his Parliament. I just came upon it." She handed him the newspaper.

Amalia looked dreadful. He didn't miss the wall that went up when he asked how she was. "I am sorry if I was too hard on you last night, Amalia. It was beastly of me." He ordered coffee and took up the newspaper.

After he had finished reading, she said, "Remember the first time we met? In that coffee house? What was it called? Der Haushahn? I asked if there was going to be a war. It seems like another lifetime. But now I am wondering the same thing."

He smiled at her with great tenderness. "I will never forget. You were so young and so earnest."

"And so frozen! I had walked miles in the snow."

Looking about him, he wondered if they were being observed. He lowered his voice carefully, leaning toward her. "And now, it is springtime a generation later, and we are at a Zürich coffee house. This time, I don't think we can doubt that there will be a war. Churchill is right. I wish Parliament would heed his warning."

"But they do not know what we know," Amalia said in a low voice. "Do you think we will really be successful in England?"

"We can only try. But we have to elude the SS first, Amalia. We may be under observation right now." He said in a natural voice, "I have made inquiries. The Swiss are accepting refugees, but we must register."

"Rudolf began the process when he sent his money here. Perhaps the bank knows what steps we should take."

"Yes. Apparently, they've been accepting money in numbered accounts since '34. Many Jews have sent their fortunes here."

All semblance of lightness deserted her and Amalia's eyes appeared sharp with desperation. "I must have something to do, Andrzej. It is essential. After Eberhard's death, there was nursing, taking care of my family, and . . ."

She stopped abruptly. He finished for her, "Me." Indeed, they had been engaged.

Lowering her voice again, she put a hand over his. "Surely you won't go off and fight again, Andrzej."

He brushed away an errant piece of her hair from her face and then, in case they were being observed, murmured as though whispering sweet nothings. "I will find some way to make a contribution. I have no faith in the Polish army or government. They seem absolutely blind to the German threat. And unless Stalin sides with Britain and France, there will be no physical way for the Western powers to intervene if my country is attacked by Germany."

Disguising the meaning of her words with a smile, she whispered back, "And the boys? You think I am going to watch my boys go to war for the British when the British wouldn't go to war for them?"

"I think you will if you think they can help beat Hitler into the ground. Rudi has all the characteristics of a good fighter pilot."

"And Christian?"

"Christian's an adventurer. Perhaps he will become a spy."

"You are probably right. He loves codes and secrets."

"Mutti?"

Amalia withdrew her hand and they both looked up at Rudi, who had arrived at their table with Christian. The boy couldn't hide his fury at what he was seeing.

"Sit down, Rudi," she said in a level voice. "And Christian."

"You are right, Rudi," Andrzej said. "No doubt, we should be speaking in private." He handed him the newspaper, one finger tapping the printed speech.

Once he had read the speech, the young baron said in a low voice, "So you were dissembling?"

Amalia dabbed at her lips with her napkin, saying behind it, "We were." Unfolding it in her lap, she said, "And where have you been?"

Chris, ever the peacemaker, gave his brother a light punch on the arm. "Rudi met his future wife this morning. She is Viennese, studying to become a biochemist."

"Oh, good heavens!" said Amalia.

"Hmmm," said Andrzej. He wondered if Rudi had his father's steadiness of purpose. Rudolf had waited years for Amalia to marry him, and even longer for her to love him. But the boy probably thought that love was an easy road, as the young were wont to think. And no one knew better than Andrzej how suddenly it could afflict one.

"Rudi," Amalia said, her brow furrowed, her voice low once again. "You don't know anything about this girl. I hope you didn't tell her anything about you."

"Only my name," her son said.

"Even that may have been too much," she said, and Andrzej silently thanked the heavens that she had said it so he didn't have to. She continued, "We agreed not to let our identity be known." Then, altering her voice to express casual interest, she said, "What is her name? Perhaps Andrzej or Max can find out more about her before you see her again."

Rudi's jaw had hardened and he didn't answer. Christian cleared his throat.

"Her name is Fraülein Hannah Gluck," the young baron said finally. "She studies at the university. And like Chris said, she's from Vienna. She has been here a couple of months." He passed the newspaper to his brother. "The only thing she knows about me is that I think the Grossmünster is an ugly church."

"The Grossmünster?" Amalia asked.

"It's very homely," agreed Chris. "Not far if you feel like taking a walk."

Andrzej knew he had to watch his step with Amalia's oldest son, but Christian did not seem nearly as forbidding to him. He liked the youngster. His emotions were uncomplicated and he was bright. By contrast, he could see Rudi was beginning to eye him with wariness.

"I think I must see this church and give my opinion," said Amalia. "I will leave you to your coffee and the check, Andrzej. It is a good thing you happened on me, you know. I had forgotten that I have no money."

He watched her walk away with her boys. She had carried that off well. Rudi threw a glance at him over his shoulder and then offered his mother his arm.

&

Max walked into the beer hall in the rail workers' quarter of Zürich, far away from the elegant hotel where they were staying. It was the lunch break, and men stood at the long bar eating their wurst and bread, drinking from foamy glasses. It smelled like a brewery and sounded like the crowd at a prize fight. He felt right at home.

Max looked for his contact. Walter Staubl would be sporting a goatee like Lenin's. He always wore a red kerchief around his neck.

Finding him without much trouble, Max offered him his hand. In it was a calling card from Vienna's Social Democatic chairman, Otto Bauer, in exile. On the back was written a line introducing Max. Staubl called for another beer for his new friend and gestured toward the back of the hall and a table.

"You arrive from Vienna," Staubl said once they were seated. "You are alone? You have family?"

"All socialists have been forced to flee or go into hiding," Max said. "I came out with a friend in the government, but he was killed by the SS. I am with his family." He put his elbows on the bar. "What is the situation here in Zürich? Are the Nazis truly without friends?"

Staubl ran a hand over his goatee. "They are not popular in Zürich. That is true. The Swiss threw the party out in '36. But they have not given up. After Hitler's treatment of Austria, they have a hard job. That is true, also." He took a long drink and Max watched his Adam's apple bob as he swallowed. "The Swiss are very independent. They are not of a mind to be annexed. That is truth number three."

"Do you know if there are any SS stationed around the city?"

"Yes. They look for refugees from Germany and now, most likely from Austria," Staubl smiled. It was not a kindly smile.

"And what is your position on these refugees?"

"Truth number four: The Swiss do not like the Secret Police. They do not like terror tactics."

"And the SS do not like socialists," Max said.

"We make trouble for each other. We do not assist them in their searches."

"Could you give me a sign if they are searching for my baron? He is only eighteen. As I told you, they have already killed his father. He was a von Schusschnigg cabinet minister. Name of von Schoenenburg."

The man threw back his head and laughed. "A proper socialist like you defending a baron?"

"His great-uncle was Lorenz Reichart."

"Ah, the Socialist icon," Staubl said with a nod. "Reichart. What a giant he was. A visionary. We miss him."

"You asked if I had family. Consider the von Schoenenburgs my family. The late baron wanted the Socialists in the government as a counterbalance to the Nazis." Max would never forget when Chancellor Dolfuss had gone against von Schoenenburg's advice and committed the shocking horror of attacking the socialist underground by shelling its neighborhoods. "He saw clearly what Hitler did in Germany, but in the end, the baron's influence wasn't strong enough to keep his government from repeating the mistake."

"This von Schoenenburg. I remember him now. He was a good friend to the Socialists. It was reported that he was against the dissolution of parliament."

Max ran a hand through his thick black hair. "I spied on his family for years for the party. I masqueraded as his butler. In the end, we helped each other escape." He paused in a moment of tribute, remembering their barge journey down the Inn River. "I can vouch for his family. A wife—Reichart's neice—and two boys. They are solid people. Particularly the baroness." And to his dying day, he would suffer because he had let her down. Her grief-stricken face haunted him: looking up at him while clasping the dead baron in her arms. "I have pledged myself to protect her . . . and her sons."

Staubl looked at him oddly. "You are in love with her. A baroness."

"It isn't that simple," Max said, looking at the man directly. "We are very good friends. Can you help us or not?"

The party leader took another long sip of beer and wiped his mouth on his sleeve. "We can let you know if we hear anything. And if we do, we can help set up an escape for you to France."

"Is it safe to register as refugees?"

"Yes. You need to do that for the government. They will be happy to have you if you brought money. Your baroness is safe from our government," he said, his voice sour. "They like baronesses and they do not share their records with the Nazis."

Max felt uneasy trusting anyone, but Staubl had been recommended and he had to admit he couldn't see the man betraying them to the SS. He wrote the name of his hotel on the back of another card. "You can reach me here. Thank you for your help."

The men shook hands and Max departed, hoping for the best.

But the SS is here. Looking for refugees.

He was very glad they had registered under assumed names at The Metropole.

{ 4 }

Hannah walked out of the biology lab, where she had been dissecting a cadaver. She wondered what that handsome young baron she had met this morning would think of a woman who made a practice of such a thing.

Grinning, she turned her steps toward the library. She hated to spend such a lovely day inside, tracking down articles on penicillin molds, but such was the path she had chosen and overall, she was pleased with her life's trajectory. Of course, it didn't take into account the possibility of marriage and a family. Thinking of the Baron von Schoenenburg again, she gave her head a little shake. She should quit thinking about him, but his name was familiar somehow.

Hannah, forget about the boy. He's handsome, yes. But not for you.

Her research in the library soon put Rudolf von Schoenenburg out of her mind. She left the building, her head full of experiments she wanted to try. She was convinced that Dr. Fleming's serendipitous discovery of the healing properties of the mold he called penicillin could lead somewhere if properly understood. There was research going on at Oxford. She would get there someday.

"Fraülein Gluck!" The words brought her out of her reverie. At the bottom of the library steps stood Baron von Schoenenburg.

"What are you doing here?" she asked sharply, confused.

"My hotel is just around the corner. What is this place?"

"It's the library."

"Ah! Will you take that cup of coffee now? I see there's a café across the street."

Her mind went suddenly blank. Hannah could think of no excuse. "I guess I could."

He offered his arm, and she took it without thinking. Once she felt the warmth beneath his pullover sweater, she realized what she had done and wanted to pull away, but knew it would be rude. As a consequence, his body heat spread through her and she recognized she had felt chilled inside the stone walls of the library.

Fortunately, they only had to cross the street and then she was able to remove her arm.

"Inside or outside?" he asked.

"Inside, please. I think a wind has picked up."

Though it had never struck her that way before, the inside of the café seemed dim and intimate. The enclosed space made her more aware of her companion, and a jolt of attraction stabbed through her.

"What would you like to drink?" the young baron asked.

"Hot chocolate, please," she said.

He smiled broadly. "Mit Schlag?"

She returned his grin. "But, of course. I am Viennese, after all!"

While he was standing at the bar awaiting their order, she studied him. He was tall and very well built. Hannah imagined that he was an athlete of some sort. His reddish brown hair grew thick and had a bit of a wave. Now that he had taken off his hat, she could see that he wore it ruthlessly slicked back, but she had noted this morning the curl escaping in the middle of his forehead. A hawk-like nose was his most outstanding feature, making him, if not precisely handsome, aristocratic looking. As he walked back to the table, she took in his easy grace—he moved with confidence.

"You and my mother would get along well, I think," he said as he delivered her hot chocolate with whipped cream.

"How do you know this?" she asked.

"She exists on Schocolade mit Schlag."

"Ah! So tell me about your family. I have met your brother, of course . . ."

His face darkened, changing so completely into a brooding mask of pain that she hardly would have recognized him. He drank his coffee.

She rushed to reassure him. "You don't have to talk about it, if you'd rather not."

The dark brown eyes under thick lashes met hers, but his head was still bowed. "There are just the three of us," he said, his voice terse. "Tell me about your family."

"Mother, Father, and me. I had a brother, but he . . . he died." She still could not talk about Josef comfortably.

Bringing his head up, he studied her face. "I would say we have both been touched by tragedy."

"Let us talk of something else," she suggested. "Are you staying in Switzerland long?"

"We plan to," he said, frowning. The look made him more interesting somehow. "But you would seem to be a permanent resident, since you are attending University."

"Yes. Although eventually, I wish to live in England. Perhaps even attend university there. At Oxford."

His frown vanished. "Why Oxford?" he asked after another drink.

"Have you ever heard of penicillin?" she asked. It was a test question. Hannah didn't think he would pass.

"Animal, vegetable, or mineral?"

"An interesting question. It is a mold. It is definitely alive."

"A mold? A vegetable, then?"

"Yes. Have you ever seen the green mold on old oranges?"

"That is penicillin?"

"Yes. And a Scottish scientist, Dr. Fleming, discovered, quite by accident, that it has extraordinary healing properties. But there are many things about it they still don't know—how to apply it, how to mass produce it, how to store it, that kind of thing. If penicillin's healing power can be harnessed somehow, it could be one of the greatest breakthroughs in medicine."

A gleam had appeared in von Schoenenburg's eye. "I appreciate people who think and imagine on a grand scale. What an intriguing project to be involved in."

He passed the test! She allowed her enthusiasm to show. "I'm not precisely involved yet. I don't have the credentials. But I'm studying all the latest articles and have some ideas for experiments I want to recreate. Maybe it will give me ideas for my own experiments."

"Brains, beauty, and a sense of adventure. What a captivating woman you are, to be sure." He removed a cigarette from a pack in his pocket and lit it. "Tell me, what is there to do in this town? Any night life?"

He offered her a cigarette, which she took. Putting it between her lips, she waited for him to offer her a light. When he did, she bent to the flame. He smelled of some exotic soap. She thought fleetingly that his hotel must be an expensive one. His hand on hers as he steadied the cigarette was warm and gentle, melting her wariness. This was a good man.

Deciding to be honest, she replied, "There are nightclubs. Some students here make clubbing a way of life. I think it is a waste of time."

"What do you prefer to do in the evenings?"

"If I go out at all, it is usually to the opera. They have a very fine opera here in Zürich."

"A woman of refinement, as well. My mother would like you."

She laughed. "I grow weary of your mother. What about you?"

"Oh, I could like you very much."

"I meant, do you like opera?"

"I can't say that I have much experience of the opera. Would you like to teach me about it?"

"Do you like music? Serious music?"

"As a matter of fact, I play the violin."

Her eyes grew large with surprise. "Now that is unexpected."

Smiling, he leaned back in his chair. "You thought I was a complete Philistine? I'm actually not a bad musician."

"Who is your favorite composer?"

"For a Viennese, I'm not terribly modern, I'm afraid. I like the musicality of Bach. It is challenging."

"So you're not a fan of Stravinsky or Anton Berg?"

"Hardly."

"I'm relieved to hear it. They revel in the confusion of the human condition. Bach tries to bring order to it."

"You have managed to put words to my own thoughts."

"There is a dance band playing tonight in the Pavilion across the river," she said. "No Bach. Plenty of Glenn Miller. Do you like to dance?"

"Of course. I am Viennese. So you do go out dancing?"

She could not stifle a giggle. "Don't broadcast it, but I love to do the Swing. This place is outside under a canopy. They serve beer and lemonade. No cocktails."

"Shall we go?" he asked.

"Why don't I meet you there? Nine o'clock?"

"Where is this place?"

"Just cross the river and continue south. You'll hear the music."

"It's a date," he said, draining his cup and standing. "Nine o'clock."

After they parted and she was running for her tram, she wondered exactly how it had happened that she had a date with an Austrian baron, of all people.

When Amalia had returned from her walk with her sons that afternoon, Max took her to the bank where Rudolf had wired his liquid assets. She transferred a sizable bit into a checking account and withdrew several hundred Swiss francs in cash.

They then went through the necessary procedures to register her family as refugees. Max had told her that according to his socialist source, it was safe to register under her own name. Her status as a refugee hinged on the threat to her life as the Baroness von Schoenenburg. Still, the process made her nervous.

When she returned to the hotel, exhaustion interceded and she took a nap instead of going to the shops to claim her new wardrobe. She slept deeply and when she woke, the sun was low in the sky, slanting weak rays through her blinds. She had the same sense of disorientation, wondering where she was and why her chest felt so heavy with dread. Then Amalia remembered and sorrow came crashing down again. Was this to happen every time she awoke? Thinking back to Eberhard's death, she remembered months of denial and then the sudden reality that was literally too much to bear. This time, she wasn't allowed that blessed period of denial, except in her sleep. She had seen her husband shot. She had seen him in the ground.

Seeking another picture for her mind to dwell on, she got up and looked out onto the street. Zürich's old town was a pleasant enough place. It reminded her of her days as a university student to see the young people riding their bikes one-handed as they clutched piles of books. The buildings were obviously old but neat and freshly painted in bold colors—red, blue, yellow, amethyst, green. However, it was not Vienna. She missed the graceful Palais that had been her home for the last nineteen years of her marriage to Rudolf.

She forced herself into recalling the speech she had read that noon. She wished she could speak in Parliament, giving the members an accurate insight into the real character of Hitler.

Somehow, Churchill had got it right. He must be encouraged in his role of "crying out from the wilderness."

Feeling more purposeful, Amalia hurried out to redeem her new clothing before closing time. Fortunately, the shops were not far from the hotel. Old Town was nicely compact.

Relieved to get out of her ski ensemble, she bathed and dressed in her black evening gown for dinner. She had purchased a basic gown with good lines that emphasized her small waist. She could not advertise her wealth or position. As far as the hotel knew, she was Frau Faulhaber, having taken her maiden name. Any associations the SS had with the name would link her to her brother Wolf, who had embraced the Nazi party.

As she rolled her hair off her neck, she fretted about Rudi. Who was this girl he had met? Was it possible her family, too, was masquerading? Could her father actually be a member of the SS?

The risk he had taken in divulging his true identity was more than worrying. When Amalia had questioned him, he said that she had not seemed to recognize their name. But if her father were SS—or even worse, Gestapo—he surely would.

Tension tightened in a knot in her middle and a headache behind her eyes. Would she ever feel safe again? Perhaps not until England, once she had delivered her message to Churchill.

At this moment, all she could think of was flight. But Max said it was important for the success of their escape to lull their watchers into believing they were fixed in Zürich. Perhaps she ought to begin searching for a flat.

Maybe Max could find out about the girl somehow. After telling her of his meeting with the Swiss socialist, Staubl, he had promised to try. She must have a serious talk with Rudi, telling him to avoid Fraülein Hannah Gluck until Max had investigated her.

She knew instinctively that her son would not take it well. It mystified her that he could become involved with a girl at all under the circumstances.

Amalia's conscience smote her. Was she being just? Was she herself not craving the comfort of Andrzej's arms? Had she not fallen willingly into his embrace just last night? She had not missed Rudi's bloodshot, heavily shadowed eyes this morning. They had indicated a sleepless night. Perhaps a pretty, interesting Viennese girl was diverting him from his grief, adding some warmth to his soul, as Andrzej added comfort to hers. She was the last person who should judge her son.

Nevertheless, the SS were here. And they were checking refugees.

As it transpired, she missed her chance to speak to Rudi privately. After dinner, he disappeared. Even Christian did not know where he had gone. She feared his absence had to do with Fraülein Hannah Gluck.

Spurred by her fears, she went to Andrzej's room. When he answered the door, she told him of Rudi's absence and her dread of what it might mean.

Drawing her inside his small room, he closed the door and encircled her in his arms. She did not resist and tried to dismiss the guilt that rose inside of her.

"You are right to be concerned, darling, but I think you are starting at shadows. Rudi is ripe for a love affair. He has just lost his father. He needs consolation. The odds are very long that the first pretty girl to catch his eye in Zürich would be the daughter of an enemy."

The warmth of Andrzej's embrace slowly chased away the chill that had invaded her as her thoughts had run wild. The length of years of knowing this man, of having his devotion was the one solid thing in her world right now. The knot in her middle unraveled as she sank her head onto his chest.

Of course, she shouldn't be here. But just now, she couldn't tear herself away from the comfort Andrzej offered her. He was a familiar quantity in this new, uncertain situation.

She sensed restraint on Andrzej's part and appreciated it. He knew her well.

Nevertheless, anyone witnessing this embrace—her sons, for instance—would think her to be heartless. She eased herself out of his arms and looked into his eyes. They were dark with desire, and she stepped away.

"I'm sorry, Andrzej. I shouldn't have come."

"I know that you are grieving, Amalia. I know that you are merely seeking comfort."

"It is not fair to you."

"I will not lie about my own feelings. You know them well. But I will not take advantage of your sorrow or your fears. I've waited too many years. I want your love."

Shame banished the warmth inside her, curdling all her self-justifications. How could they be having this conversation when Rudolf was newly laid out in that cold Swiss farmyard? Amalia bit her lip.

"Who knows how long it will be until I am ready? And I am tempting you, practically throwing myself at you. To tell you the truth, Andrzej, I am baffled by my emotions."

"I'm not. You told me about them last night, remember? Grief, guilt . . . and now, if I am not mistaken, shame. You are human, Amalia."

"But I have resisted you for years, and now . . . now, I am just collapsing."

"It is honest emotion. Just not quite the one that I hope we will have between us someday."

"You have changed," she said, forcing herself to leave his embrace and walk into the room, seating herself at the desk.

"Yes, I have. I used to demand your love as my right, didn't I?"

"Why aren't you doing that now? Why aren't you taking advantage of this situation? Another man would, you know."

"Because you're still not free. And I grew to have too much respect for Rudolf and your relationship to him. I know your love for him will not melt away overnight. It was a beautiful thing. A precious thing."

As he spoke, memories smote her that he knew nothing of—the blackness in the cobwebby rooms of Rudolf's mind, the despair he battled, the nights he struggled with suicide when he was overcome by the hopelessness of dreadful memories and feelings of inadequacy. Andrzej didn't know of her own fight to reach Rudolf, to bring him into the light. Andrzej had never known that her love for her husband had been a slowly dawning reality that came only when she witnessed the tortured man behind the mask of invulnerability he wore.

As far as her husband was concerned, Andrzej had always been the enemy. The man Rudolf never thought he could match. In the end, he had been forced to rely upon Andrzej to find his wife and save her from the Gestapo who was holding her hostage in Salzburg, hoping to entrap the dangerous Baron von Shoenenburg. Of course he had told Andrzej to care for her were he to die! He believed, in spite of everything, that he would be giving her what she most desired.

And hadn't she gone straight from Rudolf's death into Andrzej's arms? Amalia began to shake with sobs. She had honestly loved her husband. Their love had been exceptionally strong in the end. Even though she had been on the run with Andrzej at her side, posing as his wife in a shared room, her thoughts had been with Rudolf exclusively. All she had been able to think of was reuniting with her husband and sons.

"I loved him so much, Andrzej," she said between sobs. "He was so brave. So selfless."

"I know you did," he said from the other side of the room, his voice resigned. "No one knows that better than I."

Rising, she said, "I must go."

"I fear you must." He stood straight, his eyes full of regret.

{ 5 }

The band shell was down the river close to the lake. Lights were strung above and across the striped canopy. Rudi felt the brisk wind blowing off the water as he examined the crowd for Hannah. Not only the young, but people his parents' age were swing dancing to the jazz band. Seeing their hilarity, it struck him all at once how inappropriate his behavior was. Three nights ago, he had been pinned down by the SS, watching his father die, jerking in a hail of SS bullets.

Grief overtook him with a suddenness that left him weak. He didn't belong here. The entire scene struck him as frenzied, jerky, unreal. Remembering his mother's impulse to smash the glass of the hotel dining room, he sympathized. These people were dancing, celebrating, while his country was overrun with sadistic fanatics who murdered anyone they saw as a threat.

Disgusted with himself, he turned his back on the scene and began to walk away. A breathless Hannah caught him by the arm. "Here I am, Rudi."

Her cheeks were flushed, her long hair rolled on itself around her hairline, and her dark eyes large as they reflected the lights. How had he let a mere girl turn his world upside down?

"Hello, Hannah." He stood regarding her, undecided about what to do. "I'm afraid I am not really in the mood for dancing. I was about to leave."

"Has something happened? You look rather grim." A surprising look of concern puckered her brow.

It would not be fair to leave her on her own when she had come out to meet him. "I'm not good company, but if you don't mind a tame evening, the least I can do is to buy you a cup of coffee."

"You really don't want to dance?" Bewilderment rather than disappointment sounded in her voice.

"No. Maybe some other evening."

"All right," she said, falling into step with him as he walked away from the band shell.

"I'm sorry if you were looking forward to it." His voice sounded terse, even to his own ears.

"That's all right."

She didn't press him to explain, which he appreciated. Remembering the warnings he had received from his mother, he knew he couldn't tell her what was on his mind, even if he hadn't been naturally reticent about his emotions.

Pulling her hand through his arm, he put his own hands in his coat pockets as he strode firmly into the windy night. From her point of view, he must seem a strange duck.

"Tell me more about this penicillin," he said at last. "What experiments are you planning to conduct?"

As she answered his question, he caught only a few words of her enthusiastic ramble. His mind was on his family. How could he have left Chris? And his mother? Had she sought solace with Zaleski? What in the world had he been thinking, going dancing?

For a little while this afternoon and this evening, he had lived outside his dire circumstances. Perhaps because of the suddenness of everything that had happened, the old Rudi had taken over—the one who could always be counted on to react to a pretty face and a trim figure. But for now, he must concentrate on working with Max to get his family to safety. He had no time for dallying with a girl, even one as attractive and fascinating as Hannah.

"You're not listening, are you?" Her voice finally penetrated the fog of his self-castigation.

"I'm sorry, Hannah. Perhaps I should see you home. I have a lot of things on my mind."

They had reached a café and he stood outside, undecided.

"You're a refugee, aren't you?" she asked in a soft voice. "You have had a miserable time."

"Yes." Rudi felt a wave of relief at the understanding that made it impossible for him to dissemble. He looked into her espresso brown eyes, which appeared tender with empathy, and made his decision. He pushed open the door to the café.

A couple was just leaving a table in the corner. He led Hannah through the laughing, chattering crowd. The room was dense with cigarette smoke and smelled of beer. It did not suit the normally convivial Rudi. Perhaps he had made another mistake. If he had been alone, he would have walked out again, but he spared a thought for Hannah.

Once they were settled at the table and had ordered their coffee, she said, "Did the Nazis kill your father? I remembered his name. He was in the cabinet and was a noted anti-Fascist."

She knew who he was. Cold settled in the pit of his stomach. He turned on her. "How do I know your father is not SS? How do I know he is not hunting me?"

Once again, she did not react with offense, as most women would have. Instead, she beckoned him closer. "We are refugees, too. We are Socialists, and my brother was an outspoken antagonist of the Austrian Nazi Party. He was shot one day by a man on the streetcar."

Though her words were tragic, Rudi could not help the intense relief rolling through him. He bowed his head, gouging his eye sockets with the heels of his hands. He hadn't made a mistake telling her his name. He was right about her being a fellow refugee.

"We came here immediately afterward," she continued.

"I am sorry about your brother. I am familiar with the persecution of the socialists." As her explanation sank in, his relief dissolved into bleakness. "My mother tells me Vienna was not always so lawless, but for my entire adolescence, the Nazis have been terrorizing people. They nearly killed my brother, and he was only ten years old."

"They're merciless," she agreed.

Their coffee arrived. He doctored his with four lumps of sugar and stirred. After a moment, he said, "A socialist who is a close friend of the family tried to help my father escape. We all had a part in it—helping Father and trying to escape as a family. As far as my father was concerned, we failed. He was shot three days ago by the SS."

Her lips thinned, turning down at the corners. After a moment, Hannah reached across the table, took his hand, and squeezed it. "I am so, so sorry. He was a great man. Incredibly fair-minded. Though he was never one of us, he always stood up for the Socialist Party."

"Yes." Rudi sighed heavily. For moments, he was silent. When he looked up, he said, "Were you close to your brother?"

"He was years older than me and hadn't lived at home for a long time. He had a family. But losing him was devastating for all of us. So violent." She bunched her fists on the table. "So senseless. But after the Jews, the Socialists and Bolsheviks are Hitler's top enemies."

"Yes, our friend, Max, says all the Socialists are on the run."

"It is the truth. Many of them are Jews, which makes it doubly dangerous for them to stay in Vienna."

Hannah sipped her black coffee. Her eyes were shadowed with sadness.

"My great-uncle was Lorenz Reichart," he said. "My father knew him quite well through their charity work."

"He was your uncle?" She perked up a bit. "Goodness, he is legendary in socialist circles. Even I have heard of him."

He drank some coffee. Its warmth began to dissipate the cold tightness in his chest. "Father met my mother in Uncle Lorenz's flat, actually, just months before my uncle died. I understand he was an extraordinary man."

"He was," Hannah said.

"Mother was very close to Uncle Lorenz. He made her read Marx and Engels, among other things, and taught her French. You know he gave away his fortune to the poor?"

"Yes. I think he must have been that rare thing: a truly good man." Hannah smiled at him, her eyes warm and comforting.

Rudi did not tell her that though he respected Uncle Lorenz greatly, his father had thought him to be naïve about the true nature of man. In his father's mind, this had been borne out by the bloody struggle for power in Bolshevik Russia and by rumors of purges under Josef Stalin.

"I would like to hear about your father," she said. "Do you mind talking about him?"

Rudi looked into her eyes again. Now they were earnest and there was a furrow between her brows. "What do you know of him?" he asked.

"That his ideas were far more liberal than either Chancellor Dolfuss or Chancellor von Schuschnigg's."

"He was greatly influenced by my mother. She has never been a Socialist, but partly because of my great-uncle, and partly because her first husband was a Prussian officer in the Great War, she was an advocate of democracy. She wanted it to succeed in Austria. She was against any sort of union with Germany."

"I don't understand. What did her first husband have to do with it?" She leaned forward on her elbows.

Rudi settled back in his chair. "She felt her husband—Baron von Waldburg—had been betrayed by false ideals. Prussian tradition." He thought about that marriage for a moment and how it had ended up affecting his life. "Actually, it is because of him that Mother insisted I study the violin. He studied violin in Vienna, and Mother says he was very good." He sipped his coffee, then stirred it absently. "But his father was a Prussian Army Officer and raised him to be one, too. Apparently, it went against his more gentle nature. I gather he went mad out there in the trenches on the Western Front."

"How tragic." He felt her eyes on his face but kept his cast down. She continued, "I can only imagine how she feels about Hitler and his goose-stepping Nazis. What an interesting family you have."

He shook his head sadly. "It is ironic. I am sure she wanted me to take up music to keep me from wanting to be a soldier. But it didn't have that effect. I can think of nothing I want to do more than to fight Hitler."

She took his hand again. "Austria wasn't prepared to fight, Rudi. We would have been defeated."

"Not if we had had some allies—Italy, France, England. They all looked the other way."

To his surprise, at that moment, they were joined by Max.

"Good evening, Baron, Fraülein." He removed his hat.

How had Max found them? Rudi stood up.

"Good evening, Max. Where did you spring from?" Rudi asked.

"I've adopted this place. Just dropped in for a beer."

"Well, then." Rudi looked toward Hannah. "I'd like you to meet a fellow Austrian Socialist, Fraülein Gluck. Hannah, this is Max Hoffman, the friend of the family I was telling you about."

Hannah extended her hand. "You probably knew my brother, Josef Gluck."

"Join us, Max," Rudi gestured toward the empty chair at the table.

"Josef Gluck was your brother? You have my condolences, Fraülein. Another great man and good leader gone."

Max engaged Hannah in conversation about the scattered party while Rudi looked on. Was he vetting her? Was his appearance actual happenstance, or had Max been following him?

Knowing how carelessly he had acted, he couldn't blame Max. And though he had no plans to see Hannah again, he was glad Max had eliminated her as a threat.

"I have the car," Max said subsequently. "Would you like a lift home?"

"Not so subtle, Max. But you are right. It is time to cut the revelry short."

Their ride was relatively long, through the modern part of Zürich to a flat with what would be, in daytime, a view of the water. Rudi said nothing, but Hannah kept her arm linked through his.

"I don't suppose I'll see you again," she said as Rudi walked to the door. "But good luck, Rudi. Be safe."

"Thank you, Hannah. I'm sorry about the dancing."

"I enjoyed our conversation. Thank you for confiding in me. You have my condolences. Your family has suffered a tragic loss."

"As has yours. But we will defeat this madman. Good night, Hannah."

As he walked back to Max and the car, the weight of his grief pressed down upon Rudi once again.

{6}

When Amalia was picking up her newspaper from the front desk the following morning, she glimpsed a man entering the hotel's revolving door. Immediately turning her back on him, she opened the newspaper so that it concealed her profile. Her hands trembled.

"*Grüss Gott*," said the wolfishly featured man from her nightmares to the desk clerk. Amalia's heart raced as she listened to his harsh Hamburger accent. She felt the blood drain from her face, and her hands perspired freely. Though he was out of uniform, she would recognize Gestapo Colonel Dietrich anywhere.

"*Guten Morgen, mein Herr*," said the desk clerk.

"I am looking for a friend of mine who is staying here," the colonel said. "The Baroness von Schoenenburg. She has her two grown sons with her."

There was a silence while Amalia presumed the clerk studied the register. "I am sorry, *mein Herr*. If she is meant to stay here, I must tell you she has not yet arrived. We have no people of that name registered in this hotel. The Hotel Hirschen, perhaps? Across the square?"

To her infinite relief, the colonel merely slapped his gloves on the marble counter and turned to leave. She was glad she had chosen to garb herself as a commoner in an inelegant, sober black dress. Once she heard the whoosh of the revolving door, she closed the paper, her hands still shaking, and went to locate Max in the dining room.

"We must leave," she told him as she seated herself. "He was here. Dietrich was here asking for us at the front desk. He said he knew we were expected to stay here."

Max put down his breakfast roll. "He probably says that at all the hotels where he makes inquiries."

"Where is the car parked?" she asked.

"Up the hill on a side street. There are at least twenty hotels in the area."

"He is probably having it watched," she said. "We must not use it again."

"I agree." Max finished his coffee and dabbed at his mouth with a napkin. "I would advise staying inside the hotel, Baroness. This must be a personal issue with the colonel. I did not expect him to come after us himself."

"What about Andrzej? The boys? He knows them by sight." Amalia strove to keep her voice level. Had they come so far only to be discovered and killed?

"I don't know where they have gone. I must go out to find Staubl, my contact. I will take the streetcar, so I will be gone awhile. The way I see it, you can only remain here in the lobby and hope that they return soon. Act naturally. We do not want to alert the staff that there is anything untoward going on with us. After that, just wait for my return. I promise I will come back as soon as possible. Wait for me."

Standing together, they left the dining room. Using studied, careful movements, Amalia bade him farewell in the lobby and took a seat by the fireplace, where she pretended to read her newspaper.

Come back to the hotel, Andrzej, Rudi, Chris! Danger!

She kept sending her thoughts over and over like a radio transmission. Dread clenched her fists on the newspaper, damp from her hands. Amalia's head sat rigidly on her neck, the tendons tight as stretched cords.

She recalled the first time she had seen the colonel, being introduced to him only as Herr Dietrich. Her sister had made the introductions, in her own home. Amalia had not known his true identity until the day of the *Anschluss*. Was it only a little over a week ago that Rudi and Chris had escaped out the bedroom window in the pre-dawn hours?

Recalling her captivity in the temporary Gestapo headquarters in Salzburg, she knew that Max was right. She and Andrzej had duped the colonel into releasing her, posing as lovers running away from Rudolf. They had convinced Dietrich that she was the last person who would know the whereabouts of her husband.

Almost convinced. He had followed them to Innsbruck, and, if she was not mistaken, it was Dietrich who had instigated the stalking of Rudolf by the SS. If that was the case, the colonel would know that Andrzej and Max had shot Dietrich's SS comrades and left them dying in the snow while escaping in their limousine.

Yes. It was undoubtedly a personal vendetta that had brought the man to Zürich. She heard the clock in the lobby chime the hour, then the quarter hour, the half hour, and finally her sons strode in with their lengthy, careless strides.

"Rudi, Chris," she said, her voice only slightly loud. "Good morning!"

&

Andrzej noticed the reflection of the man with the martial gait in the shop window. He stiffened and pulled down the brim of his hat.

I recognize that walk. Swiss gentlemen out for a stroll in the Old Town do not walk as though they own the streets like Nazis.

As the man neared, Andrzej turned and faced down the street toward the river. Was it just that his nerves were on edge or was that really Colonel Dietrich? The Gestapo agent who had followed them all around Innsbruck and arranged the death of the baron?

The man passed him without looking and went into the hotel next door. Yes. Andrzej's heart sped up as he recognized his foe.

He waited a few moments before following him. His quarry was at the desk, his voice loud enough for Andrzej to hear him inquire in his dreadful north German accent for the "von Schoenenburgs." Waiting no longer, Andrzej wheeled about and left the hotel. That was a mistake. Before he was through the revolving door, he heard a shout follow him.

He must not lead the man to Amalia! But how was he to warn her?

"Zaleski!"

The devil has seen my face!

He slipped into the close alley between the store and the hotel and held his back against the wall, hoping cascading morning glory would hide his figure. But Dietrich went straight for the alley, and Andrzej was forced to run.

The train station. Lead him away from here.

Running down toward the river, he used every bit of speed his body could manage. His lungs burned and his heart thundered as they worked to fuel his effort. Fortunately, the colonel was not a young man either—and was cursed with short legs, to boot. When Andrzej reached the bridge spanning the river to get to the enormous sprawl of the train station, a policeman tried to stop him from crossing against traffic. Pulling himself away from his grasp, Andrzej hissed, "SS!" and the man let him go.

He did not know what happened behind him, but, dodging traffic, he gained enough of a lead to run inside the huge station and disappear in the morning crowds. Taking off his hat and coat, he pulled his jacket collar up about his ears as he stood in one of the many ticket lines furthest from the entrance. He pulled down his hat. By the time he heard Dietrich's shout, "Zaleski!" he had purchased a ticket for the earliest departure and was moving through the revolving gate. Looking at the ticket in his hand, he noted that he was going to Luzerne. He read the track numbers, ran for the correct train, and swung aboard before Dietrich could see him. There were at least twenty trains sitting in the noisy station. Andrzej had picked the right one. It began steadily to pull out. Dietrich did not appear on the platform.

When he found a seat and his breathing slowed, he tried to think. He must get in touch with Amalia at the hotel. He prayed she had not gone out. What if the man were to find her? This was Switzerland. Dietrich could hardly snatch her off the street. But he could plan something vile. The man was a complete villain.

Andrzej decided to disembark at the third stop and call the hotel to warn Amalia.

&

Max found Amalia standing by the window in her suite, looking down at the street. Rudi and Chris were gazing into the fire silently. The room was electric with tension.

She whirled at his entrance, but the hope in her eyes died when she saw him. Max felt her look like it was a blow.

"The doctor has not returned?" he asked.

"No," she said shortly. "Did you see Staubl?"

"He will have a car and a driver here for us at nightfall to take us into France. Someone may be watching the train station. I don't know if you realize it, but we are just over the border from Germany. We must drive southwest before we go north again to France. Staubl's man will take us a good way into France—all the way to Metz. But then we will be on our own. We'll take the train to Paris and from there to Calais, where we will cross the Channel."

"I have no idea what's keeping Andrzej," she said. "Do you think he's been captured?"

Max steeled himself against her obvious agony. "He may be working a diversion. I am sorry, Baroness, but your safety and that of your sons requires that we leave at nightfall."

She raised her chin. "Yes. You are right. That is what the baron would expect. Thank you for taking such good care of us, Max. I pray this will work."

The telephone rang. Rudi, sitting next to it, raised the receiver. "Yes, Herr Docktor. She is here."

Max watched as she grabbed the receiver.

"Where are you?" she demanded.

For a few moments, it seemed as though everyone in the room held their breath.

"He could have followed you in his car. Be careful, Andrzej." Max heard the anxiety in her voice, even though she was trying her best to temper it.

With the next exchange, her face softened and she turned her back to the room. "I recognized him this morning. Max has arranged for a car to take us to Metz in France. Here, I will let you speak to him."

She handed the receiver to him. Max communicated the plan to the doctor and then said, "I think to be absolutely certain you do not lead this man to the baroness, you should take a train from Luzerne on an indirect route to England and meet us there."

Zaleski said, "Right. I will telegraph my friend to expect you in a few days and tell him that I will be arriving separately. He lives in London." The doctor rattled off his friend's name and address. Max motioned to Rudi for a pen and paper and wrote it down.

When Max cut the connection, Amalia said, "We're not meeting him until London?"

"That is the safest plan, Baroness." He continued briskly, "I propose that we pay the hotel for a week in advance, in case inquiries are made again. Then the colonel will believe we are still in Zürich."

"Very well."

He watched as she walked to the window again and, standing to one side, peered down into the street. She was concerned, but the baroness knew how to keep her nerve.

{ 7 }

As Hannah rode the streetcar home in the late afternoon from the library, she fell to thinking about Rudi von Schoenenburg. Though he now knew where she lived, she was near certain she wouldn't be hearing from him again. Last night, she had glimpsed the determined man he was in the process of becoming. She sensed that he was refocusing on some goal, though she didn't know what it was. His revelations about his family had given her the idea that such a history may have planted seeds of greatness in him. Gone was the eager boy who had used cigarettes to impress her.

Though she had been more than a little interested in a night of dancing, she knew that any deeper relationship between them was impossible. Jewish girls and Christian Austrian barons certainly did not mix. That didn't stop her from being intrigued with him, however. With a little sigh of regret, she disembarked from the streetcar, walked a short block, and then put her key into the lock on the long wooden door of her flat. It was Friday, and already sundown. She was late for *Kiddush* and would no doubt be scolded.

Hannah was not greeted with a scold, however. Instead, Mama cried, "Daughter, you are safe! I was certain there had been trouble!"

Tall, slender, and beautiful in her black, high-necked dinner gown, Mama rose from the end of the table, her white face teary in the gloom. The candles on the table had already been lit, but Hannah had not yet missed the blessing of the bread and wine.

Papa sat at the head of table, his yarmulke fixed on his head in preparation for services. "Hannah, come. We will eat. I have something serious to discuss with you after services. You must not take it lightly. Your mother and I have been very worried about you."

Had they somehow found out about Rudi? Hannah's mouth quirked. She could reassure them quite easily on that score.

They blessed the bread and wine and then ate dinner in an unusual silence.

Their synagogue was the center of the small, friendly community they had come to upon their arrival from Vienna. The Glucks had followed other Jewish families to this place, a cluster of flats close to the downtown commercial center with a view of the lake.

Hannah secretly detested this part of the city. Longing for their comfortable townhouse in Vienna with its nearby park and trees, she found their flat dark and grim. But the Vienna she had loved was no more. Had they stayed, who could say what would have happened to her family now, after the *Anschluss*?

And she had the Freiheit. Papa had purchased it for her as a sort of compensation shortly after their arrival.

Now she noticed something furtive in their walk. Papa placed his arm across her shoulders, pulling her close to him, a thing he never did. On his other side, Mama clutched his arm while Papa hastened his steps, causing all of them to walk a little faster.

Looking around for the source of perceived danger, Hannah noticed other families she knew walking in similar fashion. Something was very wrong.

"What is it, Papa?" she asked.

"We will discuss it after services," he answered.

The service had never seemed so long to Hannah. They were led by a rabbi she did not know who, like Moses, appeared to be slow of speech. After an equally rushed walk back to the flat, she waited while her father hung his coat, hat, and scarf and settled himself in his armchair.

Finally, he spoke. "Hannah, something very grave has happened." He paused as though unwilling to continue, and she tried to be patient. "Last night, our Rabbi Scheelstein was shot in the back while walking down the street."

Her hands flew to her mouth. "Rabbi Scheelstein? Shot in Zürich?" Fear knifed through her breastbone. Like Josef. Like Vienna.

"There are anti-Semites even here."

"How do you know he was shot by an anti-Semite?"

"Rabbi had received threats. No one knew about them but Frau Scheelstein. And there was a threat stuck inside his overcoat. 'Jews go home.'"

Hannah gripped her hands together tightly. There must be some mistake. "Papa, you know yourself how kind the Swiss have been . . ."

Her father's voice was hard and cold. "There are anti-Semites everywhere, Hannah, and the Jew that does not remember that is in double peril. That said, you must change your habits."

Panic jolted through her. Did he mean she was to give up her studies? Life without medicine? She had already given up her home. She would not give up the life she had planned since she was twelve because of one cretinous Jew-hater. "I will not withdraw from the university. No one can make me. I would really rather be shot!"

"Hannah! You cannot mean that! Think of your brother!" Mama cried. She was weeping.

"Daughter, I understand the importance of your studies, but your life is more important. It is important to me, if not to you. I have made the decision to escort you. I think we will be safe as long as it is daylight," Papa said. "We will be home each day by four o'clock. In summer, later, of course."

Her heart swelled at the reprieve. "That is very good of you, Papa. Thank you." Indeed, his consideration for her was unusual.

She was struck by her own self-absorption. "I'm sorry for my selfishness. I am very sorry to hear about the rabbi. He was a good man."

Biting her bottom lip, she studied her lap, wondering if she dared to ask her question. It had hovered in her mind for years, but she had always been constrained somehow from voicing it.

"Why do people hate us so?" she asked finally.

"There are many reasons," Papa said. "But I choose to believe that at the bottom of them all lies fear."

She pondered this. "Why do the Jews always submit? Why do they never fight back?"

"It is not our way."

Hannah thought this a very poor reason, but she knew instinctively it was the only one her father would give.

Kissing each parent on the cheek, she walked to her bedroom, went to the desk, and tried to banish her uncomfortable emotions by studying the ligature of the human hip.

&

Amalia stepped with automatic movements into the back seat of the Mercedes Benz touring car.

"Where did this come from?" she asked Max as she sat.

"Your uncle's name still carries weight with Party members everywhere. They are eager to help you escape our common enemy. This is a very fast car. We may even be in Metz by morning."

Amalia had spent her afternoon packing her new clothing, ordering dinner for them to eat in her suite, and then speaking to the kitchen staff about foods that could be packaged for their overnight journey.

Andrzej is more than competent. He survived a war, Amalia. But will a car or a train make it faster through to Luzerne?

Somehow, you are going to have to wait until London to learn his fate. Get hold of yourself!

But she also needed to face facts. Dietrich had had no trouble finding them in Innsbruck and tracking their movements that eventually led them to that fateful mountainside. He had tracked them easily to Zürich.

The Gestapo colonel was deadly. His personal pursuit spoke of hatred, not necessity. It would be an easy thing for him to come up behind Andrzej, garrote him, and toss him off the train.

Amalia squeezed her eyes shut at the image in her mind so that her sons would not see her tears. She could go on without Andrzej—she had before—but those times, she had known he was still alive somewhere in the world. Now, would she even know if he was dead?

As the car glided majestically through the streets and finally out of Zürich, it drew into the mountain passes. Suddenly, she was filled with anger that trumped her worry. She had left Andrzej too many times in her life! The place where his soul fit next to hers had been carved out inside her for decades, always empty except for brief periods. Now the emptiness screamed and she had to use all her outward strength not to let it be heard.

The ancient trees along the mountain roads were so high and dark, she felt they were enclosed in a speeding cocoon of anxiety.

&

Rudi felt his mother's unease. Her body was rigid with tension as she sat next to him. "Mutti," he said, "we are going to get away safely. Don't worry."

She almost summoned a smile and patted his knee. "I know we will. Max has a very good plan."

"Can't you relax a bit then?"

"I'm trying, but it's a bit difficult when Dr. Zaleski has set himself up as a decoy. He could already be in Gestapo custody. They wouldn't be above torturing him to find our whereabouts."

Chris spoke up. "He seems to be able to watch out for himself, Mutti."

Max added, "He has trod a tightrope in Poland over the last few years, Baroness. If he survived that, he can survive this."

"What do you mean, Max?" Rudi asked, sliding forward to hear better.

"Like our government, the Polish government has not been wise. The doctor was very opposed to most of their decisions. He was a government minister, like your father, Rudi."

This surprised him. "I thought he was a doctor."

"He hasn't practiced medicine for a long while. You will remember that Poland has not had its autonomy for hundreds of years. It has been either part of Russia, Prussia, or the Austro-Hungarian Empire. Its geography has made it a battleground."

"He fought in the Great War against the Empire," Amalia said. "The Polish State means more to him than anything in the world."

"More than you, Mutti?" Chris asked quietly.

For a few moments, his mother did not answer. "I suppose I should tell you our story," she said on a sigh.

Rudi sat up straighter, his body rigid, as though he had just received a threat. "What story?"

"I met Dr. Zaleski a long time ago. Around the same time I met your father. It was the year before the Great War."

Though the car was speeding through a night lit only by the car's headlamps, Rudi could sense his mother's withdrawal from them all. It was as though she were taking a journey back in time.

"Things were very different then. I was a silly, young girl. There was the confused business of my engagement to Eberhard, who later became my first husband." She ran her palms repeatedly over the wool of her coat as it lay against her thighs. "He had gone back to Germany to enlist, breaking our engagement."

"Did you love Baron von Waldburg?" Christian asked. Rudi reflected how easily Chris seemed to ask the difficult questions. He had always had a closer relationship with Mutti. Rudi had been closer to their father. Which was quite possibly why he found this venture into past emotional territory so difficult.

"I thought I did," their mother said. "But I really had no idea of what love was."

He suddenly knew he could not bear to hear any more. Instinctively, he grabbed the hand that was still smoothing her coat as though he could stop her speech. "Mutti, this is too painful to discuss right now. You are too distressed."

Even in the semi-darkness, he could see her eyes were pools of sadness. "Oh, Rudi, Chris. You have no idea what a horrible thing war is. Even in your worst nightmares, you could never imagine it. It drove poor Eberhard insane."

Rudi said, "We won't talk about this any more right now."

I don't want to know anymore. I don't want to know about other people you loved.

Taking his hand from his mother's, he clenched his fist. He found himself remembering the way his father had looked at his mother—his devotion plain in his eyes. Rudi had long suspected that the baron's work as a cabinet minister had not been his choice of occupation. He had done it all for his wife.

But did she deceive my father? Did she love Zaleski all along? If so, why had she married Father?

A dread thought assailed him. What if Zaleski had forced his father out into the open there on the mountain? What if he had offered himself as a target, knowing that Father would give himself up? The baron had been in a secure position until then. They could have fought off the SS! In the end, they had succeeded in doing just that, but only after his father lay dead.

"You are right, Rudi. I am far too distraught at the moment." After blowing her nose, she gave a little shake of her head. "But there are things to be done, and we will do them. We must focus on the future. And right now, that means getting to England safely and delivering your father's message to Mr. Churchill."

Rudi's anger lowered to a slow simmer. He could deal with that challenge. But the idea that had taken hold in his head would not leave. He didn't know how he would react if Zaleski succeeded in eluding the Gestapo agent and they met up in England.

&

Andrzej was not altogether certain he had evaded Dietrich. After his arrival in Luzerne, he had seen the man pacing the platform, awaiting the train. Before he could be identified, Andrzej had reversed directions, climbing back on the train for the return trip to Zürich. Waiting in the WC until the train pulled out once more, he made his way cautiously to the hindmost car. It was third class. There were no compartments, only open seating. Scanning it, he did not see Dietrich, but that did not mean the man had not boarded.

The doctor picked up a discarded newspaper and, sitting behind a woman with a very large hat, opened it and pretended to read. He allowed his thoughts to shift to Amalia. It appeared that Dietrich had pursued their party on his own; therefore, there was no reason to suppose she was being followed. But the thought of not seeing her again until some uncertain time in the future was nerve-wracking, nevertheless. She had Max and the boys and she was far from helpless herself, he reminded himself.

His thoughts were selfish. He simply could not bear being out of her presence.

They had spent too many years apart. Despite the danger he was in, his mind strayed back to the frustrating period in his life when he had discovered the plot by his then-wife, Lilli, and Amalia's brother to keep them separated after the War. Amalia had been married for thirteen years by that time and had two children. He could not persuade her to leave them. And, truth be told, his love for her had grown as a result of her determination to honor her marriage vows. He remembered clearly the agony in her eyes, which he had watched change to resolve.

He had gone back to Poland for five years until just weeks ago, when he had learned of the approaching *Anschluss*. He had not stopped to think, only knowing that she and Rudolf were in mortal danger. Andrzej had gone to Vienna, where Rudolf had sent him off to Salzburg. The baron was leaving that night in disguise aboard a barge. But Amalia was being detained by the very Gestapo colonel, Dietrich, who now pursued him. And sometime during that five years, her resolve to not leave Rudolf had turned into a tenacious love.

Andrzej heard the door to the carriage open. Looking up, he saw his nemesis standing in the doorway.

"Hannah," her father said as they caught the noisy streetcar on the way home from the university. "I have something to tell you that will not wait. Please listen. I am afraid that for our safety, we must leave Zürich."

Her eyes grew large in disbelief. "Has something else happened?"

"Yes. There has been another shooting. Herr Mueller."

"When did it happen?" she asked with a gasp. "Where? Can't the police do anything?"

"Only this afternoon," he said. "In the square. He was doing nothing more than feeding the pigeons. His shooter escaped. Nothing could be done. There were no witnesses. At least none who would step forward."

Hannah swallowed with difficulty. There was no ignoring the threat now. Tears flooded her eyes. Herr Mueller had been a kindly old man with a wife who made Wienerschnitzel and Apfelstrudel for her homesick husband. They had lived in the flat just across the street. Once, she had even taken them for a sail in the Freiheit.

"We must take Frau Mueller with us when we leave," she said, blinking back tears.

"Yes. She is packing. So is your mother. We leave tomorrow."

After the rabbi's death, Hannah had not been willing to panic or change her plans. But Herr Mueller was different. His death was so random, it frightened her. If anti-Semites could shoot their harmless neighbor, they could shoot anyone. Her own father, for instance. Sudden fear made her palms moist and her heart gallop. There was no guaranteeing one's safety against random acts of hatred.

There were other universities in the world. She pushed away her regrets at leaving Zürich.

It was their stop. She stepped off the streetcar for the last time.

"Where are we going?" she finally thought to ask.

"It is important for you to continue your studies. We are going to England. I should like for you to attend Oxford."

Oxford! Someday is arriving more quickly than I planned.

"Will it be safe in England?"

"One can only hope, Hannah. These are bad times for our people." He pulled her hand through his arm and patted it reassuringly.

Amalia was too anxious to sleep well during their brief stop in Metz. Visions of Colonel Dietrich taunted her. She hadn't liked him from the first time she had seen him in her sister's drawing room. As soon as the *Anschluss* became reality, he had lost no time whatsoever in appearing before them in his Gestapo uniform, shocking even Antonia. He had taken Amalia into custody, questioning her long and hard about the whereabouts of her husband.

She recalled the gray whiskers that sprouted out of his nose and ears. The heavy eyebrows that overhung the small, beady eyes. Mostly she remembered his sadistic smile as he beat his baton into his open hand while he strutted in front of her.

Andrzej had rescued her just in time. The colonel had not been able to afford to offend a "fascist Polish minister" who claimed to be the lover who was taking her back to Poland with him, away from her "misguided" husband. After all, for the time being, Poland was an ally, and Herr Doktor Zaleski an influential man.

Now, the fact that she and Andrzej had misled the little tyrant would make him all the more determined to kill the doctor. How could a people relish being ruled by such bullies? Amalia twisted in her sheets. The dull ache of exhaustion was fixed behind her eyes and her ears were still ringing from their hours on the road. She wasn't living well with this uncertainty.

Anger suffused her suddenly, chasing her anxiety. Hadn't she lost enough to the Third Reich? Her husband, her country, her safety? Rudolf should be lying next to her, not dead in the ground! And now, they were on the run again. Was one hate-crazed man going to wipe out Andrzej and her family? She pounded her pillow and let the tears of anger and frustration flow.

Finally, she exhausted herself and, as dawn approached, Amalia surrendered to a brief slumber. It seemed like mere moments before Chris came in to wake her for the journey across France to Calais.

{8}

Andrzej was extremely grateful they were in Switzerland, where mob rule did not grant the Gestapo the right to shoot private citizens on railway cars. Coolly folding his newspaper, he stood and walked straight to Dietrich. When he reached the colonel, he faked a stumble, grabbed the man's shoulder seemingly to steady himself, and gave a hard pinch to the nerve in his neck that Andrzej's knowledge of anatomy told him would cause the man to collapse.

Simulating concern, the doctor bent over him. "*Entschuldigen Sie, mein Herr*! Are you hurt?" Looking at the startled passengers, he said, "This man is ill! I will go for the conductor!"

Andrzej began moving into the next carriage, calling the conductor in agitated tones while passengers encircled the fallen man.

Once he was past the connecting carriage, Andrzej consulted his wristwatch. They should be arriving in Zürich in fifteen minutes. Again, he hid in the WC, lest any concerned conductor or passenger should come looking for him. The odds were great that Dietrich would revive sooner rather than later.

Leaping off the train the moment it halted in the Zürich train station, he bought a ticket for a sleeper compartment on the overnight train to Paris, climbed aboard, and entered the dining car just as the train was pulling out of the station.

He hadn't killed a man since the War, and never at close quarters. But if ever a man deserved killing, it was the Gestapo colonel who had engineered the murder of Baron Rudolf von Schoenenburg. Andrzej considered it unfortunate that he wasn't carrying a weapon.

&

A day and a half after they had set out from Metz, the ferry carrying Amalia's family and Max across the English Channel arrived in Folkestone. Though she was exhausted, the sight of the port town with its busy fish markets bordered by heavily wooded walks down to the sea filtered into her mind, carrying the knowledge that, at last, she was in England. The journey had seemed endless and at times, she had completely lost sight of their destination. Now, just knowing that they were within hours of reaching London put new heart into Amalia. This had been Rudolf's plan. She, Max, and the boys, were over the second great hump.

Her feeling of accomplishment dimmed, however, as it pressed in on her that they were without Rudolf. A wave of pain assailed her. He should be standing next to her and his sons here in England. Her eyes clouded with tears. Standing against the stiff wind off the channel, she looked back toward France, trying to stifle her anguish and her fears.

I must be optimistic for the boys' sake. We must go on and do the best we can. Rudolf would expect me to be brave and competent. He always brought out the fighter in me.

Anthony Fotheringill's London residence was far grander than Amalia had expected. Through the fog and steady rain, she could see that it was large and imposing—three stories of gray stone on a street across from a large park. They had come by train from Folkestone, taking a taxi from the train station to their destination through the confusing streets where everyone barreled down the wrong side of the road. This must be the right address.

Amalia felt not only exhausted but unkempt and unready to make anyone's acquaintance after thirty-six straight hours of travel. She had to remind herself that Mr. Fotheringill was expecting refugees. She prayed that he spoke some German.

A butler opened the door. She had no calling cards, and her lack of umbrella had left her drenched. Pulling herself up into her Baroness persona, she said with all the firmness she could gather, "Baroness von Schoenenburg für Herr Anthony Fotheringill."

Mercifully, the butler didn't hesitate to let her party into the black-and-white-tiled vestibule; however, he left them standing there, dripping, while he went to the back of the house. Moments later, a man of middle age with thick blond hair and a limp walked into the hallway, supporting himself with a cane. He held a hand out to her, bidding her into the hall. "Baroness! Wilkommen in England!"

Amalia summoned a smile in her relief. He spoke at least some German. Taking his hand, she asked, "Thank you. You are so kind to have us to stay with you. Have you heard from Herr Doktor Zaleski?"

"Only the message that you were to arrive separately. These young men belong to you?"

"Oh, yes. Excuse me. My sons, Rudi, the new Baron von Schoenenburg, and Christian. And this is our dear friend Max Hoffman."

After shaking hands with the boys, their host said, "Andrzej related your recent tragedy, Baroness. You have my sincere condolences. You are a very brave woman to come on to England under the circumstances."

"We really had very little choice," she said.

He raised an eyebrow. "I am eager to hear your story, but first, you must get out of your wet things." He looked at the three suitcases. "This is all of your luggage?"

"Yes. We weren't in Switzerland long enough to buy many things."

"Stinson will show you to your rooms. The chambermaid will have fires lit directly. It is chilly and damp, but that is England for you." Grinning, he gave a shrug. "We'll have tea in the drawing room on the first floor when you're ready. I am anxious to hear an account of your journey."

Amalia would much rather have had a nap, but she was so grateful to have found their host welcoming and genial that she readily agreed to tea. The bedroom she was shown was spacious, with heavy, old-fashioned mahogany furniture. The walls were hung with cream wallpaper figured in brown, matching the drapes, bedhangings, and counterpane. It was not a cheery room.

&

Andrzej arrived in Paris having slept heavily throughout the night. He felt the need of a shave and fresh clothing acutely.

The morning was beautiful and clear, with a breeze blowing pink blossoms about on the wind. It was not Andrzej's first time in Paris. He had been there as an emissary when he was attached to the Polish government, and he loved the city.

Looking up at the clear periwinkle sky, he wished Amalia were with him. He had wished it every time he had visited the place, with its bold, tree-lined boulevards, neo-classical architecture, and romantic walks along the River Seine. God willing, he would be with her again tomorrow in London. Proceeding to the ticket stall, he purchased passage through to Rennes on a train leaving that afternoon and went off in search of a barber and haberdasher. Though he was proceeding to London by an indirect route, his confidence was growing that he had eluded Colonel Dietrich. Though he hated the man intensely, he didn't want to have to kill him. Just on the off chance that he was still being followed, he took a taxi to an *arrondissement* on the other side of Paris. Finding a barber's quaint but clean establishment, he tried to relax as he was shaved.

How was Amalia faring? Had she and the boys reached England yet? Had they been able to find Fotheringill without difficulty?

He ached with the knowledge of what she must be enduring. Going to England without Rudolf had certainly never been the plan. And now she had the added anxiety of Dietrich's pursuit. He longed to take away her grief with his love, but knew it was impossible. She had to endure this soul-wracking torment. As the barber placed a steaming towel over his face, he prayed that he could be patient.

After his shave, he purchased fresh linen. During a late breakfast, he perused the newspaper. Someone in the offices of the tabloid was clearly championing Churchill, as his speech to the House of Commons upon the invasion of Austria was reprinted in there, as well.

Andrzej folded the newspaper and decided he must stay away from the train station until the very last moment in case Dietrich was lurking. Hopefully, the man had no clue that he was headed for London ultimately, but Andrzej couldn't take the chance that he might be followed.

Andrzej clenched his fist as he reflected on the Nazi barbarism. How could the world look on as thugs and bullies rose to power and threatened to take them back centuries to a time before modern civilization?

{9}

Mr. Fotheringill's drawing room was large and daunting, with its heavy wood paneling and enormous fireplace. The drapes and carpet were dark ruby, the only light being provided by the small electric bulbs in two chandeliers. Amalia preferred things to be light in color and had refurbished the von Shoenenburgs' town Palais in ivory and gold leaf. Now, with the gloom outside and the darkness within, she was feeling very out of her natural element.

Her host was exceedingly kind, however. The tea was lavish—scones, cream, raspberry jam, both ham and chicken sandwiches, as well as lemon biscuits. Rudi and Chris, though very polite, managed to eat several sandwiches apiece as well as a good portion of the scones and cream. Fortunately, Mr. Fotheringill seemed to have no antiquated notions about Max eating in the kitchen, which would have set them off entirely on the wrong foot.

They spoke only briefly of Rudolf's death, but at some length about his career in the ministry and the gradual descent of Austria into fascism.

"Zaleski has written that you have some information that you think Churchill ought to have."

Amalia squirmed uncomfortably. "Yes, we do." She felt reluctant to speak of the Berchtesgaden conversation with this man she didn't know. Andrzej trusted him, but Amalia had been badly betrayed before—by those in her own family.

"Never mind. I won't press you for it. I realize you still need to learn to trust me."

Stinson entered the room holding a silver salver. "A cable for the baroness."

Amalia rose hastily and met him partway across the room. Thanking the butler, she slit open the cable and read it, her back to the room.

AM SAFE IN RENNES STOP HOPE TO CROSS TOMORROW STOP LOVE A STOP

Relief flooded Amalia in a wave. Blood pounded in her ears. Safe! But why in Rennes?

Turning, she saw four faces staring at her. "Dr. Zaleski is safe in Rennes. He hopes to make the crossing tomorrow. Where is Rennes?"

"It is the capital city of Brittany. Not far from the coast. Curious," Mr. Fotheringill mused. "I wonder what he is doing there?"

Max said, "I encouraged him to take a circuitous route with that Gestapo colonel on his tail. He must be trying to elude him."

"A devious route, to be sure. It will take a good portion of the day for him to make it to Calais tomorrow for the crossing," Anthony said. "Anything but main railway routes are devilishly slow in France."

&

Rudi observed his mother's white face and her eyes as they darted about distractedly. Her anxiety was clear. Though he was jealous on his father's behalf, he couldn't bear to see her so unstrung.

"Mutti, come have some more tea. I am certain all will be well. I feel sure the doctor has nine lives."

"Hah!" exclaimed Mr. Fotheringill. "In the trenches, we nicknamed him 'The Cat.' He used up at least five of his lives when I was serving with him. Took the most potentially disastrous chances but always landed on his feet. You are right, Baron. He does know how to handle himself in a crisis."

Rudi watched as a tiny smile formed on his mother's face. He was positive she was lost in some memory.

Chris asked, "What are you smiling about, Mutti?"

Her eyes took on a faraway look. "When I was a girl, we had a black cat with green eyes that used to crawl along the garden wall. For the longest time, Dr. Zaleski reminded me of that cat."

Mr. Fotheringill said, "You know, Zaleski never told me how you met."

His mother reseated herself between himself and Chris. "We met at a coffee house near the University in 1913. I asked him if he thought there would be a war. He said he was not overly concerned or interested in the subject. The only thing he would talk of was Poland."

Fotheringill laughed. "How very like him. We all thought him a dreamer, you know. We never thought there would be another Poland."

Chris asked for an explanation, and as the doctor's friend gave him a short history lesson on the origin of the modern Polish state, Rudi's mind drifted. He took his mother's slim hand in his. It was her left hand. She still wore her wedding ring—a broad gold band. It heartened him that she hadn't removed it.

Later, when they went upstairs, he lingered outside his mother's door as she entered.

"Rudi?" she asked. "Did you wish to talk?"

"Did you love Father?" he blurted, still standing in the doorway.

She walked to him and grasped his hands, her brow puckered as she looked into his eyes. "What a question! You know I did. Very much, darling." She paused. "I think you had better come in and sit down."

When he did as she asked, she continued, "You have no idea how much it pains me that you would have to ask such a question. If you are wondering about my relationship with Dr. Zaleski, it dates from another time in my life. It was over before I married, and I loved your father completely. Never doubt that."

"I remember the doctor coming to the house when Chris was clubbed by the Nazis."

"I sent him away then, Rudi."

"But you won't send him away now." Even he could hear the hollowness in his voice.

She rose and switched on the bedside lamp. Turning, she faced him squarely.

"Your father knew there was a chance he might not make it to Switzerland. In that event, he wished Dr. Zaleski to look after us. This business with Churchill . . . even a baroness and former cabinet minister's wife would not be taken seriously. And I speak no English."

Rudi paced the room, unsure what he wanted to say. Things would be difficult for a woman alone, it was true.

"He loves you, Mutti," he said finally.

Walking over to the window, his mother parted the drapes and looked down to the street. This action had become a habit with her. After several minutes, she turned to face him again. "At the moment, my feelings for him are all associated with an earlier time in my life. That is only natural. He was my first love, Rudi."

Agitated by this declaration, he rose. He could not look at her.

Walking to him, she placed her hands on his shoulders. "You also have to realize that our world has changed completely over the last week. So many life-changing events have happened and we are all reeling. My grief for your father is very deep and very real." She drew him close and lowered her head to rest on his chest. "I, at least, was somewhat prepared to lose him, though I wonder if one can ever really be prepared for such a loss. You were not prepared at all." She hugged him fiercely. "The fact is he is gone. So is our home, our country. It is hard to take in. Almost impossible."

Raising her head, she looked him in the eye, and he saw determination there. "But one thing I have learned in my life is that the days go on, whether we want them to or not. Time is relentless. And our family still has a purpose. We must regroup, here in England. We must hope that someone will fight Hitler and win—that someday we will at least get our home and our country back."

His heart heavy, Rudi nevertheless tried to rise to her expectations. "I will do what I can, of course. But right now, I feel so helpless."

She let him go and walked a short distance from him. "So do I, darling. But there are things I have to do. Things your father wanted me to do. Do not blame me for going on with my life. I feel rather as though I am groping in a heavy fog at the moment, but this is not the first time I have lost everything."

For a moment, Rudi found he was able to view his mother as a person in her own right. Not simply his mother or his father's wife. Suddenly he saw himself as he was—a self-centered child. His mother's life had been fraught with trials. The trials had not broken her.

She continued. "We will never lose the good memories, and we can only hope that the horror of the night on the mountain will dim with time. We must try to find hope, Rudi. I am trying, but I admit it is terribly difficult." For a moment, she stopped, and he saw tears fill her eyes. As they spilled over, he quietly offered her his handkerchief.

"I don't think anything tries the soul more than the death of someone you love," she said as she gained some control. "Even though we are struggling in darkness now, we have to believe there is light out there somewhere."

Rudi's jaw hardened in an effort to restrain his own tears. He admired his mother tremendously for what she had overcome, but when he looked into the future, he did not see light.

In fact, he hoped this meeting with Churchill would bring them nearer to war. He wanted to be the one to put a bullet through Hitler's power-mad brain.

6

Hannah first saw Oxford through the rising morning mist and thought the city must be enchanted. Fairy-tale-spired towers rose as far as she could see in the foggy dawn. Though they were roofed variously in gray slate, the colleges were all constructed using golden-colored stone. Each of the many buildings had a garden of bright flowers.

As the mist evaporated, the town transformed into a throbbing center. A plethora of bicycles thronged the lanes, and loud red buses charged through the streets, seemingly mindless of the automobile traffic. Bells chimed from the chapel towers all at once.

Hannah was thrilled to her toes. She could never be happy about the shootings that had necessitated her leaving Zürich, but she was very happy to be here.

Her family checked into the glamorous Randolph Hotel, and Hannah set out immediately to explore. The first college she ducked into was Christ Church, with its enormous bell tower and cathedral. On the right-hand wall when she entered the church was an impressive and very tragic list of all those scholars of Christ Church who had been killed in the Great War. Hannah felt suddenly ill and, for some reason, guilty. Hundreds of young men!

Were they headed for another war? Rudi's visage flashed into her mind. Would he fight? She was almost certain he would. The thought of seeing his name inscribed on a wall like this somewhere made her clutch her fists in anger. Why should young men have to die like some offering to whet the appetite of older men who wanted an empire? Kaiser Wilhelm, Hitler, Mussolini. Gentile Men! Perhaps there was something in the new field of genetics that would explain the reason why, ever since

Cain and Abel, the male of the species, sought violence and domination.

The thought of scientific research recalled Hannah's goal to mind. If there was another war, penicillin could save thousands, perhaps millions of lives. But not in its current state of development. Someone needed to come up with a way to culture it and deliver it so it could be put to use properly.

Maybe that someone would be Hannah Gluck. Her heart lifted a bit. Maybe that was why she had come to Oxford. Drawing herself up, she made a promise to the young men on the wall that she would give it her very best effort.

{ 10 }

Andrzej just missed the 2:00 p.m. ferry to Folkestone. The train from Rennes had been a local, stopping at too many towns between that city and Calais. Frustrated, he found a quayside café with red-checked tablecloths and ordered onion soup. He ate gazing out at the docks. The savory, cheesy broth restored him somewhat.

All day as he had traveled, his mind had been occupied with thoughts of Amalia. He had come to realize that it was good they had this time apart because he had needed it for the sake of clarity. Ever since Rudolf's murder, he and Amalia had been together almost every waking hour. He had loved Amalia so deeply and for so long that it was difficult for him to see her so distraught with grief without trying to offer her the comfort of his love. But he knew she needed space to grieve in.

Rudolf had been there, years ago and had picked up the pieces of the heart Andrzej had unknowingly broken. She had been grieving then—over him. But in time, she had reconstructed her life around Rudolf. The man had known full well he wasn't her first love, had known she didn't even believe in love any longer. But he had a virtue that Andrzej was only now learning. He was patient with her, and she had learned to love again, once her sorrow over Andrzej was manageable. Andrzej had seen evidence of that love.

Now the irony, of course, was that she was grieving for Rudolf, and Andrzej was the one who needed to cultivate patience. He hoped and believed that there was one important difference, however.

For him, their love was a *grande passion*, simmering just below the surface of their lives. His memories of the time they had spent loving one another with whole hearts had distilled and become an enormous part of his personal history. He prayed it was the same for Amalia,

He knew that, to begin with, neither Eberhard nor Rudolf had ever received the kind of love she had given him, and he had certainly never given it away to another.

Amalia had shared every thought and dream with Andrzej, had loved him without restraint in every way except the giving of her physical body. Eberhard and Rudolf had known her physically, and that had driven him close to madness at the time. Now he continued to hope that she still reserved knowledge of her deepest self for him, as he did for her.

Did she realize how much he had changed? Did she know that he could be patient and loving at the same time? Or was her spirit so damaged that she never wanted to put it at risk again? He would not really blame her if that were so. He had been responsible for hurting her greatly. And losing two husbands left deep wounds.

Getting up, he paid for his meal, left the café, and began walking. Rudolf was a remarkable, heroic man. He deserved to be mourned properly, and Andrzej's presence was not making that easy. He needed to keep his distance more than he had been.

Now, he cast about for ways to spend the next two hours. A street of bordellos held no appeal. The run-down nature of the quayside district reminded him uncomfortably of the War, so he decided to stroll into town. Happening upon an antiquarian bookshop, he walked in, jingling the bell above the door. Two stories high, the inside was dimly lit, with a rolling ladder upon which perched a portly shopkeeper in a black waistcoat. The smell of dust and leather was calming and welcoming.

"Bonjour, monsieur," the man greeted him.

Andrzej nodded and greeted him in return. Wondering if he could perhaps find a gift for Amalia, he stepped to the shelves and began examining the spines of the aged volumes. No, she probably would not appreciate Voltaire.

He had just reached the poetry section when the room darkened slightly. Absently, he looked toward the front display window and stiffened. The unmistakable form of Colonel Dietrich was plainly visible, blocking the light as he squinted into the shop.

Andrzej swore under his breath. He had been certain he wouldn't see the Gestapo colonel again. The man must have guessed his destination and been waiting for him here in Calais, checking every train and ferry load. Andrzej had been so preoccupied in the restaurant, he hadn't even noticed the man. But he was getting entirely too close to Amalia. The time had come to dispatch Dietrich for good, much as Andrzej disliked the idea.

He moved toward the back of the shop, hoping to find another entrance. An untidy office sat through an opening in a dark hallway. In the light of a single bulb hanging from the ceiling, he spotted a gleaming letter opener on the desk. Just the thing. Slipping it into his jacket pocket, he left a handful of Swiss francs on the desk as payment and proceeded further down the hallway.

There was a back door. Sliding out noiselessly, he found himself in an alley. Perfect. There was another alley beside the shop, leading him back out into the streetfront. There he spotted Dietrich as he was about to open the shop door.

Andrzej gave a sharp whistle, which arrested the colonel.

"Looking for me?" the doctor asked.

Dietrich narrowed his eyes and began striding toward him. Andrzej retreated into the alley and pressed himself against the back wall of the bookshop.

When the colonel appeared, he was waving a pistol. Andrzej sprang upon him, chopping the man's wrist with the edge of his hand. But Dietrich unaccountably managed to hold on to the pistol. Swinging toward Andrzej, he said, "If you don't want me to kill you, you will tell me the whereabouts of the Baroness von Schoenenburg now."

"You will kill me anyway," said Andrzej. He focused his eyes on an imaginary man over his enemy's shoulder and stifled a smile. As he had hoped, Dietrich jerked his head around, looking for the doctor's phantom accomplice. But when Andrzej grabbed for the pistol, the colonel looked back at him and, grinning his hideous grin, wrested the weapon out of reach.

"Tell me," he said. "Or I shoot." He aimed high, at Andrzej's shoulder.

The doctor merely shrugged, then swiftly ducked and grasped the colonel at the knees, bringing him down. The pistol went off, but the shot was wild. Andrzej slipped his hand inside his pocket, grasping the letter opener.

Dietrich fired again. Scorching pain raced through the doctor's left arm. He couldn't wait another second. Rolling on top of the colonel, he pinned the man's gun arm with his left hand and, using his right, he brought the letter opener up under Dietrich's ribs with great force, straight into his heart.

The man grunted in surprise. Andrzej, losing strength in his wounded left arm, used both hands to pin the Gestapo agent's pistol hand until his eyes glazed over.

The doctor staggered to his feet, pulling off his jacket. The wound was deep in his biceps and bleeding copiously. He had never taken a life in hand to hand combat, and it revolted him that his knowledge as a surgeon had made it possible for him to do so. But he couldn't have allowed this monster anywhere near Amalia.

With no other choice available to him, he walked through the shop's back door. The black-waistcoated man stood before him, his eyebrows near his hairline.

"*Sacre Mere!*" he said.

"I will be needing a doctor," Andrzej said.

&

When night fell at Fotheringill House, Amalia prepared to receive Andrzej with the help of her host. They ordered a large dinner featuring both guinea fowl and beefsteak. His room was prepared, and it was there, awaiting her dinner, that Amalia kept her vigil. It was another bleak room, furnished in unrelieved dark olive green with the same heavy furniture as her own.

Now felt much like the time she had waited for Andrzej to come home from the Great War. They had been engaged when he had gone off to fight, over a year before the war's end. Six months after the armistice, he still hadn't arrived in Vienna. He had been fighting for Austria's enemy, so there was no official telegram or mail. She had concluded he was dead until a mutual friend wrote of seeing him in Warsaw. Disbelief, pain, and anger had made up her terrible grief. It was years before she had learned that her brother had confiscated Andrzej's letters and her own. By then, she had been married to Rudolf for thirteen years.

Amalia had imagined horrible things when he didn't come home from the war, and now her mind was working in the same manner. She had just lost her husband. She hardly had her feet under her. Andrzej was the great love of her youth. Perhaps, given a while, they might love again, but they were living in different times.

As long as Dietrich was out there, she knew Andrzej was not safe. Her anxiety was exquisite, but just like last time, she had no choice but to live through it.

Even in the whirl of her anxiety over Andrzej, she still grieved over her husband's death. It wasn't so long ago that she couldn't feel his strong, dependable body and his arms about her in the final waltz they had enjoyed, not knowing it was to be the night he died. She needed him here now—solid and steady—to see her through this frightening time as he had seen her through so many others.

With tears in her eyes, she wandered impatiently to the window, as she did every five minutes, to look down into the street, willing Andrzej's taxi to appear. She felt like two different creatures. Andrzej and Rudolf were as unalike as two men could be. Whereas Andrzej had always been very frank, her husband had been loath to express feelings. For all but the last five years of their marriage, he wouldn't admit to loving her or even needing her. Only after reaching through Rudolf's tremendous reserve had she been able to find a man she could love. His dedication to her political causes in spite of his own reservations had long proved his bear-like devotion.

Unlike Rudolf, Andrzej was handsome and dashing, possessed of great physical strength—a panther: sleek but powerful. She had loved him practically from the moment they met.

Both men were heroic in their own individual ways. How could love for both of them co-exist in her grieving soul? She was so confused.

When the doctor hadn't arrived by dinnertime, they ate without him. The tension was thick, though Mr. Fotheringill kept up a lively discussion about the British royal family and the abdication of Edward VIII.

"Heaven only knows what the attraction of Wallis Simpson is. She is very masculine looking and by all accounts quite pushy. Add to all that her questionable politics," Fotheringill grimaced. "Perhaps it is as well for the country that he abdicated, for now that they are the Duke and Duchess of Windsor, it is said that they are supporters of Hitler and the Nazi movement," he concluded.

"How dreadful. Just how popular are the Nazis here in Britain?" Amalia asked.

"They have their enthusiasts. Many people sympathize with the Germans because of the inequities of the Versailles Treaty. And they think Hitler has brought much-needed order to the country. Order and purpose some of them wish to see here. They see him as a bastion against Bolshevism. And, of course, no one wants another war."

Rudi said, "Father used to say that that treaty was to blame for much of Hitler's appeal. It emasculated Germany, and their Führer is offering to restore the Fatherland."

Mr. Fotheringill agreed. "I have always feared that that treaty made another war inevitable. There was no way Germany was going to buckle under it."

Rudi asked, "Are you allowed to tell us about where you work?"

"I'm one of the undersecretaries to Lord Halifax, our Foreign Secretary. That's how I've been able to keep Zaleski in the picture about what is taking place in Britain these days."

"How does Lord Halifax feel about Hitler?" Amalia asked.

"He thinks there's more to him than a raving maniac. The problem is that our ambassador to Germany, Neville Henderson, is feeding Halifax and the Prime Minister pap. Henderson considers himself an expert on the German people and doesn't believe they will tolerate Hitler for long. It's a subject I'm not quite reasonable about."

"I can certainly understand that," Amalia said.

She digested this information with discomfort. If the Foreign Ambassador to Germany wasn't giving his government the true picture, it was more understandable that Britain had done little to stop Hitler.

"How discouraging," she added.

"How can Henderson so misjudge Hitler?" Rudi asked.

"He thinks he understand the Germans in a way no lesser being is capable of. Do you know what he wrote Lord Halifax following the *Anschluss*?"

"I've no idea," said Amalia.

"I believe I can remember exactly. Halifax had asked Henderson to protest the German action to his good friend Goering. Instead, Henderson reported to the Foreign Office that he quote agreed with Goering that Chancellor von Schuschnigg had acted with precipitate folly endquote."

Amalia gritted her teeth. Finally, she said, "I suppose that was meant to refer to the very legal plebiscite he meant to hold about whether Austria should join Germany? And what was the Foreign Office response?"

"Halifax was furious," Fotheringill said, frowning. "This is typical of the problems we have with Henderson. Halifax wrote back that Henderson's reaction had substantially diminished the protest he was instructed to make."

Amalia clenched her fists in her lap. Her country was cannibalized, her husband was murdered, and a proper protest had not even been made by Britain.

"Would it be possible for me to get in to see Lord Halifax? I would like to tell him the true story of the *Anschluss*."

Fotheringill said, "I was going to suggest it, actually. I think he would be very interested in your view of Germany. Henderson has repeatedly tried to convince the Foreign Office to tread lightly—that the German moderates, supposedly represented by Goering, have a real chance of dominating policy making. He really believes Hitler to be without support from the majority of the people."

"How can the man be so blind?" Amalia protested. "Hitler is Germany! And Goering not only worships him but defers to him in everything!"

"Well, I can see I definitely must get you in to see Halifax."

"Will he listen to a woman? Does he speak German?"

"I will translate for you. And you are not just any woman. You are the Baroness von Schoenenburg."

Amalia gave a tight smile. She was growing agitated with the conversation. She glanced at the door. "What can be keeping Andrzej?"

Christian said, "He may have had to make another detour, Mutti, if that Gestapo colonel is on his tail."

"If he doesn't arrive tonight, we will get another cable, Mutti," Rudi assured her. "He will not let you worry."

A cable did indeed arrive. Amalia alone was awake, in the drab brown and gray sitting room at the front of the house, mending a tear in Rudi's shirt, when the door knocker sounded near midnight. His master at a Foreign Office reception, Stinson had been instructed to wait up for the doctor. The butler brought her the message on his silver salver.

She fairly snatched it up, opening it hastily.

"HAVE BEEN DETAINED STOP DIETRICH DEAD STOP LOVE A."

Amalia took a long slow breath. He was safe. It took a moment for the reality to sink in that the colonel was dead. It took a further few minutes to realize Andrzej must have killed him.

Detained. That suggested the police. Who else could detain him? Worry gnawed at her stomach once more. The cable originated in Calais. He had gotten that far, at least. But should she not go to him? If he was being held, her witness in his favor against Dietrich and his persecution of her family would be necessary.

Amalia walked in circles about a room that had grown cold with the death of the fire, kneading her hands together.

I've got to do something! Perhaps I can convince Mr. Fotheringill to go with me. He fought alongside Andrzej in France. That has to stand for something.

&

Andrzej had bribed his jailer to send a cable to Amalia. That worry off his mind, he turned his thoughts to his wound. His arm was bound with a dirty linen towel, which was all the bookseller had had on hand. Though it was no longer bleeding, it was damnably sore. He guessed the bullet was lodged next to the bone.

The bookseller had not been well disposed toward Andrzej and had phoned for the police rather than a doctor. Apparently the letter opener had been an heirloom. Monsieur Guison had taken umbrage at its theft and subsequent use as a murder weapon.

Murder. Andrzej had to face the fact that he had just committed murder, though it had been in self-defense. He wasn't some swashbuckling hero. He was a surgeon. He saved lives.

Then Amalia and her sons came back into his mind, and the reality that he had saved their lives revisited him. He had not written Dietrich's agenda. The bully had brought his death upon himself by going after those Andrzej loved. And, yes, he would kill him again if he had to make the choice.

Nevertheless, the police interrogation had not gone well.

"You have an accent," the Sûreté officer had said. "What country are you from?"

"I am Polish."

"You say this man was an agent of the Gestapo. Why would he be after a Pole? He has no identification. How do we even know he was who you say he was?"

"He probably has a Gestapo tattoo on the inside of his arm. He orchestrated an ambush a week ago in Austria, killing a former member of the Austrian cabinet whom I was helping to escape."

"Not an easy story to check. Why would he want to kill you?"

Deciding to keep the explanation as simple as possible, Andrzej answered, "I was a witness to the murder of the Cabinet Minister Baron von Schoenenburg by the Nazis."

The police officer gave a Gallic shrug. "And who cares about that? Austria is ruled by the Nazis now. I suppose they can kill whom they like."

In the end, they had escorted him to this cozy cell with a filthy cot, a washstand, and a bucket.

Perhaps the cable should have gone to Fotheringill. If anyone could get him out of the mess, it was his former comrade-in-arms.

Now, hours later, as he lay on the disgusting mattress, Andrzej's teeth chattered with an overwhelming chill. A fever was setting in. He covered himself as closely as he could with the thin, rough blanket.

When he finally fell asleep, nightmares plagued him. He was upstairs in his childhood home in Poland. A snowstorm blew in through the open window. Amalia was at his side as he shot at a platoon of Nazis assaulting his house in waves. As soon as one machine gun was empty, Amalia would hand him another. But they kept coming. And coming.

{ 11 }

Amalia had noted that her host tended to breakfast early. She was there to meet him the next morning with the cable she had received the night before.

"Detained?" Mr. Fotheringill asked, one blond brow raised.

"I think he must be being held by the police for the murder of Dietrich, the Gestapo colonel. It is my idea to go to Calais at once."

He gave a short nod. "He undoubtedly needs a character reference. I think I should go, as well."

"Do you mind if my sons remain here?"

"Of course not. I believe it would be best." He finished eating his boiled egg and threw down his napkin. "How soon can you be ready?"

Relieved that he saw the seriousness of the situation, Amalia said, "I have already packed a small suitcase."

Within the hour, they were on their way to Folkestone in Mr. Fotheringill's Bentley. Amalia had acquainted Rudi and Chris with the situation, and they assured her they would find plenty to do exploring London. Both had wished their mother good luck.

Now that she knew Andrzej was alive, she had more attention to spare for her host. His face always seemed somewhat vacuous, though she guessed he was in pain much of the time. His conversation the night before had shown him to be perceptive.

If she could make some headway in getting to know him during this journey, it would certainly give her something else to think about.

"Are your parents living, Mr. Fotheringill?"

"Unfortunately, no. They both died of the influenza after the War."

"That was a ghastly time," Amalia said. "I'm so sorry. Have you siblings?"

"Two. My sister is Warden at Somerville, a women's college in Oxford. My brother lives at the family seat in Somerset. He takes care of the estate. I'm the middle child—the only one to prefer Town."

"It is very nice of you to offer us a place to stay. The boys and I shall have to find one of our own, I suppose."

"You plan to remain in London, then?"

"Yes, I believe so. That was Rudolf's intent, if Zürich did not prove safe. Your sister must be quite a scholar," Amalia remarked. "I had no idea there was a women's college at Oxford."

"Irene is a classicist."

"I hope to meet her someday. I went to University for a while. I studied history."

"I thought Zaleski said you were a nurse."

"I trained on the job for that, during the War. I found University to be a disappointment. No one had a modern vision specifically for what was left of Austria."

Mr. Fotheringill glanced over at her. "But you did. Zaleski wrote that you wanted a democracy. That you convinced your husband to go into government to back the idea."

So Andrzej had written of her. What else did the man know about them? Thinking of Rudolf, she sighed heavily. "I did. It seemed the only government plan that would save poor Austria from a war or a revolution from the right or the left. I wanted us to stand with the Western powers. That obviously didn't work out so well."

"Where did you come by your ideas?"

She found herself telling him of her unusual background as the daughter of a middle-class burgher, the great-granddaughter of a count, and the niece of a famous socialist who encouraged her to think.

"I was also married to a Prussian officer during the Great War. I became very opposed to the Prussian war ethic that Hitler has taken as his model for his army. I hold it responsible for the misery we all suffered in the Great War and may suffer in one to come."

"It is very important to understand that, I agree. English people tend to think all rational people think like they do. It is an affliction, I feel. The British, the French, the German—each people thinks it is superior."

For a while, they remained comfortably silent, viewing the spring green of the lush Kentish countryside. Finally, Amalia asked, "Have you ever been married, Mr. Fotheringill?"

"Yes, Baroness. I am married, as a matter of fact. But my wife has never appreciated being married to an amputee. We have lived apart since the War."

"Oh! I am sorry!" Amalia was appalled. So many men had died; how could the woman not be grateful just to have her husband alive? Their conversation foundered. He rescued it by asking her, "I would really like to learn more of your husband, Baroness. If it doesn't grieve you to speak of him."

She thought for a moment. How would she describe Rudolf to a stranger?

"If you had met him, you would undoubtedly think him stern and rather stuffy. But he had a softer side. As a matter of fact, I met him through one of my uncle's charities. For years, the von Schoenenburgs had been principal patrons of an orphanage for boys in Vienna. My uncle gave a large part of his fortune to them, and they met when Uncle Lorenz sat on the board."

"Your uncle sounds a generous man."

"He was wonderful. I have never known another human being like him." Amalia smoothed her gloves, thinking of Uncle Lorenz and how much she had loved him. He had been like a father to her and had understood her better than either of her parents. "He introduced me to Rudolf. I was a silly young debutante without enough to do, so Uncle thought I might like to have a story hour for the orphans a couple of times a week. We used to see each other at the orphanage."

"That is a unique story."

"He used to call himself my 'maiden aunt.' He was always watching out for me. I married him after the War." Those few words skipped over so much: Rudolf's management of her brother, one of his officers, when Wolf was in a deep depression over losing his leg, his championship of her going to University, his solace and understanding over the break with Andrzej.

"And he served in the government as a cabinet minister," her companion added.

"Yes. He tried to be the voice of reason when no one would listen. It wasn't an easy job. The Nazis and the Socialists were at each other's throats, and the government stood in the middle."

"And the Nazis finally used the Red threat to trump the Socialists. That must have been very rough for you, Baroness."

"Yes. It wasn't hard to see the writing on the wall. It was the identical strategy Hitler used in Germany."

For a few moments there was silence, then Mr. Fotheringill said thoughtfully, "The great empires left a power vacuum. It is the curse of our age that we allowed it to be filled by dictators."

She didn't tell him that Rudolf thought he'd failed her and failed Austria, that he had gone to his death as a martyr. It was far too painful a subject to discuss with this man she was only beginning to know.

Folkestone was a hive of activity as the next ferry prepared to cast off. Amalia and her companion scarcely had time to drive the Bentley on board. She was very glad they had gotten one of the last spaces, as the next wasn't due to leave until noon.

&

After making inquiries at the Radcliffe Infirmary, where patients from Oxford were treated, Hannah learned that research with penicillin was going nowhere at this point, but researchers were having some luck with sulfonamide drugs at the William Dunn School of Pathology down the road at Oxford. Hannah was given the name of Dr. Norman Heatley.

With some trepidation at her boldness, she walked in the heavy door of the red brick facility and asked to speak to Dr. Heatley. A medium-sized man with short black hair wearing large glasses and a lab coat met her in the lobby of the school.

"Miss Gluck?"

She extended her hand to shake his square one and spoke in English, which she had studied intensely in preparation for her career. "Thank you for seeing me, Dr. Heatley. I have been following your articles in various medical journals and am a great admirer of yours. Someday, I hope to join you in your research of the development of penicillin. I intend to study biochemistry here at Oxford."

He looked her up and down. "You are a German?"

"Austrian."

"You have followed the development of Protonsil?"

"That is the sulfa drug you are working on now."

"Yes. If you are truly interested, you might as well come back and see what we are doing. It doesn't have the properties I hope to find when we unearth a way for the wide distribution of penicillin; however, we are having a lot of success with its strong protective action against infections caused by streptococci."

As he entered the lab, which was far grander than anything Hannah had seen, he quizzed her about her background. She told him about her private research and her undergraduate work as a biochemist at University of Zürich.

She had brought a folder documenting some of her own experiments, and after Dr. Heatley glanced over it, he showed her a seat and talked to her about the direction of her research and what steps she might take in the future.

"I am very impressed, Fraülein Gluck. "I would like to hire you as a lab assistant. We are creeping up on these phenomena and they are demonstrating their powers to us. I feel almost like an old-fashioned alchemist. Imagine! Protonsil started out as a dye. Penicillin as an orange mold. How many other elements in the universe are hiding healing properties? I must admit I am alternately intrigued and frustrated by the process. We discover the most surprising things by trial and error."

Hannah had never imagined she would be welcomed with such open arms with only her scanty qualifications. She was overwhelmed by the man. "Thank you so much for the opportunity. I assure you I appreciate it."

"I am determined to launch a new study on penicillin next year with a group of scientists right in this lab. I do not like the way the political wind is blowing. We will be greatly in need of these ways of treating infection in the next ten years, if not sooner."

"I feel certain you are right."

"Well, then. As it happens, I am shorthanded. Can you begin today?"

Hannah agreed with enthusiasm.

Andrzej heard Fotheringill's voice coming from the front of the police station late in the afternoon. At first he thought it a fever dream, but soon, his friend was shown to his cell. To his surprise, Amalia accompanied him. His heart lifted at her appearance. He only hoped she was not a hallucination.

"Andrzej!" she said, putting her hand through the bars. "What has happened to your arm? That's a filthy bandage." She shifted her hand to his forehead. "You are burning with fever!"

Her hand was blessedly cool, her face drawn with concern for him. The demons in his mind fled in her presence. She was real. Thank God.

The arresting officer accompanied his visitors. Andrzej decided it would be *politik* to speak in French. "Dietrich must have figured out where I was headed. He was waiting here for me at the docks. He was looking for you and evidently decided to shoot me to gain my cooperation." He looked at his arm in disgust. "I go through the War without a scratch and then let that joker do this. Unfortunately, since I wasn't talking, he turned lethal, and I had to kill him or be killed."

"Well, this could be plenty lethal if you don't get it taken care of." She turned to the Frenchman. "I am the Baroness von Shoenenburg from Vienna," she said. Andrzej almost smiled as she assumed her most imperious air. "I am also a nurse. Please let me into Dr. Zaleski's cell at once. He is suffering from a high fever." She strode closer to the man so she looked directly into his eyes. "He is no murderer! Now, go immediately and bring me hot water and first aid supplies. I know you must have some here."

The Frenchman gave a short bow and scurried away.

Though his arm felt it was on fire and his head was drumming like an oompah-pah band, Andrzej managed a smile. It was good to see Amalia's baroness persona reemerge after all her recent travails.

"Don't worry, old man," Fotheringill said. "I'll get you out of here. Tell us what happened."

Andrzej managed to stumble to the washstand, splashed his face with water from the sink, and, holding a bit of water in his curved palm, drank it. He repeated the action until his throat felt as though he could do more than croak. He related the story of the demented Dietrich, the poisonous bookseller, and his benighted letter opener.

Finally, the officer returned with a bowl of hot water and a first aid kit. Handing the bowl to Amalia, he unlocked the cell. When she had entered, he gave her the kit and locked both of them in.

"Now, then," Fotheringill said to the jailer, removing something from his pocket. "Do you recognize this, my good man?"

Andrzej watched the scene as Amalia unwound the bandage.

The Frenchman's eyes grew large. "It is the Victoria Cross, the highest medal of honor for valor in the British army."

"Yes. You are correct. I am Major Anthony Fotheringill. The only reason I was alive to receive this medal is because of this man you have imprisoned. Doctor Andrzej Zaleski is Polish, but he fought alongside the British and the French in the trenches. He saved my life, carrying me out of No Man's Land on his back. He is a great hero. He has medals of his own."

As Amalia probed his inflamed flesh for the bullet, Andrzej clenched his teeth, but in the end was powerless to prevent himself from fainting. When he regained consciousness, he was lying on the cot, neatly stitched up and rebandaged. The cell door stood open.

"I wish you could have heard my account of Dietrich's sins," Amalia said in German. "But that bullet was deep, so it is just as well you swooned."

"Milles pardones, Monsieur le doctor. You are free to go. I am sorry you had this ordeal," the French police officer said with a bow.

However, as Andzrej attempted to rise, his head spun and he fell back against the cot in weakness. He was drenched in sweat but shaking with cold.

Amalia spoke to Fotheringill in quick German. "We must get him to a hotel where at least it is clean. You and the Frenchman will have to carry him between you to the car."

Andrzej grimaced with pain as he was hoisted between his friend and the policeman and dragged out to the street.

"This is absurd," he murmured once he was settled in the front seat of the Bentley. "It is only a bullet wound in the arm."

"That rag you were bound with was filthy." Amalia's voice was stiff with anger. "I don't know where it came from, but there were rat droppings in the folds. We'll get you some broth at the hotel, and a good night's sleep. Then we'll leave this blighted country in the morning. Imagine! Locking you up when you clearly had a defensive wound!"

&

Amalia had nursed many types of wounds during the war, particularly when she lived in Germany. She knew a serious infection when she saw it, and Andrzej's wound caused her more concern than she demonstrated. Rarely had she seen a wound fester so terribly in such a short space of time. Blood poisoning was most often lethal. She did not intend to lose Andrzej to such an affliction. She would not even allow herself to consider it.

Mr. Fotheringill chose a fine, elegant hotel situated away from the docks. They managed to get Andrzej up to a well-appointed room, and she breathed a sigh of relief once his friend had taken over the removal of Andrzej's soiled clothing and settled him in between crisp, white, ironed sheets.

While that was taking place, Amalia went down to the desk and arranged to send a cable to Rudi and Chris.

DR WOUNDED BY DIETRICH STOP DANGEROUS INFECTION STOP MUST REMAIN HERE STOP CONTACT US HOTEL GRILLON IF NEEDED STOP LOVE MUTTI

After ordering clear broth for Andrzej and a beefsteak dinner for Mr. Fotheringill to be brought up to the room, Amalia went back upstairs. Andrzej was sleeping, his cheeks flush with fever.

While she awaited their food, she couldn't resist stroking his face, which showed a stubble of dark, heavy beard. She reflected that in the time she had known him, he had gone from a hardened society flirt to a brilliant surgeon. From there, he had apparently become a courageous soldier fighting for his beloved Poland. When he returned from war, he had thrown himself into helping to establish his new state, suffered a painful marriage to a woman who had deceived him, and returned to Austria to try to win Amalia back. But leaving her husband was never an option for her. After saving Rudolf's life during a brief period of hostilities in their country, Andrzej had shown his respect for her wishes and returned to Poland—until he knew her family to be in danger. Then, with the devotion that had grown so steady over so many years, he had returned and risked his own life not only for her, but for Rudolf, Rudi, and Christian.

Now, she must not indulge negative thoughts. He was going to pull through. They had things to accomplish.

"How much has Andrzej told you about our past, Mr. Fotheringill?" she asked his friend, who was sitting in an easy chair near the window.

"Enough to know that there will never be another woman in his life," Mr. Fotheringill said. "And I think by now you must call me Anthony."

"And you must call me Amalia." She smiled a little. "I am very concerned about him, Anthony. That rag he was wrapped in was poisonous to his system. This infection is serious."

At that moment, there was a knock on the door and their dinner arrived. Anthony had the table set up at the foot of the bed.

"Amalia, you must eat. You've had nothing since breakfast."

"I'm stronger than I look. I am more concerned about getting Andrzej to take some broth. He needs his strength."

With a cold cloth on his face, she woke him gently.

"Amalia . . ." he said. "My love . . ."

"You must take some broth, Andrzej. You need to fight this."

She succeeded in getting him to sip most of the bowl of liquid. Then she checked his bandage and settled him for the night.

"I'm going to stay with him," she told Anthony. "I need to wake him at intervals to take some liquid. He is becoming very dehydrated."

"How about if you take the first watch?" Anthony asked. "I'll come in at one o'clock and relieve you."

Amalia agreed, but had no intention of going to bed when Anthony came. As a nurse, she knew these hours were critical. The progression of the infection was frightening and, despite her determination to save him, she had seen nothing to reassure her that it was not going to end in death.

She could not share this with Anthony. She couldn't say it out loud. It would be too like giving up. Looking down at Andrzej's face, pasty white and shiny with sweat, she summoned all the hope of which she was capable.

Oh, God! Don't take him, too!

{ 12 }

Rudi and his brother had come in from a morning horseback ride in Hyde Park, enjoying two Fotheringill geldings that their master had obligingly lent them, when he received the disturbing cable from his mother. They had not seen it lying on the table in the vestibule before they went for their ride. It had apparently arrived in the night.

Rudi's reactions upon reading it were a surprise to him. He was very uneasy.

He tried to tell himself that it was because Mutti's mission with Mr. Churchill would be compromised without Zaleski's help. His mother was a formidable woman, but she was a woman. He knew nothing about Churchill. Would the man even grant her an audience?

Of course, there was Fotheringill, who probably carried a far greater amount of influence than an unknown Polish doctor. So that reasoning did not really explain his unease. Grimacing to himself, he went out the French doors into Fotheringill House's back garden. Bees buzzed about the clump of sweet peas and stalks of hollyhock. He sat on a white bench next to the koi pond, focusing on a lily pad.

No. The truth of the matter was that he did not wish his long-suffering mother another loss. And Zaleski was a decent sort. Fotheringill had told him that if it weren't for the doctor's heroics in the war, he would have been left dead on the doorstep of the German trenches.

Rudi couldn't reconcile that fact with his fleeting idea that perhaps Zaleski had set his own father up for murder. It was far more likely that he was a hero. And hadn't he just been shot keeping the repulsive Colonel Dietrich from finding them? That fact alone gave him hero status.

It didn't mean that Rudi didn't still harbor feelings of resentment. But it did mean that he hoped they would fade in time.

His mother, apparently, was an unforgettable female. It was difficult for him to see her in that light. In fact, the whole idea made him uncomfortable. Somehow, she had had the power to keep Zaleski in love with her since years before Rudi had even been born!

Then for some reason, he found himself thinking of Hannah. He had a feeling that someday, she too would be a formidable woman. He had expected that thoughts of her would fade, as thoughts of the girls he had left behind in Vienna had faded. Now he was thinking of her uniqueness and admitted that it was too bad he would never see her again. She didn't share Mutti's timeless elegance, but she was beautiful, intelligent, and assertive. He had no doubt she would achieve her goals and become a biochemist.

He stood, thrusting his hands in his pockets and walking around the small pond. Maybe he would see her again in a few years' time, when she came to study at Oxford. But he knew himself well enough to know that another woman would undoubtedly have caught his eye by then. And perhaps they would be in the midst of a war.

He was really at a loss as to how he had even come to think of her again. Something had put her in his mind. What was that drug she was so passionate about? Pen . . . something. When they had been walking between the dance pavilion and the café, he hadn't really been listening all that closely, but hadn't she said something about it being a potential breakthrough wonder drug for the treatment of infections?

Oxford! She had said they were doing experiments with it at Oxford. How far was Oxford? Maybe if he could get there somehow, they could give him a bit of it. Wasn't there at least a small chance that he could get some to treat Zaleski's infection?

Undoubtedly, it was a hare-brained idea. But Rudi owed the man something. What if he died having killed Dietrich for them? Picking up his steps, he walked into the house in search of Stinson.

Half an hour later, Rudi had followed the butler's hand-drawn map to the train station and was boarding the next train for Oxford. He had remembered the name of the drug. Penicillin.

Max was appalled at what he was hearing from the German ex-pat socialist who had lived in the English capital for five years. They were lunching at a working man's pub in the city's East End. He could hardly credit what he was hearing.

"The aristocrats, they're all for this Hitler."

"That can't be true," Max said. "Don't they know he despises the upper classes?"

"They're scared of the Bolshies, and they think he's done great things for Germany. They've seen films. All his parades, all the flags, all those soldiers marching. *Triumph of the Will*, one of them's called."

"I've seen that film. It's terrifying. Don't they realize those soldiers are being trained to goose step right over their country? It won't be anything like the last war. They're building airplanes and tanks by the hundreds. Don't they understand why?"

"Nein. They live in their own little world. They think they can reason with him. They figure he'll let them rule this island themselves and they'll get to wear the smart boots and carry the flags."

"They must be insane," Max said, shaking his head.

"The government, now, that's a different story. They lean more toward our line of thinking."

"But they're just as blind. They let Germany rearm, take back the Rhineland, and invade Austria. What about this Churchill?"

"He's an old Imperialist. He recognizes he and Hitler are on a collision course."

"Except Hitler envisions his empire to be Europe and Britain. I don't think that Churchill's mind is going in that direction."

"No, he's still thinking about India and Singapore. But old Britain's not the same as it was before the War. Too much hard liquor, too many drugs. My feeling is it's become a playground for the rich and when they feel that they need to think seriously about anything, it's either communism or fascism. Crazy world."

"It'll come about," Max said. "Remember the dialectic. Pendular swings."

"I think it's going to take something pretty sobering to bring that about. I only hope it is not a war. But then, again, someone's got to stop Hitler."

"There will be a war, all right," Max predicted. Draining his beer, he left the pub and his friend and took a walk down by the docks. He wished very much at that moment that he possessed a crystal ball.

Rudi found Oxford much to his liking. Old and honey-stoned, with both delicate spires and bold Romanesque towers, it was bustling every bit as much as London, but on a smaller scale. Its architecture soothed the part of him that missed the decorative, grand Vienna.

A sense of purpose and direction appeared to motivate bicyclists and motorists as they charged through the narrow lanes. He inhaled both diesel fumes and a particular sweetness he couldn't identify. He crossed over a bridge and looked down. The river ran with small, flattish boats navigated by young men in white trousers and navy jackets. The men wielded long poles while women reclined at their feet. His mind flashed back to Hannah and the Freiheit. She would be at Oxford someday. For just a moment, he forgot the purpose at hand, imagining the two of them taking their leisure on the river. Hannah would be lovely reclining in the bow of one of those oddly shaped boats. Shaking his head to dismiss the vision, he began looking for some place to have a quick meal.

The Miter was the first place he saw. Entering the hostelry and smelling lamb, he realized how hungry he was. He ordered chops and fried potatoes. All around him sat undergraduates in their black college gowns, laughing, drinking, and enjoying tearing spirits.

As he ate, Rudi wondered what his group of friends was doing at that moment in Austria. Probably being goose-marched through the streets and trained in the dogma and ritual of the Third Reich.

Employing a mime, he enquired of his waiter about the local hospital. The man drew a map, using a page from his order pad. Rudi thanked him.

An undergraduate heard him speaking German and laughingly gave him a Nazi salute, accompanied by a "Sieg Heil!" Rudi frowned and, getting to his feet, walked swiftly out of the restaurant.

Stupid people. They think it is all a joke.

Following the map in his hand, he found his way to the Radcliffe Infirmary. There, by using the word "penicillin," he was given another map, this one directing him to the William Dunn School of Pathology. He had been in such a hurry when he set out on this mission, he had given little thought to the difficulty of making himself understood. His request was going to take more than a mime was capable of conveying.

He found the redbrick building and let himself in. When the porter addressed him, Rudi asked, "Sprechen Sie Deutsch hier?"

Excusing himself, the man disappeared behind a door. As Rudi wandered around the small vestibule, he wondered if he had acted too impulsively. This expedition was more in line with

Chris's personality than something he would do. But all Rudi could think of was his mother's anguish.

Moments later, the door opened again and he saw a familiar face. His heart jolted and he exclaimed, "Hannah! What are you doing here?"

"I work here," she said with a broad smile. "The question is what are you doing here?"

"We just arrived in England a few days ago. Someone close to us has a very bad infection. I remembered what you said about Oxford and penicillin. I thought it was worth a try to see if I could get some."

Her brow puckered. "It must be very serious for you to resort to this. Come back to my office. You must explain everything to me."

Hannah's office was little more than a cubbyhole with a gray metal desk covered in loose papers and medical journals. She sat down behind it, and he took the only other chair.

"What kind of an infection is it?" she asked.

"It's a long story. May I rely on your discretion?"

"Of course, Rudi." Her eyes were worried now.

"There was a Gestapo agent, a Colonel Dietrich, who has been following us with intent to kill my mother and perhaps me and Chris, as well. He nearly found us in Zürich. A friend of our family, Herr Doktor Zaleski, has been traveling with us for protection."

"Not the man I met at the café in Zürich?"

"No. That was Max. At any rate, we escaped while Zaleski led him away from us, but Dietrich caught up with him in France. I don't know the whole story yet, but I would guess the colonel threatened our friend. The colonel is now dead, but Zaleski is wounded. I presume a gunshot, although it could be a knife wound, I suppose. Mother cabled that his infection is serious. She was a nurse, so she knows what she is talking about."

"Oh, dear. How dreadful. So he is in France?"

"Calais. He was just about to make the crossing."

She bit her lip, and in spite of everything he was feeling, he was distracted by her beauty—her long black hair pulled behind her in a knot, accentuating her high cheekbones and large coffee-brown eyes.

"Unfortunately, penicillin research isn't advanced enough that it would be of any use in this case, but there is something else that we are working on that would probably help. There is another class of drugs that can cure many bacterial infections. That is what I am working with now. Sulfa drugs. I can give you some powder. You are supposed to sprinkle it on the wound."

"And it works?"

"I can't tell you from personal experience. But they have been using it here at the hospital and have seen good results."

"That sounds excellent," Rudi said, feeling a rush of relief. "If I can buy some, I must be on my way if I am to catch the night ferry. But I promise I will come back to see you. I wish to find out more about your work."

"Yes. I will look forward to it. I'll just go see Dr. Heatley and explain the situation to him. You don't need to buy the sulfa. We will call it an experiment, though I am ninety-percent certain it will work."

After she had gone, a man who looked to be in his mid-twenties with sandy hair and a red face poked his head in the office and said something in English. Rudi recognized his accent as German.

He replied in his own language, "She has gone for a minute."

The man frowned heavily then entered the room, extended his hand, and said in German, "Reinquist. From Düsseldorf. You are Austrian, ja?"

Rudi shook the man's hand. "Ja. Von Schoenenburg."

"What is your business with Gluck?"

Startled at hearing Hannah referred to in this careless way, he said only, "We are collaborating on some research. I have known her some time."

At that moment, Hannah reappeared in her office.

"Reinquist, I see you've met the baron."

"Ah, Baron, is it? Well, I will leave you to your business."

The scorn on the man's face made Rudi uncomfortable—as though he were a mere youngster.

Hannah brushed off the encounter. "Reinquist is rude. Don't let him bother you."

"Do you happen to know his politics?"

"He isn't fond of Hitler, if that's what you're wondering."

"He isn't fond of me, either."

"He's not fond of many people. That's why he's a scientist. The molds and dyes don't take offense."

She handed him a small pillbox which she had taped shut.

"Now, the sulfa powder is inside. You can use it quite liberally. If I were your mother, I would actually reopen the wound and sift the powder inside."

Rudi stood. "Hannah, I don't know how to thank you. You may have saved my friend's life, just as he has saved my mother's. I am greatly in your debt." He had a strong urge to kiss her in his exuberance, but he restrained himself. Instead, he extended his hand and shook hers. "God bless you in this important work. I am sorry I must hurry away."

"Thank you, Rudi. I will look forward to seeing you again."

"This is far too strange to be coincidence," he said. "Go with God, Hannah."

{ 13 }

Amalia had sat at too many sickbeds in her life. This morning, Andrzej had begun to be delirious, and she realized her nerves were far from steady. He was getting worse. This was not like tending patients during the days when she worked professionally.

The last time she had sat at the bedside of someone she cared for anywhere near this much was when her uncle was dying. Andrzej had been there, treating Uncle Lorenz for what proved to be a fatal heart attack. She had barely known Andrzej then, but she was already in love with him. It had all happened very fast. Amalia had hoped that love would last a lifetime, but she never could have guessed the long and circuitous route that their relationship would take. Looking back at her younger self, she remembered fierce love and perhaps even fiercer heartbreak. Was that love reviving in the midst of her grief, or was she only caught up in the emotions of her younger self, yearning for more uncomplicated times?

While Fotheringill was present, she managed to seem strong and capable, but when he was out of the room, she allowed her memories free rein while bathing Andrzej's face. Her tears fell.

"Do you remember our first waltz, Andrzej?" she whispered. "At the von Altwald's ball? It was our moment. You saw through me and my debutante posings as though I were made of glass. And I saw through you the same way. It frightened you." She gave a little sigh, remembering his discomfiture at having his true, gallant nature exposed.

Amalia hoped her words were registering in some part of his mind. He thrashed between the sheets as the fever worked in his brain.

"Remember the orphanage? How we scrubbed and painted that little room where I told stories to the boys? Then we combed the parish book sale and found all those old books with the marvelous colored plates of the fairy tales. You framed them for me."

Those were the good memories. Then she was swamped by remembered scenes of working next to him in the University Hospital during the war, trying to save the lives of horribly maimed soldiers that came in from the never-ending trains.

As she gazed down at his beloved face, a thought visited her that had never come before. "Do you know that the time we spent working side by side in the hospital remains in my heart as the most satisfying time of my life? Isn't that strange? We hardly spoke, but we worked as one—always anticipating one another's needs and actions. Before that, I knew you only in the social realm. Your skill and compassion as a surgeon were a revelation to me. And you accepted me as a necessary part of your work." Casting her mind back to capture her long-ago feelings, she said with wonder, "I do believe you saw me as an equal in your task, Andrzej. I loved working with you."

She broke off her conversation as she continued her train of thought. She had known during that time that Andrzej loved her not just as a woman, but as a person. He loved her strengths and was not threatened by them. At her times of sorrow or weakness, he showed true empathy, not condescension. Loving Andrzej had made her whole.

Dampening another flannel, she continued washing his face, neck, and chest. Tenderness flooded her, tempered by guilt that she should feel so strongly and, most of all, anxiety over his recovery.

"Andrzej, it is only an infection," she said bracingly. "You survived a war. You can survive this. You must! Don't let Dietrich win. We have too much fighting left to do."

Night fell and Anthony insisted that she go down to the dining room for a meal. "You need a rest from nursing, Amalia. You can be sure I will send for you if there is a change."

Her dinner of Veal Français, *pommes frites*, and spring peas, though well-prepared, was tasteless to her. Every muscle in her neck and shoulders was clenched with tension. Pushing her plate aside, she ordered hot chocolate, hoping it would help her to relax.

Feeling more tired than she could remember, she returned to Andrzej's bedside. Anthony took one look at her and insisted that she go to her room to get some sleep.

"But I feel he is approaching a crisis," she said. "I cannot be away from him, Anthony."

"Then I will watch out for you while you watch out for him."

"That is really not necessary."

"I feel it will take some of the burden off you to know that I am here," he insisted.

"Very well. Thank you."

She spent the next hours making and replacing cold compresses for Andrzej's head. Bathing his chest and arms with cool water, she tried without success to bring his fever down. When she replaced his bandage, she was not surprised at the appearance of greenish-yellow pus oozing from his wound.

God, please! What we need here is a miracle.

Anthony was asleep by the fire in the armchair when Amalia raised her head from a prayer. The clock on the mantle told her it was midnight. Behind her, a door opened.

Surprised, she swung her head around to see her son.

"Rudi! Darling, what are you doing here?" Her mind raced. "Is it Christian? Is he all right?"

Without preamble, he took a small box out of an inner pocket and handed it to her. "Christian is well. I brought you this, Mutti. It is a new drug. You need to reopen the wound and sprinkle this powder inside. The scientists at Oxford have had great success using it to treat infections. It is a bit of a wonder drug."

She looked from the box to his face. "Scientists? Oxford? What are you talking about?"

He pulled a chair up next to hers and threw himself into it. Lines of weariness showed on his young face.

"Do you remember Hannah, the girl I met in Zürich?"

Amalia was only more confused. "Yes? What has this to do with her?"

"She is a biochemist. She told me the latest research on drugs for infection was taking place at Oxford. So I went there today. I was surprised to find her there." He ran a hand through his hair. "I still don't know that story, but she is working with a man who is developing what she called 'sulfa drugs.' As I said, they have had great success. She gave me some for Dr. Zaleski."

She didn't know what was more surprising—the fact that Rudi had cared enough to go to such lengths, or that his efforts had produced results.

Amalia looked at the pill box in her hand. How she wished Andrzej were in a fit state to ask if he consented to the procedure.

From behind her, Anthony spoke. "Well done, Rudi. I have read about these trials. They have been very successful, Amalia. I do think it is worth a try. I think it is what Zaleski would want."

Could this be the miracle I prayed for?

Utterly astounded, she hugged her son as he sat in the chair next to her. "I can never thank you enough for your concern and your actions. God bless you. Dr. Zaleski is very, very ill. I believe I will try this at once."

The procedure was a grisly one. She unwound the bandage and reopened the wound after sterilizing Anthony's penknife. It was a sickening, angry sight. Tapping the edges of the box, she sifted some of the powder into the wound. Because she lacked a sewing kit, she could only tightly re-bandage the site with a fresh strip of linen she had torn from a pillowcase.

It had gone against her training to open the wound. Her hands felt thick and clumsy. But she was strangely hopeful. It was very odd to have Rudi there looking after her. When had he become a man?

"Mutti, how long have you been awake?" Rudi asked when she was finished.

"Don't tell me to rest, darling. I couldn't close my eyes." Turning, she looked at him. "We owe him our lives, Rudi."

"He is a heroic man. He has all my respect and gratitude."

Surprised yet again by her son, she saw the softness in his eyes. "I am glad."

He put his hand over hers. The warmth of her son's concern helped to calm Amalia. She rested her head on his shoulder for a moment. Before she realized it, sleep overtook her.

After seeing how ugly his wound was, and how close to dying he had come, Amalia couldn't believe Andrzej's fever was down by morning. She was almost overwhelmed by the miracle.

There is going to be a future. Andrzej is not going to die.

She watched him wake up clear-eyed, if exhausted. Though he did look better, he had charcoal-gray rings deep under his eyes. His face seemed gaunt; his lips were dry and cracked.

"Andrzej, you have passed through a terrible ordeal, but you are going to be all right now." She resisted the need to caress his face, instead washing it with one of her cold cloths. "And it's all due to Rudi."

"Rudi?" He looked confused.

Her son moved forward to the side of the bed. "Herr Docktor, I am so glad you are feeling better."

"But where did you spring from?" Andrzej asked.

"Oxford. We put sulfa on your wound. Have you heard of it?"

"Yes," Andrzej said. "I've been keeping up with the studies. But where the devil did you get hold of sulfa?"

Rudi related his story, and Amalia felt the ache of unshed tears of relief in her throat. She gulped them down with determination.

When he was finished with his tale, Rudi said, "Mutti, you need to get some rest. You have been awake for days."

Andrzej said, "Amalia, I can't think what would have happened to me if you and Fotheringill hadn't come to France. But I feel terrible to have put you through all this at such a time. You must rest now."

Amalia felt tears close again but quelled them, saying, "Well, you are very fortunate that wound didn't kill you. I think the bookseller who put that filthy rag on your arm must have been in league with the Nazis."

Turning to Rudi, Andrzej said, "I appreciate your actions. Thank you. You and your mother have saved my life between you."

Rudi seemed pleased by his words. "I would have been in a tight spot if I hadn't found someone who spoke German," Rudi said. "As soon as we're back in England, I'm enrolling in an English course."

"I think I'd better do the same," Amalia said.

"But for now, you are going to your room, Mutti. You must rest." Rudi led her out of the room and into her own. As soon as she saw her bed, she collapsed onto it, not even bothering to change her clothes. Rudi pulled the feather quilt over her and drew the drapes. She tumbled into sleep.

When Amalia had left the room, Andrzej noticed Anthony sitting in the corner in a large armchair. He came forward. "How about a shave, old man?"

"That sounds wonderful, but I am weak as a newborn kitten."

"I should probably be getting back to London," said Rudi upon reentering the room.

Fotheringill objected. "You've had no sleep yourself. I insist that you take my room." He handed Rudi a key. "It's freshly made up. Go get some sleep."

"Thank you, Mr. Fotheringill," Rudi said, taking the key. "First I think I'll go down and have some breakfast."

"Splendid!"

Andrzej fully enjoyed the shave his friend gave him. "Never did I anticipate such a dramatic reunion. How have you been, my friend?"

"Working. Not much else. Louise still won't have anything to do with me. She has a new lover, I've heard."

"How rotten. I can't understand why you won't divorce her."

"The job mostly. Divorce is frowned upon, you know." Anthony finished up his shave. "Amalia is quite a woman. She's offered to speak to Halifax. About the *Anschluss*."

"Do you think it will do any good?" Andrzej asked, taking a long drink from the glass by his bed.

"One can hope. With Henderson as our foreign minister in Germany, I doubt if we'd even hear if Hitler was going to declare war on us." Fotheringill removed clippers from his pocket and began clipping Andrzej's fingernails. "When are you going to marry her?"

"Amalia? Don't be deceived. The fondness she has for me is left over from long ago. It's not for the Zaleski that you are acquainted with." He sighed heavily, thinking of the tired angel he had awakened to find tending him so anxiously. "I used to be a remarkably selfish chap, and her husband was a man who will be hard to follow in her affections. She is in the middle of serious grieving."

"You didn't see her when she was nursing you through your delirium. I think if you had died, it would have been all up with her."

"These last weeks, she has had rather a lot of drama, not to mention tragedy in her life. I love her, Anthony. More than you know. But I won't take advantage of her emotions at this juncture. I want her to love the man I am now, not the memory of a demanding, selfish egotist I once was."

He watched Anthony study his face. "Understood. But I still think you're acting too nobly."

"I have a lot to make up for." Every time he remembered what life had been like for her in Vienna after the War, thinking he had deserted her, he cursed himself anew. How could he have been so prideful? Why had he believed Lilli's lies? Why hadn't he gone to Vienna to investigate her situation?

&

When Amalia woke, she had no idea of the time. Her thoughts flew to Andrzej. Then she remembered the sulfa and relaxed.

Would she need to reapply it? She should go check on him, but she felt grubby in the clothes she had worn for she didn't know how long. Time had collapsed on itself like a telescope and she didn't even know what day it was. She needed a bath.

Running the water in the tub, she stripped off her clothes. Ugh. What a mess she was!

As she lay soaking in the warm water, she tried to sort out her emotions of the last few days. She remembered her frenzied pleas for Andrzej's life. Struck, she realized there hadn't been any time to plead for Rudolf's life. The SS had appeared and minutes later, he had been dead. She had spent the last couple of days, or however long it was, agonizing over her former lover. Amalia hadn't even thought of Rudolf during that time.

Instead, she had been overtaken by memories of her past with Andrzej. She had felt her love for him revive. Turning suddenly cold, she climbed out of the tub and rubbed herself down briskly with the bath towel. How could she feel these feelings? Rudolf was scarcely dead!

She should go back to London, leaving Anthony to care for Andrzej. She should. But she couldn't. What if the fever and infection should return? She had no idea how often the sulfa needed to be applied.

Amalia had no choice but to act like the professional she was and put the welfare of her patient before her personal desires. Professionalism was the key. She would have to reinsert the distance between herself and Andrzej that she had put there back in Vienna when he had appeared in the children's playroom that day so long ago. He had appealed to their past, to their overwhelming passion for one another. And she had used every mite of her strength to put Andrzej behind her.

But Rudolf is gone now.

The fact of his death bore down on her, and she was almost relieved to feel the pain. Summoning a vision of him lying asleep in his library after one of his night-long tussels with the dark memories that obsessed him, she welcomed the return of her tenderness toward her husband.

I am not, and never was, a faithless wife. My feelings for Andrzej were only triggered by his illness. I will be able to maintain my distance now.

But the effort of dragging out her armour was too much.

Face it, Amalia. You nearly lost another person you love.

Wrapping the large towel around her thin body, she dissolved in sobs of confusion that wracked her body. She stumbled to her bed, pulling the quilt over herself. Kaleidoscoping before her were pictures of her husband's bullet-riddled body, Andrzej's septic wound, and his fever-ravaged face as he had emerged from his delirium. The feelings were all jumbled together—almost more than she could bear. She felt as devastated as though she were lying bleeding on a battlefield. All the emotions of the last five years were separate wounds, each of them lancing her with their special variety of pain. Amalia wept as she had never allowed herself to weep.

After all the tears were gone, she lay still, staring into the gloom until she heard a light tap on the door.

"Who is it?" she managed to call out.

"Rudi. Did I wake you?"

"No. Wait just a minute."

Climbing off the bed, Amalia pulled her dressing gown out of her suitcase, threw it on, and went to the door, glad of the dim light in the room.

"I brought you something to eat," Rudi said. Behind him stood a waiter with a tray. Suddenly, Amalia was ravenous.

"Oh, thank you, darling. I am simply starved." She let the waiter in and led him to the table in her suite, where he set down a plate of sandwiches, a bowl of cheese-encrusted onion soup, and a pot of tea. "Thank you so much," she said to the waiter in French. Then, "Rudi could you open the drapes?"

Soon she was eating and, by exerting tremendous effort, managed to chat with her son as though the last hour had never been.

"Doctor Zaleski is sleeping, but his fever doesn't seem to have returned," he said.

"Oh, I am glad. Rudi, you are a true answer to prayer. I know he would have died without that sulfa. Do you know how many times it needs to be applied?"

He looked chagrined. "I never asked. I assumed once would be enough. But it makes sense that it would take more than one application."

"Your father would be very proud of your resourcefulness. You are just like him, darling." Tears welled in her eyes again. "I miss him so much. But thank God I have you and Chris."

"And Zaleski," he said in a low voice.

She looked her son in the eye. "The doctor is a good man, Rudi, but your father's place in my heart is unique and secure. I want you to know that."

"I think I understand, Mutti. Doctor Zaleski is a good man, but he and father are very different."

She reached across the table to where Rudi was sitting and covered his hand with hers. "That's right."

"I think you need some exercise and air when you are finished eating," Rudi told her. "Would you come for a walk with me?"

"I am still very tired, but I think you are probably right. You have designated yourself as my caregiver, I see." She smiled at him.

"Someone has to be," he said. "It's what Father would want."

When Andrzej woke up, it was early evening. Amalia was sitting by the window and Anthony was gone. He struggled up onto his elbows. "Hello."

"Oh!" Amalia exclaimed, putting down what appeared to be knitting. "You're awake. Wonderful. I must check your wound again."

He recognized her professional briskness. If what Anthony had said was true, she must be regretting the forbidden byways through which her fears for his life had led her.

"I could eat something," he said as she unwound his bandage. He waited patiently while she probed it.

"Amazing," she said. "It looks as though you are continuing to mend without any further infection."

"Sulfa is very effective medicine," he said.

"So it would seem. A true miracle drug." She kept her eyes off his face. "I will order you something to eat. What would you like?"

"Meat. Lamb chops if they have them. Thank you, Amalia." He put a hand on her wrist. "I can only imagine what tortures you suffered so soon after losing Rudolf. Anthony says you were splendid. I apologize for putting you through all this."

She smiled gently. "You were wounded on my behalf, Andrzej. I will be forever grateful. However, if you are still progressing well in the morning, I think I had better return to England with Rudi."

"Yes," he said with as much encouragement as he could muster. "I understand."

Amalia ordered his dinner on the telephone and then went back to her knitting.

"What are you knitting?"

"Rudi and I found a yarn shop a few doors down when we went walking this afternoon. This is marvelous Shetland wool. Light as down. I am making a shawl. Anthony is very kind, but his house is dreadfully cold and damp."

When his meal came, Andrzej tucked into it like a starving man.

"Tell me about the time after the War, Amalia," he said. "I want to know how Rudolf rescued you. I have never known the details."

Looking at him sharply, she ceased her knitting. "Why do you want to talk about that?"

"I would like to understand Rudolf better."

Tilting her head on one side, she studied him for a moment. "Very well."

She proceeded to tell him a story of Rudolf's saving her from a life of drudgery, poverty, and abuse by her brother, Wolf, that nearly broke his heart. She left out any mention of Andrzej himself and the anguish she had gone through because of him.

"Can you ever forgive me?" he asked when she was finished.

"It wasn't your fault. You were misled by Lilli. I can't even blame her. She loved you, and between us, we broke her heart when we got engaged in the first place. Besides," here she held up her head, "I don't regret marrying Rudolf."

"Of course you don't," he said softly. Suddenly, he was exhausted. With the dinner tray still on his lap, he closed his eyes. He didn't even notice when she removed it.

When he next woke, it was morning, and Amalia, dressed for travel, was examining his arm.

"I declare you well on the road to recovery," she said, giving him a smile. Turning to Anthony, who stood behind her, she said, "You must start getting him up and walking around the room. Before he undertakes the journey to England, be sure that he can walk a fair distance outside."

Andrzej smiled at her. "You are my angel of mercy. Thank you so much for coming to my aid."

She patted his hand and squeezed it. "Of course. Now mind Anthony, and I will see you in London."

His heart ached as she walked out the door. There was a new wall between them. He would give her space to grieve, but he fully intended to disassemble that wall, brick by brick, rebuilding her trust and love no matter how long it took.

{ 14 }

Amalia and Rudi took the boatrain from Calais to London. Most of the way, Amalia dozed. Every time she woke, her mind and heart rebelled, choosing sleep rather than dwelling on the experiences she had passed through since she had left Vienna just two weeks before.

They arrived in London late in the afternoon. She was still tired and the unfamiliar city seemed hostile to her with its foreign language, strange buildings, and general lack of elegance. Rudi hired a taxi, and soon they were at Anthony's townhome once again.

Max greeted them with some unwelcome news. "Christian took a notion to do some spying. He left earlier this afternoon and hasn't returned."

Amalia sank onto one of the red couches in the cold drawing room. Of course, it was raining.

"Spying? The wretched child. Whom is he spying on?"

"It seems one of the footmen here is German. We were playing chess yesterday in the sitting room off the butler's pantry. We heard this young man—his name is Langen—on the telephone with someone he called 'my lady.' They were speaking German."

Max seemed nervous as he paused to light a cigarette. The webs of drowsiness still clinging to Amalia's consciousness dissipated. What was this all about?

"Langen seemed to be reporting on the events taking place in this house."

"What events?" Amalia asked, suddenly alarmed.

"Nothing about Zaleski. Be at ease about that. He was talking about your arrival and your political leanings. Especially the fact that you were going to be speaking to the Foreign Secretary."

Amalia considered this. It was certainly disturbing. "Where does Christian come into the story?"

Max drew on his cigarette. "He decided to follow Langen when he left the house this afternoon for his half-day. He had an idea that he might be calling on 'her ladyship.' He wants to find out her identity."

Rudi broke in, "Of all the hare-brained schemes!"

Amalia tried to still her trepidation. "Why did you let him go, Max?"

"He said he just wanted to see where he went. I didn't see the harm in it."

Amalia put a hand to her forehead, trying to stop the ache that had formed there. She wouldn't snap at Max. But where could Christian be? Had he been caught in some Nazi web? It seemed far-fetched that that could happen here in London, but if not that, where was he?

Rudi cursed. "None of us speaks English, so we can't even question Stinson about Langen. This is damned frustrating, to say the least."

"How did you leave the doctor?" asked Max.

"Well, but only just," said Amalia. "Rudi saved his life, I think." She told Max the story.

"Well done, Rudi!" Max said. "Imagine Miss Gluck being at Oxford!" He turned to Amalia. "I am sorry you had to return to this news, Baroness. I never thought of Christian as irresponsible."

"He's an adventurer, which can be the same thing," said Rudi. "What in the world did he think he could prove by this behavior?"

"It would be a good thing if he could find out the name of an aristocrat with Nazi leanings," Max said.

"But not at the risk of his own safety!" Amalia snapped. Rising, she left the room and, climbing the stairs, went to her own suite, where she could be alone. The headache was raging and she simply could not process the idea that something might have happened to Christian.

"Rudolf! What am I to do?" she cried. "There is going to be a war. If I can't endure this, how can I manage to let Rudi and Chris go fight Germans? How can I go on without you?"

Depression descended on her, separating her from her surroundings like a dirty scrim falling between her and reality. Everything took on threatening proportions and for the first time since Rudolf's death, she questioned whether she could go on. There were not many times in her life that she had felt helpless, but this was certainly one of them.

As had become her habit, she walked to the window and looked down into the street. The rain had ceased, finally, blown away by a wind that set the leaves shivering on the trees outside. She brought her hands up to her arms and hugged herself in the cold of the room.

In Vienna, it would be warm. Spring was a glorious season—flowers abundantly spread throughout the city in window boxes and gardens, women in delightful spring frocks promenading the *Ringstrasse*, children screaming in glee as they rode the giant Ferris wheel in the *Prater*. Would she ever see her city again?

Will I ever see Chris again?

At that moment, Rudi knocked on the door and, without waiting for a reply, he entered.

"Mutti, Christian has returned. He is safe."

Taking a deep breath of relief, Amalia drew herself up. "*Gottseidank*!"

"Come downstairs. He is terribly repentant, and he has a story to tell."

"I will be there in a moment."

Rudi looked a question, but after a second's hesitation, shut the door. Amalia went to her bathroom and ran the water until it was warm. She splashed her face until it was no longer rigid with cold and despair. Drying it vigorously, she told herself that Christian was here, that he was safe. She thanked God over and over, but she still felt numb.

Finally, grabbing a wool sweater, she descended the stairs to the drawing room. Christian ran to her and enveloped her in an embrace. "Forgive me, Mutti. I wouldn't have added to your worries for the world. I had no idea you would be home today."

"You wretched child, what have you been up to?" she asked.

Dressed as a street urchin, he pulled a grubby piece of paper from his pocket. "I have obtained a list of Nazi sympathizers.

Langen came to Mr. Fotheringill from the Marchioness of Sievers. She's a German. A Nazi."

"And how did you find this out?" Amalia asked, feeling suddenly breathless. She sat down hard in the closest chair.

"I followed Langen and made up to the housekeeper. She thought I was a poor German immigrant down on his luck. She fed me a meal and gossiped freely. Unfortunately, she was quite ugly, with a giant mole on her nose."

"Christian!" Amalia admonished.

"She came to this country as the marchioness's maid. She's a Nazi as well, and was in raptures over der Führer."

"What about the Marquis?" Amalia asked. "Is he a Nazi, too?"

"He's British. Works for the government, as a matter of fact. But he's definitely 'pro,'" Christian said. Handing his mother the list, he said, "Those are his cronies—other pro-Nazis who are coming tonight for a big dinner party. Frau Wilhelm was tremendously puffed up. Evidently, some of these men are high in the government, and their recruitment is quite a coup for the Marquis and Marchioness."

"Surely you didn't take the names down as she was speaking!" Rudi said.

"Of course not!" Christian responded. "I did an association technique with my memory and wrote them down at a pub on the way home. The spelling's phoenetic, I'm afraid. I'm hoping Mr. Fotheringill will be able to figure out who they are." The boy beamed at his own cleverness. "Speaking of Mr. Fotheringill—he didn't return with you? How is the doctor?"

"Your brother saved the doctor's life. He can tell the story."

Amalia was weak with relief. She studied the list Christian had given her as the boys talked. It was written with an unsharpened pencil on the back of a handbill advertising something she couldn't translate. Her son might actually have accomplished something useful after all.

She wondered how Anthony would respond to having a Nazi spy in his household. He must be an influential man in the Foreign Office to rate such attention from the enemy.

However, any hope of her going incognito among the pro-Nazi contingent in London was lost. Thanks to Langen, all would know that the Baroness von Schoenenburg was an avid opponent of the German leader.

Rudi wanted to see Hannah to report on the success of Zaleski's cure. However, remembering his encounter in the Miter, he was self-conscious about his German. He decided the first priority was to set about learning at least some English.

So he settled for writing a letter:

My dear friend Hannah,

I wished to let you know the outcome of our experiment. It was miraculous! My mother reopened the wound and applied the drug. She closed it and rebound it, and his fever was down by morning. In a few more days, he will be able to start for England. Our injured friend, who is a medical doctor, imagines he will be fit in a week's time.

You are indeed our good angel. I have never been more grateful in my life to see anyone than I was to see you at the laboratory.

I imagine we will be here until the scourge of Hitler has been wiped from the Continent. I have decided to learn English. When I have mastered it to some extent, I wish to attend Oxford.

But I want to know of your circumstances. How did you happen to come to Oxford so quickly? By what miracle did you manage to obtain your job in that lab? I know you are, of course, brilliant, but I assumed you meant to try for it after you graduated..

I am to begin my English studies this week. Please write to me and tell me your story of how you came to leave Zürich.

I look forward to seeing you once again, and perhaps taking you down the river in one of those flat-bottomed boats! I imagine you miss the Freiheit. I will never forget seeing you for the first time on the dock by the Limmat. That was a sad and anxious day for me, but you made it bright.

With friendly greetings,

Rudi von Schoenenburg

Hannah was delighted to receive Rudi's letter. She had made no acquaintances in Oxford other than Dr. Heatley and his lab assistant, David Reinquist. She was not invited to participate in their after-hours libations; however, Reinquist found reasons to be constantly at her elbow.

She wrapped up her letter, but not before he had seen the address.

"Ah, the Baron von Schoenenburg. You have correspondence with him. Tell me, does he know you are Jewish?"

She hid her surprise. How had he guessed? "He doesn't know much about me at all. We are chance acquaintances. He didn't even know I worked here when he came."

"But he'd like to know you better."

"Perhaps." Hannah did not want to discuss Rudi with Reinquist. "Did you have any results on the experiment today?"

"If he finds you are Jewish, he will drop you flat. Barons do not consort with Jewesses."

"And what business is it of yours?" she asked.

"I could make it my business."

She dismissed him. "You're nothing but a bully. Please leave me alone."

As soon as he had gone, Hannah sat down to write back to Rudi. Reinquist's point made her uncomfortable. Should she confide her religion to this young man she was feeling increasingly friendly toward? Even though he was younger than she, there was something about him that attracted her—she could very much picture him on a white charger. Rudi was unusual in this uprooted society of cocaine and alcohol and easy sex among their generation. Her father had told her that after the Great War, non-Jews had, for the most part, cast away most traditional notions. Rudi was an anachronism, and she could see him becoming a sort of touchstone. Hannah hoped the fast and loose aristocratic society wouldn't dull his gallantry.

My dear friend Rudi,

I am so glad that between us, we were able to help your friend. That is wonderful news indeed. Sulfa helps many infections, but nothing that is not on the surface of the body. On the other hand, penicillin could have greatly helped if we had had it in the influenza epidemic that killed so many millions of people after the War. However, we still have to find out how to deliver it to the body, how to package it so that it keeps its potency.

I approve of your plan to take English lessons. I hope they will go well for you. I am starting up my classes again, a few at a time while I am working at the lab.

The people you saw on the river were doing something called punting. The bottom of the river is very muddy and they stick their poles in and punt their boats along. I should love to go punting with you! But you must get a straw boater hat, white trousers, and a navy blue jacket. That is the uniform! I shall have to wear some silky flowery thing.

Have you thought what subject you will read when you come to Oxford?

Friendly greetings in return,

Hannah

The fact that she was Jewish just didn't come up in such a letter. In fact, she realized she had completely failed to answer his question about how she came to leave Zürich and to be in Oxford.

{ 15 }

Andrzej and Anthony arrived at Fotheringill House a week after Amalia had left them. Amalia tried unsuccessfully to dampen her excitement at seeing Andrzej again. He wore a sling, but was, of course, freshly barbered and handsome, though a little pale.

She examined his wound in the butler's pantry.

"Well, you managed to avoid reopening it, I am relieved to see. It is healing nicely."

"I am glad you are pleased," he said with a straight face.

Without thinking, she pulled his shirtsleeve back over his arm and began to button his shirt. When she was halfway done, she pulled back in embarrassment.

He grinned at her. "I'll take over, shall I?"

She scowled at him. "It may interest you to know that we had some excitement while you were in France."

"More excitement?"

She related Christian's adventure.

"I told you he was cut out to be a spy."

"What is it about men that makes them act like little boys when there is a possibility of war?" Amalia said irritably.

She left Andrzej sitting on the chair in the butler's pantry and went to her room. She studied the gloomy wallpaper, finally identifying the brown figures on it as dragonflies, and reflected that she had to find a house of her own. Amalia clutched her hands in fists. She wanted to run away somewhere and grieve in peace. Andrzej was distracting, to say the least. Just seeing his face again stirred her. How could she love two men? The feelings surfacing for Andrzej were not new. Her longing for him was disturbingly familiar. Had she never stopped loving Andrzej despite her marriage? She was inclined to think she had shoved her feelings for him down deep inside her, ceasing to feel anything at all for a time. It was years before a love for Rudolf had begun to develop. And when Andrzej had returned and told her how both of them had been deceived, she had had to exert every bit of her strength to keep from leaving her family and going off with him.

Sitting at her vanity, she felt sick at this self-knowledge. It helped only marginally to remember that Rudolf had known she loved Andrzej and married her anyway.

At dinner that night, she took her first step toward independence by asking Anthony's advice on the matter of an English teacher.

"My daughter would be happy to teach you. She often works with the families of diplomats who are stationed here. I will get in touch with her tonight. When would you like to begin?"

"Tomorrow, if possible. Also, is there any chance of locating an estate agent who might speak German?"

Andrzej spoke up. "I speak both languages, Amalia. I will be happy to help you locate a house."

If the others had not been in the room, she would have been able to tell him no, but that response would raise red flags with Anthony and the boys. After dinner, she excused herself with a very real headache and went back up to her very dreary room.

The following morning, she came down to breakfast and tried to present a professional front.

"Have you thought how different things would have been during the war if we had had sulfa?" she asked Andrzej as he ate his boiled egg with difficulty, his arm still in a sling.

"It would have spared us many an amputation and lives without number if we'd been able to stop the infections."

Rudi said, "If they make the advances they expect to in the next few years, there will never be another flu epidemic like the last one, either. The thinking is that penicillin can be taken into the system and heal the bacteria that cause inflammation of the lungs, and pneumonia."

"What an age we live in!" Amalia said with wonder.

"Yes, that we do," said Anthony. "Only with modern communication like radio, film, telephones, and telegraphs could we have dictators with the reach of Hitler, Stalin, and Mussolini. Christian, would you mind letting me see that ill-gotten list of yours? I'd like to check it for familiar names."

Christian stood and handed over the crumpled piece of paper. "The names are written phonetically. I hope you can read them."

Anthony nodded over several of them, exclaiming over others. "Hmm. Viscount Wembly's politics are going to be a shock to the Home Office. So are Redfern's. None here in the Foreign Office, though."

Chris said, "I have no way of knowing if those are all the invited guests. It looked like Frau Wilhelm was preparing to receive an army. There are only six couples there, but I am sure there were more invited."

"Well, Amalia, what do you say? Are you willing to risk a truthful presentation to Lord Halifax? Even knowing there could be someone of questionable politics present?"

"By all means," she said.

"I've spoken to my daughter, and she will be able to begin your English lessons this afternoon, if you like, but for your meeting with the Foreign Secretary, I will be honored to be your interpreter."

"I accept the gallant offer, Anthony. Thank you."

"You'll open the man's eyes," Andrzej said with confidence.

As Amalia borrowed from Andrzej's confidence in her, she realized it was a familiar sensation. She had done it many times in the past when they were surgeon and surgical nurse. Andrzej had always expected a lot of her.

Anthony arranged her meeting with Halifax for the end of the week. When the time came, her principal impression of the man was that he was long. Long face, made longer by a balding head, long nose, long fingers, long body. He sat at the head of a long mahogany table, one hand encased in a black glove. Anthony had told her Halifax had a withered hand.

Fotheringill translated his formal greeting. "It is a pleasure to make your acquaintance, Baroness."

Amalia responded in kind, drew off her gloves, and seated herself in the chair indicated in the darkly paneled room. There were some seven or eight people around the table. As she studied faces, she wondered if any of them were carrying information to the Nazis. One or more of them could have been among the anonymous men Christian could not name at the Marquis of Sievers' dinner. Knowing this, she felt uncomfortable but determined. Men thought women emotional creatures. She was determined to keep her temper.

"Perhaps you might tell us about the *Anschluss* from your point of view, Baroness. Your husband was in the cabinet, I understand?" Fotheringill translated.

"Yes. For many years. He advised both Chancellor Dolfuss as well as Chancellor von Schuschnigg. He was murdered by the SS when we attempted to leave Austria following the *Anschluss*."

"You have my condolences, Baroness. The SS murdered him because he opposed the new regime?"

"He always stood for democracy. He was against the German and Austrian Nazis from the beginning. He had certain knowledge dangerous to their cause."

"And what would that knowledge be?"

"I am not free to discuss it at the moment. He entrusted me to disclose it only to a certain party."

Halifax grinned ruefully. "Churchill, I suppose." Then he said, "Pardon me, but I was under the impression that the majority of the Austrians favored union with Germany."

"We will never know, will we?" Amalia asked, just barely holding her bitterness in check. "Hitler's invasion prevented Von Schuschnigg from holding his plebiscite on Austrian independence." Folding her arms on the table in front of her, she leaned forward, looking Halifax in the eye. "It was precisely such British and French misconceptions from as long ago as 1933 that aided the Fascists in the winning of Austria. Dolfuss and von Schuschnigg were facing a cult of personality in Hitler's Germany. Neither of them were charismatic men. But they both wanted an independent Austria. They sought allies to help defend them against Hitler. But no one was interested except Mussolini. His requirements drove them even closer to fascist dogma."

"Perhaps we didn't offer support because Austria was ruled by a dictator, not a democracy."

"It is a matter of which came first, the chicken or the egg. You have no idea how hard my husband fought to maintain parliament, to maintain a democratic government. He could not interest the West in our cause, even when we had a democratically elected parliament." She drew herself up, remembering their disappointments. "The failure of democracy came in the wake of the duel for power between the Socialists and the Fascists in 1933. Exactly as it did in Germany. We did not have a democratic tradition, as Britain and France did. But in 1933, our democrats, the Christian Socialist government, stood crushed between Red Socialism and German Nazism. All three parties had private armies. It was a dangerous situation. To my and my husband's great sorrow, in order to stave off revolution, Chancellor Dolfuss dissolved parliament, thereby establishing a *de facto* dictatorship. He thought it was in Austria's best interests to avoid civil war and the victory of either the Reds or Hitler's Nazis. Under his rule, we remained independent, at least."

"I see," Lord Halifax responded. He bridged his long fingers. "I think we in the West did not have that perspective. I must say, Baroness, that you are very well informed."

"I was in my husband's confidence."

"That is quite obvious. You must have been very anxious when Dolfuss was murdered."

"I was, as a matter of fact. But I was relieved that the attempted coup by the German Nazis failed. Didn't you see the handwriting on the wall then? If Austria was desirous to be part of Germany, why was the Nazis' first act in their Putch to murder our Chancellor? Why did we defeat them then and still continue to remain independent for the next five years?"

"What is your explanation, Baroness?"

"I think you did not see, did not stop him because all of you are spellbound by Hitler. You make the mistake of believing that he is only trying to redress the unfairness of the Versailles Treaty." Though she remained cool on the outside, anger was bubbling within her.

Halifax countered, "I think, to the contrary, that you attribute far more power to the man than he actually possesses."

Amalia drew herself up and took her gloves off the table. Proceeding to put them on, she said, "Then you do not know Hitler."

"You are misinformed. I met him last year in Germany. Along with Reichsmarshal Goering."

"To know Hitler, one must live in his shadow," she said. "And I must warn you that should you continue to remain blind, that day lies in Britain's future." With great restraint, she avoided telling him exactly how she knew this fact. That knowledge was for Churchill alone. "He understands you far better than you understand him. He knows exactly what to say to appeal to your desire for peace. But if you read his manifesto, you will clearly see that your view of the future and Hitler's view are on a terrible collision course. Austria is but an example. You should at least learn from it." Standing, she bowed her head in his direction. "Thank you for your time, Lord Halifax. I wish you could have known my husband. He was a great man."

The Secretary for Foreign Affairs stood and bowed. "Again, Baroness, I am grieved at your loss. You are very emphatic, and I appreciate your coming to tell me your views. Thank you."

{ 16 }

Andrzej spoke to Fotheringill late that night over whiskey in the library.

"How did Amalia do today?"

"I think Halifax was impressed in spite of himself. She was regal and informed. And she wasn't afraid to tell him the truth as she saw it about the years leading up to the *Anschluss* and about Hitler. She has good reason to be angry, but she kept a cool head. She let Halifax know that Britain and France had let Austria down when it counted. I was deeply impressed, Zaleski. She is quite a woman."

"Her understanding is superior," Andrzej agreed as he proceeded to light his pipe. "Her uncle, though a socialist, taught her to think independently. Her brother, brother-in-law, and sister all succumbed to fascism, but she and Rudolf fought it to the bitter end, even though Austria was essentially a fascist state by the time of the *Anschluss*."

"You interest me." Anthony poured himself two more fingers of whiskey. "What form did her resistance take?"

"She counseled with her husband, and he counseled with von Schuschnigg and before him, Dolfuss. There was rough patch in their marriage over Dolfuss's dismissal of Parliament in '33." He recalled that time vividly. "As is happened, I was in Vienna at the time, trying to convince Amalia to leave Rudolf. She was devastated by the end of the Austrian democracy, and I gave her some personal news that shook her world, as well." Drawing on his pipe, he remembered the anguish in Amalia's eyes when he told her of Wolf's treachery in destroying his letters to her after the war.

"But von Schoenenburg managed to convince her that the state of the government would be far worse if it weren't for his influence in the cabinet. Her loyalty stayed with him and her sons. And, if you will recall, Dolfuss was murdered that year in the attempted German Putsch."

"Did she ever really love von Schoenenburg, or was he just a means to an end?" Fotheringill inquired.

"I wondered that. But Amalia's heart is very large. She loves fully despite flaws in the beloved. Rudolf became a great man, a man who was willing to die for his beliefs. I think Amalia loved him into being that man." Andrzej stretched his hand out for the rest of his whiskey. After a sip, he said, "Now she feels tremendously guilty about it all."

"I can see why she is so unforgettable," his friend said.

"The first time I lost her, it was because I was such a selfish beast. The last time I lost her was because of my pride. If she should give me a third chance, I hope I will be worthy of it. She has loved me into a better person, as well. I actually came to admire her more for staying with her marriage. It was the right thing to do."

The following morning, he approached Amalia at breakfast. Since the emotionally fraught time surrounding his illness, he had not been blind to her attempt to keep a distance between them. "I feel like taking a walk in the park today," he said.

"You are certain you are strong enough?" Though there was real concern in her voice, he read panic in her eyes.

He said, "You can't keep me an invalid forever, my dear. Come with me?"

"I shall invite the boys to join us," she said. "If they ever arise."

He had expected this. He insisted gently, "I would rather go just now," he said.

A frown appeared between her brows. "Very well."

It wasn't long before they were out of the house and across the street in the park. Though she wore a rather uninspired frock from Zürich and a hat covered her marvelous hair, she moved with her accustomed grace, and the exercise brought gentle color and animation to her face. Even after twenty years, his heart still caught in his chest when she smiled.

As they strolled the banks of the Serpentine among blooming pink peonies, she said, "It seems an age since I have simply walked in the park."

"Lovely, isn't it? How are your spirits, Amalia?"

"I am feeling a bit hollow, to tell you the truth. London feels very foreign to me most of the time. My old life has completely disappeared with scarcely a blink."

"Yes. London is very different from Vienna. There seems not to be a Baroque building to be had." He pulled her hand through the crook of his arm. "But it wasn't a blink of an eye that stole your old life. It was a succession of traumatic occurences. You would not be human, darling, if you weren't somewhat depressed."

"You are right. But I preferred Zürich to London. Londoners are so impersonal, so businesslike, and I don't speak the language."

"There will never be another Vienna, my darling."

Tears formed in her eyes. "I know. And I fear my Vienna is gone forever."

"We have a piece of it between us—our memories." He patted the gloved hand. "Do you remember Theresa von Altwald?"

"How could I forget her? Her protégés, her outlandish clothes, the trouble she always tried to stir. She is vintage Viennese. When you were so ill, I was remembering her Christmas ball."

"The one where we danced the fated waltz?"

"Of course. You were so angry with me that night!"

"Was I? That is not what I remember. I remember being absolutely carried off into another place. Populated only by the two of us.You were the first and last person to ever make me feel that peculiar sensation."

"You were very unhappy to be taken to that place when all was said and done," she said.

"I was put out of countenance. Mostly because you were off limits. Remember, I thought you were engaged."

"I was so vain and foolish, not to let everyone know that engagement was broken," Amalia said. "But it did make you very irritated not to have what you wanted."

He stopped and, taking both her hands, he looked into her eyes. "I hope you know I am not that man anymore, Amalia. I have learned, the hard way, how to live without you."

"I am not that silly girl anymore, Andrzej. How different things would have been if I had been honest."

"Life has taken some strange turns," he reflected. "The Greeks might have something to say about it."

"I have never read the Greeks, Andrzej," she said, dimpling at him.

"In Western literature, they invented the idea of the tragic character flaw that determines destiny. My flaw is obvious—pride. It has kept me from having the woman I love twice in my life."

"But, Andrzej, you are not alone. I was equally prideful on both occasions. I did not want anyone to know Eberhard had broken our engagement. I went to absurd lengths—even to chasing after him to Berlin and marrying him! Now, that was what you call truly tragic."

"But the second time we were engaged, I should not have believed Lilli when she said you were in love with Rudolf. My pride kept me from going to Vienna and investigating the situation."

"But Wolf confiscated my letters to you, as well! The scenario Lilli painted fit. It was not your fault, Andrzej."

He remembered the pain of her supposed betrayal as though it were yesterday. "Perhaps if I had not loved you so much, her words would have hurt less."

"And if I had hurt less, I would not have ceased to believe in love," she said.

Knowing the pain he had caused her was the worst ache he had ever known. It filled him. "I cannot bear to think of what you must have been through."

Her eyes looked troubled and she frowned slightly. She did not look away and for a moment, the air between them was thick with memories and meanings. Her slightest touch or even just the sight of her caused him to yearn for her with an intensity that rendered him nearly breathless.

Lowering her eyes at last, she took her hands from his. "Well, I did marry Rudolf, and Greeks or not, that was not a bad thing. I did come to believe in love again, after a time."

His desire to declare himself, to kiss her there in the park was so strong, he mastered it only with great effort. Rudolf would lay between them for some time. How long, he could not guess. Taking her elbow, he said briskly, "Let us return. Your boys may take this opportunity to infiltrate the government this morning if we don't hasten."

"Now that's a frightening thought." She looped her arm through his and chattered about inconsequential subjects during the remainder of their walk.

&

The outing unsettled Amalia. Andrzej's desire for her was clear in his eyes and his burning touch, but Amalia wasn't ready to confront it yet even though she couldn't deny the sweetness that resided inside her at his presence in the same house, at meals, and in the drawing room. There was a rightness, a familiarity about it that was nearly impossible to resist. She tried to quietly enjoy his presence without wishing for more.

To her mystification and frustration, Anthony was not successful in gaining an appointment with Churchill. Excuses were put forward by his office secretaries. A personal letter that Amalia addressed to the man himself was answered by one of these secretaries, as well, begging her to understand that there were many people from Eastern European countries who requested Churchill's time and that he had to be judicious in granting interviews.

This letter angered Amalia so much that she determined to find a way to meet the man publicly, introduce herself, recall her husband to his mind, and request a meeting in private. She was certain that such a plan would not fail. To this end, she perused the newspaper for announcements of possible public appearances among his constituency.

One morning, Anthony brought the second section of The Times to her. He pointed out an advertisement. Churchill was an amateur painter, apparently. A gallery in Soho was having an exhibition of his French Seaside Collection that very evening.

"I think this would be just the thing," Anthony said.

Amalia, Andrzej, and Anthony appeared at the gallery halfway through the reception. She wore her black suit with an ivory chiffon blouse and tried to calm her nerves with stern self-talk.

This is Rudolf's mission. He is beside you in this. You will not fail.

The crowd was actually far more sparse than she had expected. Mr. Churchill himself was invisible, however, ringed by a group of people. Amalia and Andrzej circulated about, studying the surprisingly interesting paintings of beach scenes in the South of France. Anthony positioned himself near Churchill, waiting to intercede with him on their behalf.

Amalia said, "Maybe this was not the best idea."

"I feel certain he will see us. There has been some kind of miscommunication in his office, I am sure," Andrzej answered.

Half an hour later, Anthony approached them, the shorter, plumper Churchill in tow. The latter struck Amalia as having a face like an aging, ill-tempered baby with a cigar. For some reason, his appearance chased away her nerves.

In German, Fotheringill said, "Baroness, Herr Doktor, I would like to present to you the Honorable Mr. Winston Churchill. Mr. Churchill, allow me to introduce the Baroness von Shoenenburg and Herr Doktor Andrzej Zaleski."

Mr. Churchill bowed his head formally and Amalia extended her gloved hand to shake his.

"Baroness, Doctor, it is a pleasure to meet you," the man said in heavily accented German. He then added in English, which Anthony translated, "Fotheringill has told me you have no designs to assassinate me."

Startled, Amalia's eyes grew large. "Assassinate you? We have come all the way from Austria just to speak with you!"

When he heard the translation, Mr. Churchill waved his cigar. "Never mind. An anonymous caller frightened my secretaries. It seems someone did not want our meeting to take place. "

"Someone said I was going to assassinate you?" Amalia asked.

"You are meant to be a very dangerous woman!" Churchill said with a smile. "What you have to say must be important."

"It is," Amalia said. "The SS murdered my husband to prevent him from getting to you. I am his messenger."

Mr. Churchill's eyebrows came crashing down and his bottom lip shot out. He grasped her hand. "My dear Baroness, what a dreadful thing. You have my heartfelt condolences." He squeezed her hand and for a moment, his eyes drooped with sadness. "The SS is a monstrous blot on the planet. It must be dealt with. I am eager to hear this message. Shall we rendezvous at the bar of the Savoy once this little gathering has finished? Say ten o'clock or thereabouts?"

The Savoy Bar was elegant, crowded, and loud. Probably a good place for a confidential conversation. Amalia's party took a booth, ordered drinks, and awaited Mr. Churchill.

"He's not what I expected," said Amalia.

Anthony laughed. "You'll get along with him. He's very personable."

"Lord Halifax looked more the part," she said.

"Halifax hasn't even a portion of the charisma. Or anywhere near the grasp of affairs. You've never heard Churchill on the floor of the House. He's a very persuasive speaker," Anthony assured her. "I'm certain he will be glad of anything you can tell him of the situation in Austria. He has feelers out all over Europe, gathering his own intelligence since at this point, those in the government do not tell him what he wants to know. You'll know he really takes you seriously if he gives you an assignment. He is fond of running his own show."

Rudolf's hope for the salvation of Europe rejoined them shortly, immediately ordering a large whiskey. He sat across from Amalia, smiling at her with the cigar still between his teeth. "Baroness, my German is very bad. It would be helpful if Fotheringill here could continue to translate for me."

"That would be good," Amalia said. She wanted to make sure her message was clearly understood. Turning to Anthony, she said, "You don't mind?"

"No. It will be my pleasure."

She had given much thought to what she would say and had decided that she should begin by establishing common ground. "I have read your speech to Parliament about the *Anschluss* in the Swiss papers. I was very relieved to find that one politician, at least, understood what Hitler had done."

Fotheringill translated and then Churchill began to speak. His voice lost all hesitancy and gained a powerful fluency, which Amalia recognized even though she could not understand him. She was reassured. She saw Andrzej relax and knew he felt as she did.

Anthony translated, "From time to time, people such as yourself have come to me, most of them German. They have told me enough to make me aware that the Hitler the world wants us to see is far divorced from the Hitler of Mein Kampf. I believe his manifesto represents his true agenda."

"I agree," said Amalia, further heartened to hear that he saw this point so clearly.

"However, you cannot underestimate France and England's horror at the idea of another war," the leader said. "They want to take Hitler at face value. They want to see him as a reasonable human being who is also against another war. But nothing, unfortunately, can be further from the truth. I am convinced he has been preparing for war at least since 1933."

At last! Rudolf had not been wrong about this man. He had not given his life for nothing.

"I can see that my husband was right about you. I am very relieved, Mr. Churchill. You obviously need no convincing about Herr Hitler."

Removing his cigar, he leaned toward her, not troubling to lower his voice. "Indeed, I consider the *Anschluss* to be part of his overall strategy. It is a great tragedy for your country, but I think it holds greater significance than His Majesty's Government can conceive of at this point. You are familiar with the 'Little Entente?'"

"Of course," Amalia said. She had followed this union of former subjects of the Hapsburg Empire with interest. "It is a treaty between Czechoslovakia, Yugoslavia, and Rumania—primarily for trade purposes. There are no tariffs. They operate principally as one country. Rumania provides oil, Yugoslavia offers minerals and raw materials, while Czechoslovakia is the manufacturer and provider of munitions. It is very profitable for all of them."

Churchill beamed. "You are very knowledgeable, Baroness. I wish members of His Majesty's Government were equally well apprised! You are no doubt aware that with Austria now part of Germany, her geographic position offers the Nazis military and economic control of the communications—road, river, and rail—of all of Southeastern Europe! A wedge has been driven into the heart of the Little Entente. All one must do is study a map. With Austria in his pocket, Germany can cut off any trade between Czechoslovakia and Yugoslavia. Czechoslovakia is now isolated. She, I believe, is Hitler's next target."

"What about your government?" asked Andrzej in English, entering the conversation. "You're saying it doesn't realize this?"

"I think they do not. Recently, they declined the Soviet proposal for a Grand Alliance between our country, their country, and France to secure the integrity of the countries of Central Europe. To my utter regret, Chamberlain has brushed such an alliance off as being 'inimical to the prospects of European peace.' He thinks it smacks of conspiracy against poor misunderstood Germany."

"My country is also hopelessly blind," Andrzej said. "They are crushed between the Soviets and the Germans, and yet it seems they do not perceive their own danger. All they can think of is regaining the province of Teschen, which is now part of Czechoslovakia. Any German aggression against that country would be welcomed by them as an opportunity to make a grab for it."

There was a pause in the conversation while Anthony translated the gist for Amalia. She watched Churchill study Andrzej. "Zaleski, your name is?" asked Churchill. "I did not make the connection at first. You are related to August Zaleski, the Polish Undersecretary for Foreign Affairs?"

"You have a remarkable memory for names. Yes, he is my cousin," said Andrzej.

At this, Amalia observed Churchill's wooly brows lower as his expression turned thoughtful. "Zaleski is not a name one forgets. And what exactly is your role in this meeting with me this evening?"

"I came to support the baroness. I have been a close friend of the baron and the baroness for many, many years. For a time, I was associated with the Polish government, but no longer."

As soon as Anthony translated Andrzej's words, Amalia felt ashamed that in her preoccupation with Austria's dire fate, she had not considered Poland's concerns. Those would, of course, be closest to Andrzej's heart.

Churchill said, "Very interesting. I may have a job for you. Before we discuss that, however, I must hear what the baroness has come so far to say." He inclined his head toward Amalia. "I am sorry to tell you that I sometimes get carried away in my own rhetoric, which can only be regrettable."

All eyes were on her once more as she prepared to deliver Rudolf's message.

"Czechoslovakia may be the next target," she said. "But she will not be the last." She explained to Churchill about Rudolf's mission to Berchtesgaden. "While von Schuschnigg was arranging a doomed compromise with Hitler, von Ribbentrop, who was on leave from his post in England, was making conversation with Reichsmarshal Goering in the hall outside the anteroom where Rudolf was sitting. He was very bold, laughing at the naivete of all the governments of Europe. He called them weak and gutless." She paused for Anthony to translate, then continued. "He praised Hitler's vision and unstoppable will. Finally, he said that even the German army would be surprised when the day came that Germany was the master of all Europe. Rudolf said, 'They dismiss the Führer as a madman. Little do they know that he is the most clear-sighted man in the world today. He knows exactly what he wants and he has a clear idea of how he is going to get it.'"

Churchill leaned forward eagerly. "Bravo, Baroness! Here is the confirmation of my own view! 'Til now, I have been founding my view on estimates of armaments build-up and a gut distrust of Hitler." He slapped the table in triumph as Anthony translated. "I tell the Prime Minister that he must read Mein Kampf. But he continues to believe that the German people will not tolerate a war. That Hitler's goals are absurdly finite. That he can be appeased! Thank you, Baroness, for your courage in coming to me. In the larger scheme, it is regrettable that I have been proven right, of course. But it redoubles my sense of purpose."

He ordered another whiskey. Amalia felt great elation as a load left her mind. She could not have asked for a better reception of her news. This remarkable man deserved to have his instincts confirmed. He was fighting a lonely battle among his peers. He must be victorious, or people such as herself and Andrzej would have nowhere left to run. She pulled Christian's list from her small evening bag.

"My son, Christian, is an amateur spy. He recently visited the house of the Marquis of Sievers, posing as an urchin. The marchioness, as you may know, is German. They were entertaining a group of Nazi sympathizers. Perhaps none of these names will surprise you, but I think you should have them, just the same." She handed over the names her son had garnered, which Anthony had transposed into their proper spellings.

Sticking out his lower lip, the politician read the list. "Misguided idiots!" he said, folding it up and sticking it in his breast pocket. "Unfortunately, I have come to realize there are many such in Britain in all walks of life. Thank your son for me, Baroness. He is a brave soul. This is valuable. Several of these men work in the government in some capacity."

Sipping his whiskey, he gave Andrzej a speculative glance. "Fancy a trip to Germany?" As Anthony translated, Amalia's heart lurched.

"Perhaps," said the doctor. "In what capacity?"

"I am not unaware of your government's preoccupation with Teschen. I am also cognizant that our Foreign Minister in Berlin is not giving our Prime Minister a true view of what lies ahead. He is far too sympathetic toward Germany."

A crystal of icy fear was forming next to Amalia's heart. Was this man going to challenge Andrzej to perform some kind of dangerous mission? They had just gotten away from the Nazis!

"Let us just pretend for a moment that you are doing your cousin August a favor," Churchill continued. "That you are anxious for the German invasion of Czechoslovakia for reasons I have stated, and that you are nosing about unofficially. Testing the wind, shall we say."

Anthony translated for Amalia in a low voice. The man with the cigar continued. "If you can get me some advance warning of the reality of the threat of invasion, perhaps I can budge His Majesty's Government."

Andrzej's pulse quickened. Here was something he could do rather than sit around like a lazy aristocrat. "It could work," he said.

Then he caught sight of Amalia's face. Her eyes had widened with alarm. "You just killed a colonel in the Gestapo!" she said, her voice low and urgent.

Churchill's eyebrows rose. "Is this true?"

"Yes," Andrzej answered. "But we have reason to think he was alone and that no one knows of my actions. His vendetta against us was personal. The man followed us from Austria, where he had engineered the shooting of the baroness's husband, but we escaped."

"Ah, you are a man of action, I see." Churchill gave a satisfied smile. "Better and better."

Amalia's anguish touched him. She had just watched as he almost died, and the nature of this proposed mission dictated that he not make contact with her while in Germany. He didn't deceive himself that it wouldn't be dangerous, either. Thoughts of her anxiety when he left for the Front years ago came rushing back. However, he felt the need to do something concrete to prove Hitler's intentions to the people of this island. Perhaps if he aided this man, another war could be avoided.

"I will get in touch with my cousin," he said. "I will tell him what I am supposedly doing. He will be all for it, I am certain."

"That is excellent," declared Churchill. "He will vouch for you should the Germans contact him?"

"Yes. That is the idea," said Andrzej.

Churchill removed a card from his breast pocket and noted a number. "I am about to make a trip to France to sound out the situation there. But I will tell my appointment secretary to expect a telephone call and to make an appointment for you upon my return. We need to discuss this in further detail." He turned to Amalia. "Baroness, I cannot stress too much what it means to me and hence to Britain that you would travel all this way in order to deliver your husband's message."

"Do you really suppose Dr. Zaleski will be able to determine anything useful by the visit you propose?" she asked, a touch of arrogance in her tone.

Andrzej smiled. Churchill raised his eyebrows. "I wouldn't propose such an unorthodox mission unless I thought it might be instrumental in preventing a disastrous war, my lady."

"You think Chamberlain is prepared to go to war over Czechoslovakia?" she asked.

"I think he must," said Churchill.

Amalia said no more, but rose. The men got to their feet. The informal conference was over.

Everyone remained responsibly silent during the taxi ride to Fotheringill house. Then Anthony tactfully left Andrzej and Amalia alone, sitting in the gloomy red drawing room.

"Amalia," he said, holding her hands in his. "I know you are already grieving. I don't want to add to your angst, darling. But you know as well as I do that times are desperate, and I am particularly suited to this job because of my connections with the Polish government."

She bit her lower lip. "Is Poland really so crazy that they think they can gain something from a German invasion of Czechoslovakia? What is Teschen?"

Andrzej shook his head. "Sadly, Poland is indeed deluded. One look at their history should tell them they are the next target. Teschen is a disputed duchy that has a mix of Polish and Czech citizens. It has been a sore spot for hundreds of years."

He tweaked her chin. "You should have heard of it, you know. It was the only part of Silesia to belong to the Hapsburgs. After the Great War, there was a war between Czechoslovakia and Poland over it. It didn't solve a thing. Presently, the duchy is divided between the two. Families are divided. Obviously, it continues to be a sore spot."

"What do you think you can possibly do in Germany? You have no contacts there!" she protested.

He tried some humor, putting his arm around her shoulders. "Can it be that you will miss me?"

Shrugging off his arm, she said, "Be serious!"

He doused his grin. "Actually, I was attached to several missions to Berlin over the years. I do know some people, as a matter of fact."

"But are they people who would be helpful?" Desperation was clear in her eyes and voice.

He made his gentle. "I met a German general high in the Wehrmacht Command at a birthday party for Hitler that I attended with our Foreign Secretary. I thought he would be a good man to be close to. I made it a project to cultivate him." He took her hands in his, making circular movements on their backs in an effort to soothe her. "His name is General Beck. We saw each other socially the times I was in Berlin. Chess and that sort of thing. I even attended a dinner party at his house, where I met his wife and several other members of the military."

Amalia shivered, and he put his hands on her shoulders and looked directly into her eyes. "Rudolf would not hesitate to do this were he asked," he said.

"Yes," she replied dully. "And Rudolf is dead. I cannot bear to lose you, too."

"Amalia, if there is a war, millions could die. I could not live with myself if I refused this mission."

"You will take the greatest care?" She lowered her eyes and fingered his lapel.

"Of course." He desired nothing more than to kiss her full, lovely mouth, but knew that to do so would be to take unfair advantage of her anxiety. Leaning down, he kissed her forehead instead. She pressed her cheek to his chest, and he called it progress.

{ 17 }

Rudi was aware that his mother had finally been successful in her bid to meet with Churchill the night before. However, as they sat together at the breakfast table, her face was troubled.

"Did your meeting not go well, Mutti? After all the trouble we have taken to come to England?"

"It went very well, Rudi," she said, smiling at him.

"You have been looking very grim," he said.

Taking her time, she seemed to concentrate on buttering her toast. "Mr. Churchill may send Dr. Zaleski to Germany with a special commission for him. Apparently, he is fond of sending people about on missions."

"Ah," Rudi nodded. "It is safe to talk to me about it if you like. Remember Langen is gone." Putting his hand on her elbow, he led her to an ugly red plush divan in the morning room.

He listened as his mother spoke to him of Churchill's desires for Zaleski to uncover information from highly placed Germans regarding a proposed invasion of Czechoslovakia.

"War may come soon, then, Mutti."

"Yes. But only if Chamberlain can see the danger." She shook herself slightly and looked up into his face. "If he cannot, then war will probably come later and be more deadly. The more time Hitler has to prepare, the more weapons, airplanes, and tanks he can produce. Therefore, the sooner he is stopped, the better." She seemed to notice his apparel for the first time. "What are you up to today? You look very dapper."

He was dressed in white slacks, a navy blazer, and bow tie. In his hand, he carried a straw boater. "I think I shall travel to Oxford to see Hannah. I am bored with the English lessons. Chris is a whiz, of course."

"Then you must take her a note from me expressing my gratitude for her help. Thank goodness she speaks German. I am not coming along as fast as I would like with the English, either."

"Write your note then, for I am off. Do not fret about Dr. Zaleski. We'll send some sulfa along with him."

"That is hardly encouraging, Rudi," she said grimly.

"No one in Berlin is going to know of his connection with us," he said.

"He is presumably going as part of the Polish government. He is to be observant, however. In a word, he is to spy. Spies are never completely safe."

Rudi did not know what to say. He had grown to have confidence in Zaleski's powers, but that wasn't enough to reassure his mother.

"I think we must come up with a project for ourselves while he is gone."

"We must begin house hunting," she said. "After meeting Mr. Churchill, I think that England is the best place for us to stay at present. He has an extraordinary grasp of the European situation. If there is a war, he will be at the helm. I am certain."

"House hunting will not occupy all of our time. Nor will English lessons. I will think on it." Rising, he kissed his mother on the cheek. "To your desk, Mutti. Your letter to Hannah."

He found his friend in listless spirits. Her brow was furrowed and her eyes did not have their usual sparkle.

"Is your work not going well?" he asked once he had greeted her.

"It is going perfectly well. It is the association with the other lab assistant that has me down." She looked into his eyes, her own earnest. "Let's get out of here for a while. My boss is gone for the week. It will be all right."

"Of course. Where would you like to go?"

"We'll go for a late lunch at the Bird and Baby."

"The Bird and Baby?" he asked, amused.

"A pub near here. Actually, it's The Eagle and Child. They have the usual pub snacks—pickles, cheese, and bread. Will that do?"

"Sounds just the thing. Then I propose we go for a punt. You notice I am wearing the proper clothing," Rudi said. "I came prepared."

She smiled and her mood seemed to lighten. "I will disgrace you in my practical clothes." She looked down at her navy blue skirt and white blouse. "I should be wearing something slinky and seductive." Striding to the door of the clinic, she opened it. "Tell me about your family."

"My mother wrote a note for you." Once they were outside, he pulled it out of his jacket pocket and handed it to her.

She read as she walked. "That is very sweet of her," she said, smiling the bright smile he had become used to. "I am so delighted your friend is all right. If you don't mind my asking—you were terribly concerned about him—what exactly is your relationship? His name sounds Polish."

"Yes. He is someone my mother was actually in love with at one time. Back before the Great War. I don't know what went wrong, why she didn't marry him. He loves her still. But she married my father after the war, and swears to me she loved him."

"And having this Zaleski around doesn't make you uncomfortable?"

Rudi hesitated. "It did," he said finally. "But the man killed a Gestapo agent to protect our safety. He has proven himself to be a good man to have around. He is very different from my father in many ways, but he is an honorable man. A good man."

"Is Max still with you?"

"Yes. Another good man. Our escape wouldn't have been successful without both of them. Max used to pose as our butler."

She laughed. "Pose? Don't tell me he was a socialist spy?"

"Yes. But he and my father became very good friends. They were escaping together when my father was killed."

They had reached the small pub. Opening the door for Hannah, he looked inside. It was very welcoming, with high, sloping ceilings, cream-colored walls, and dark woodwork. Rudi ordered a standard pub lunch for both of them and two glasses of lager.

They sat at a table in an inglenook near the back, away from the few mid-afternoon customers.

When they were seated, Rudi said, "All right, what's got you down, Hannah?"

She played with the ringed napkin. "Let's not talk about it and ruin the day. Tell me what you've been doing."

He made a face. "English lessons. Riding in the park. Trying to keep up with my mother. You know, she is the most extraordinary woman. She actually faced off against the Foreign Secretary."

"Halifax?"

"Yes. I gather from Fotheringill, the fellow who translated for her and with whom we are staying, that she told Halifax he didn't understand Hitler."

Hannah clapped. "I wish I had been there."

"As do I. I feel restless, Hannah. As though there is something I should be doing. Even Christian did a bit of spying."

Laughing, she said, "Oh, do tell me all about it!"

Their lunch was served, and Rudi paused to bite into his cheese and pickle sandwich. He was ravenous, as usual.

"He infiltrated a household of Nazi sympathizers. He came home with a list of a half a dozen couples—all of them pro-Nazi, and some of them in the government. Churchill was impressed, apparently."

"Churchill?" Hannah asked. "What are you not telling me?"

"Hmm. Sorry, I let that slip. You must keep it to yourself, but it was my mother again. She actually came to England to give Churchill a message from my father."

"She is the most amazing woman!"

"Yes," Rudi said. "She is."

They ate for a while in silence.

"You know," Hannah said. "You're amazing, as well. I consider you a bit of a hero for what you did for your mother's old love."

"Why?" Rudi looked at her in surprise.

"No matter what you say, it must be difficult to have him so close, with your father only recently killed. And you went to great lengths to save him. You didn't know I would be here. And you had only some vague notion of penicillin. Yet you exerted yourself a great deal on his behalf."

Rudi brushed off her praise. "He had just been shot and was badly infected because he was protecting my family. It was the least I could do."

"It was heroic just the same," she insisted.

He shook his head, smiling. "You must meet my family," he said. "You had a great role in Dr. Zaleski's miracle, as my mother is calling it. I am sure they would like you."

"If I come to London to meet your family, you must promise to do something for me." She grinned a saucy grin.

"What is that?"

"Play the violin for me."

Rudi was taken aback. "But I have no violin! It was left behind in Austria. And besides, I am very certain I am not up to your standards."

"After our punting expedition, I will take you home to my house and make you a present of my own violin. I still have it, but I haven't played since I was twelve. I was no good. That means I will be in a position to appreciate your playing. I know how difficult it is!"

"But I have no music!" Rudi was panicking. "Besides, I'm certain your parents will never let you give your violin away."

"They are gone for the day. To London, as a matter of fact. They will never miss it. And Blackwell's is just around the corner. I believe they carry some music books. If they don't, they'll know who does. You told me you like Bach?"

"Yes, but . . ."

"Consider it payment for the sulfa."

"You would put it like that!"

"I'm counting on your sense of honor."

He smiled at her reluctantly. "I think it's time for us to go punting."

As it was a lovely spring day on the Cherwell, the river was a bit crowded. Hannah draped herself becomingly across the prow of the little boat and proceeded to giggle as Rudi attempted to master the punting pole.

He wished he owned a camera. He wanted to capture a picture of Hannah with her uninhibited grin and come-hither pose. She was the real reason he was having trouble with the punt. Soon, however, he mastered it and they were proceeding slowly down the river. The spring sun sank through the cloth of his navy blazer. But the warmth he felt had little to do with the sun.

"But Andrzej! I insist. You must take Max," Amalia said over afternoon tea. "He can be your valet. And he can watch your back."

"But August will be sending me papers as a Polish diplomat. Max has no papers," he replied.

"Have your cousin send a set of papers for your servant," she said, pouring his cup and adding two sugar lumps.

"Max would abhor the idea." He loved watching Amalia pour tea. She did it with such grace, her gold bracelet sliding up and down her arm.

"Nonsense. He masqueraded as a butler for years."

He had to admit it was a good idea. Max always came in handy. Though the idea was tempting, it was not wise. "Darling, I am counting on Max to watch out for you. Christian has identified people who are your enemies, right here in London. You are in danger."

"Then I will leave London. It is that important to me that you take Max. You will be in far more danger than I am."

"You would really leave London? But where would you go?"

"Perhaps Mr. Churchill will have a mission for me, too," she said, smiling teasingly. Then her face straightened. "I am dead serious about Max, Andrzej. I know how Rudolf always counted on him. I am worried enough about you going. Please take Max for my sake, if nothing else."

"You promise you will leave London?"

"I promise. The boys will go with me."

"All right then. I am writing August today. I will ask him to send papers for Max, as well."

Delicately, Amalia sipped her own tea. "The whole idea of you consorting with Hitler's cronies is giving me nightmares. However, I must tell you that I have come to accept that it is a good idea. I agree that it will be worth it if you can change the Prime Minister's outlook."

Chris walked in to tea in time to hear this comment. He said, "Remember, Mr. Fotheringill says Dr. Zaleski has nine lives."

"And he's used up at least eight," Amalia said.

"Five, actually," Andrzej reassured her with a grin.

For a moment, everyone concentrated on their macaroons and sticky buns. Andrzej would miss Amalia more than he wanted her to know, but he was anxious to be doing something concrete to further their goal."The Times is predicting Premiere Brun's government will fall shortly in France."

"Who will replace him?" Amalia asked.

"Monsieur Daladier. We don't know whether he will offer the same promise to back the French treaty with Czechoslovakia or not. Presumably, Churchill is meeting with him over there and he will be able to tell us."

"If he does," Amalia said. "And if France fights, Britain will surely follow, won't they?"

"One would think so," said Andrzej.

Suddenly, Amalia stood. "I have the fidgets. The gloom of this house is driving me distracted! Is there a museum or something in this city?"

Chris answered, "Madame Tussaud's is awfully nice."

"It sounds like a bordello!"

"It's a wax museum. It has figures of all the great murderers in history."

"Christian!"

"There is the National Gallery, darling," Andrzej said. "Do you really want to go look at paintings?"

"What I really want is go to work at the hospital. I'm out of sorts with nothing to do. But I can't speak English! It is all horribly distressing."

"The Opera is doing something light tonight, I believe. Shall we go?"

"It would be a nice diversion," she admitted.

Andrzej had never seen Amalia in this mood before. Their time together had always been fraught with anguish of one type or another. She wasn't used to being idle. Plus, from his own experience with mourning for his family's deaths, he knew that depression was an inevitable part of grief. She definitely needed something to do.

"Go out and find something to wear," he suggested. "I will buy tickets."

&

The opera was La Traviata, and it was a good diversion. Amalia felt her tense muscles uncoil. Gradually, she relaxed. She forgot for a few hours that Rudolf was dead and that she was not in Vienna.

Andrzej took her to a nightclub after the opera. Very chic, it had a large dance floor surrounded by a waist-high partition of glass bricks. A live orchestra played on a dais, and round tables, clothed in Art Deco pink and mint green, hugged the walls.

"Ah, a Tango," said Andrzej. "Tell me you dance the Tango."

Amalia sent him a broad smile. "I adore the Tango."

Fortunately, her gold tissue evening gown was slit up the side, so she was able to take the dramatic dance steps and perform the abrupt turns. She and Andrzej played to a crowd that was gathered. It was great fun. Possessed of keen reflexes and an uncanny mutual timing, they had always danced well together. Amalia's spirits rose. The Tango was stagey and dramatic, just what she was in the mood for—breaking out, living in this moment, separate from past and future.

"You have definitely recovered your stamina, Dr. Zaleski!"

"Feeling better?" he asked as they sat down after their performance.

"Much," she said. "I never realized I was such a shallow creature."

"There is nothing shallow about a good Tango. It is a dance of strong emotions, like those you have been feeling lately."

"It is a lot of fun. But not as romantic as the waltz." She turned to him, suddenly solemn. "Andrzej, I want you to know that I support this mission of yours. Rudolf would do it, you are right. He was far more stuffy than you. You are very svelte, very charming, you appear wise and trustworthy. You fit the mission better. But remember, the men around Hitler—they are fanatics, bullies. And I can't believe they have enough respect for Poland to take you into their confidence about anything."

"The army is not enamored of Hitler," Andrzej said. "They see themselves as the real power in Germany. It is an illusion, but perhaps it will be useful." He clasped her hand and kissed it. "Amalia, it is not easy for me to leave you. Don't think for one moment that it is. But this is a critical time. It is going to take nothing less than a war to unseat Hitler. If Britain, France, and Russia fight over Czechoslovakia, it may be over quickly." Letting go of her hand, he sipped his vodka martini. "I need to try to determine Germany's military strength. If they are not up to full strength yet, the last thing they want is a two-front war. They will not have enough troops to level Czechoslovakia and fight on the Western Front as well. Remember, France and Britain have beaten Germany before. And if Russia comes to Czechoslovakia's aid, it will not be easy to defeat her."

"Surely someone else is already checking on these things for Britain?"

"Not so as you'd notice."

Amalia sipped her wine and then wet her lips, biting her lower one.

The feeling of dread that had shrouded her since Mr. Churchill had outlined his assignment revisited her. It was familiar in an awful way. Just thinking of Andrzej sitting shoulder to shoulder with brown-shirted Nazis with swastika armbands made her ill. She pushed her wine away. "Max has agreed to go?"

"Yes. As we speak, he is using his faithful contacts to obtain British passports for us in alternate identities, should we need them." Leaning toward her, he caressed her cheek. "Darling, nothing will prevent my returning to you. Nothing. I want you to know that I love you now more than I've ever loved you."

She looked steadily into his eyes. His resolve was strong, and she felt her fears recede a bit as the knowledge of his love blanketed her with warmth. She did not question the feeling. She couldn't face that self-scrutiny tonight when she ached to be held in his arms. "I believe you do," she said huskily. "Dance with me, Andrzej."

They remained on the dance floor after that. There was no more talk of Germany. No more talk of Nazis or war.

&

Amalia woke the next morning to the sound of someone playing Bach on the violin.

Throwing back her bedclothes, she drew on her dressing gown and walked into the hallway. Anthony should be at the Foreign Office by now. It could only be Rudi. She peered over the banister. Where had he gotten hold of a violin?

Dressing quickly, she brushed her hair and fixed it with combs. She needed to get to the hairdresser. Her mirror showed she was pale from her late night. But it had been so marvelous to forget everything dire for a few hours.

Downstairs, she found her son playing a beautiful-looking instrument, his brow furrowed as he studied the music on the stand before him.

"Darling, forgive the interruption, but where did you get the violin?"

Rudi seemed to emerge from a dream. "Hannah. She loaned it to me. It's been in her family for generations, but no one plays it now. She claims that she wants to hear me play. I bought this piece of Bach's yesterday at Oxford."

"I never thought you would take it up again. But I'm so glad you have. Bless Hannah! I would like to meet this girl."

"She is coming up to town on Saturday and is anxious to meet you, as well."

Amalia seated herself on the sofa. "Go on practicing, Rudi. This is just what I need right now."

Rudi set the bow on his stand. "You look anxious. What is wrong, Mutti?"

"It's true that I'm not myself, Rudi. Maybe it is because England is not my home. I miss your father terribly, and I am worried about Dr. Zaleski's clandestine mission to Germany. I seem to have misplaced my bravery."

"I envy him being able to take some specific action. I am fearfully bored."

"As am I. But what if he gives himself away somehow? What if he's arrested and shot by the Gestapo as a spy?"

"Mutti, remember we have always been determined to do whatever we can to fight against Hitler. Dr. Zaleski will be careful. I am certain he wants his mission to be a success."

"You are right. Play some more Bach, darling. I will be brave."

Andrzej was in for luncheon, but both boys were out riding. When the footman had laid their luncheon, he put a hand over hers. "It is a pity the pro-Nazis already know who you are. Otherwise you could be a spy like Christian."

"Wherever I settle, I am going to overcome my frustration with English and learn it in record time. Anthony's daughter says it is a Germanic language, so why is it so difficult? If there is a war, they will need nurses. I must buckle down and learn it."

"Perhaps if you ask him, Anthony can speak nothing but English to you. That is the way I learned it. Total immersion. You will pick it up in no time."

When Hannah returned to work after her day with Rudi, she found Reinquist making himself at home at her desk chair.

"What are you doing?"

"Looking for your notes on that last experiment. Ah! Found them." He held up her report. "Spend the afternoon with the baron?"

"Yes. I will work late tonight to make up my hours," Hannah said.

"See that you do."

"You are not my employer," she said icily.

"Does Dr. Heatley know that you are a Jew?"

"I don't imagine he cares," she said. "Go away."

The man moved off. His stiff posture made it clear she had offended him, but she could not make herself care.

{ 18 }

Churchill had suggested that he meet with Andrzej at Fotheringill House to avoid having their conversation overheard. After securing Anthony's consent, the doctor invited him for luncheon.

"I don't expect a meeting with Hitler to come out of this," Churchill said at the beginning of the meal. "You wouldn't get the truth out of him anyway. I want you to see the way the wind is blowing with the military. Troop movements would be an added bonus, but what I really need is any evidence that they are dissatisfied with their Führer." Churchill sliced his chop and mashed a piece onto his fork, together with a bit of potato and some peas. "How much power does he have over them? Are they taking his orders? Are they likely to obey or balk if he proposes an impossible military position? Who calls the shots?"

"He has appointed himself commander-in-chief, I believe," Andrzej said.

"Yes, that is true. But I am having trouble believing that the Wehrmacht has a large enough army to risk exposing their western border to England and France and their eastern flank to Russia over a handful of Sudeten Germans in tiny Czechoslovakia. And Hitler is a bully. He's just as capable as Stalin of having his generals shot if he thinks they are conspiring against him."

The discussion vitalized Andrzej. After years of dealing with those who were blinded by Hitler, it was inspiring to work with someone who really understood the man and wasn't afraid to air his views. "I shall try to see General Beck. We have an acquaintance."

"Marvelous! I knew you were the man for the job! I shall have you and the baroness down to Chartwell when you return."

"I don't suppose you have anything for her to do here in England? I feel she needs to get out of London for her safety. She is known here. The pro-Nazi German community has been forewarned that she is not an émigré but a refugee from Hitler. Together with which she is bored but handicapped by only speaking German and French."

Churchill tilted his head to one side as he considered the matter. "That is unfortunate. Do you suppose that knowledge is had beyond London? There are other enclaves of would-be Nazis in this country. There is something about the architecture in the spa town of Bath, for instance, that breeds them."

"How far away is Bath?"

"Close by train. Only a few hours' journey." Having made his suggestion, the man resumed eating.

"That would be excellent!" Andrzej said. "She can spin herself a cover story and take one of her boys along."

"Yes. That is a good plan. "

The weight of his worry over Amalia's safety, as well as her state of mind, lifted. Andrzej was even happier for her assignment than he was for his own. Her funk worried him. Between her mourning, her dislike of London, and the language barrier, he was afraid she would fall into a serious decline. That the woman with the "spine of steel" who had been through more than he could imagine could be undone by these things was not really hard to understand. She was at her best when responding to a challenge.

"She will be very pleased to have something to do."

The Polish identification papers for Andrzej and Max arrived by afternoon post. Andrzej was instructed by his cousin to try to determine Germany's timetable in moving against Czechoslovakia. It was all working out for the best. In performing Churchill's reconnaissance, he would be able to get the information to his cousin, as well, even though August's agenda was not precisely his own.

"Thank heavens for Churchill," Amalia said when Andrzej told her of her assignment. "That idea suits me completely. I shall shop this afternoon for clothes other than widow's weeds. We will leave for this Bath—why is it called that, I wonder?—when you leave for Germany."

After her English lesson, but before leaving for the shops, she took Christian and Rudi into the red sitting room. She reflected how glad she was going to be to leave this gloomy house.

"How would you like to accompany your widowed mother on an undercover assignment?" she asked Christian.

His blue eyes sparked with interest. "What will we do?"

"We are traveling to a town called Bath, where there is apparently an enclave of pro-Nazi Germans living. We are to insinuate ourselves among them, pretending to share the same politics, and find out whatever we can."

"It sounds fun. Better than sitting around here," he said.

"You need to come shopping with me this afternoon to buy clothes appropriate to your station."

"What am I to do?" Rudi asked.

"I have been thinking." Indeed, Amalia was beginning to feel herself again, full of plans. "Do you imagine there might be pro-Nazi students at Oxford? It might be a good thing for you to go there to see what you can find. Hannah knows English, doesn't she?"

"Her English seems to be excellent," Rudi said with pride.

"Then she can be a good help to you."

"What a splendid idea!" Rudi said. "When do we begin our various charades?"

"I know that this must appear to you two in the guise of a lark," she said. "But it is actually serious business. We must remember that these people are dangerous. The situation here is not quite as bad as Vienna before the *Anschluss*, but you both know how bullying and underhanded these people can be. They live according to their own creed and believe themselves to be superior to anyone else."

Rudi said, "Do you think we can forget that when they killed our father?"

"We are not at war with them yet," Amalia said. "And their presence in this country is not illegal. Mr. Churchill wants us to observe and report back."

"To spy," said Christian.

Amalia sighed. "Just remember this is real—not something out of *Boys Own Adventure Magazine*. I believe that Dr. Zaleski will be leaving for Germany on Saturday. We will begin our journeys that day as well." Full of zeal, Amalia said, "Come, Christian. To the shops!"

"One moment, Mutti," Rudi said. "Hannah was to have come here on Saturday. Shall the three of us travel to Oxford together? I would like for you to meet her. You could go on to Bath from there. I will check the trains and have it all arranged."

"That would be lovely, darling. I should like to meet this young woman. She sounds quite unique. I am interested in her work, as well."

Amalia felt more alive than she had since Rudolf's death. She and the boys had a purpose. And what they were going to do was important. Add to that the fact that she was going to get out of London, and it all seemed a very good plan to keep her occupied while Andrzej was gone. The scrim of her depression raised slightly.

At dinner, Anthony approved their plans. "Rudi, you should have some good hunting at the university. You may even bag yourself a professor or two." He smiled at Amalia. "I am glad you have something to challenge you, Baroness. I am certain you will take to Bath. It is a perfect gem, and at its best in the spring and summer. It was built up during Georgian times but sits on an old Roman site. The waters are said to be medicinal, but I must warn you, they are certainly foul tasting."

"Is there any district you would particularly recommend for us to take rooms?" she asked.

"I would recommend finding lodging in the Royal Crescent. It is rather splendid. All the architecture is neo-Classical."

Andrzej said, "Churchill remarked with a bit of humor that something in the architecture draws the Germans there."

"Yes, it is very regular, unlike the hodgepodge of most of our cities and towns," Anthony agreed.

Though Amalia was happy to have a purpose, her Saturday morning leavetaking of Andrzej at the railroad station was still difficult. Among the loud clanging and hissing, she looked into the dear, handsome face she had left so many times. "Another good-bye," she said.

Doubt and worry assailed her again as huge swastikas crowded her imagination. Would he be safe? Would she see him ever again? A sense of impending loss settled on her like a grey cloud.

She could not see past this moment. Giving into sudden desperation, she joined him on the lower step of the train, cupped the back of his head with her hand, and pulled it down for a lengthy kiss. The feel of his lips on hers made her long for a deeper caress, and she prolonged it far beyond was proper in public. In spite of all the years since she had kissed him, it was a familiar sensation.

"Amalia!" he said, his eyes full of concern. "Darling, don't worry. I'll be back."

Dropping his bag, he took her face in his hands and, lowering his mouth to hers again, kissed her gently several times.

"God go with you, dear Andrzej," she said, caressing his cheek with her gloved hand. "It may not seem so, but I am determined to be brave."

"You are the bravest person I have ever known. I will join you in Bath, darling. I shouldn't be gone more than a few weeks." He looked at her with his intense green eyes, as though trying to memorize her face. "*Aufwiedersehen, Liebchen.*"

She watched him turn his back and board, a handsome figure in a black coat and Fedora hat. Biting hard on her lower lip, she was planted in place, waiting until the train at last pulled out of the station. In the short time since Rudolf's death, Andrzej had wound his way back into her soul and now his leaving was tearing it apart. She pulled at her glove, ripping it off and putting her bare fingers to her lips where they had melded with his. Standing for a moment with her eyes closed, she let the crowd eddy around her. Finally, she walked away slowly, wending her way eventually until she met her boys at the track for the Oxford train.

Hannah met them at the train with a bouquet of spring roses for Amalia. She was a lovely young woman, just as Amalia had expected—fresh-faced, with an intelligent forehead and large, steady brown eyes. Her hair was worn up in an attractive chignon, and she smiled a brilliant smile as Rudi introduced her.

"Mother, I should like to present Fraülein Hannah Gluck. Hannah, my mother, the Baroness von Schoenenburg."

"I have looked forward to meeting you since Rudi first told me about you," Hannah said. "From his stories, I think you must be a woman in a million."

Amalia laughed a bit self-consciously. "Life has a way of putting me in the middle of interesting circumstances."

Then Hannah turned to Christian. "It is nice to see you again, Chris. I understand you have proven to be a competent spy."

Watching her younger son color up, Amalia decided the girl was charming as well as intelligent.

"My parents are still away in London, I am afraid, so it will only be the four of us for luncheon. My father has met an old friend from Vienna there and they are enjoying an extended visit, seeing the sights."

When all their luggage had been accumulated on the platform by the porter, Rudi hailed a taxi.

Once they had boarded, Christian in the front and the other three cozily sharing the back seat, Rudi said, "I have a surprise for you. I shall be putting up at the Randolph Hotel for a while until I find some lodgings."

"Splendid!" Hannah said. "How long will you stay?"

"The summer, perhaps. Then I shall join Mutti and Christian in Bath."

"Excellent! I shall put you to work in the lab."

Amalia was entertained by this exchange, and also very taken by the lovely city of medieval colleges with their gothic architecture racing by outside the taxi window. Already, she liked Oxford a great deal more than London. It had both granduer and elegance. It was entrancing to think of the many years that intense learning and discovery had been taking place on this spot. Like Vienna, it was the repository of great minds.

Hannah's home was a cottage on the Woodstock Road, very quaint, with vines growing all over it. A profusion of pink roses decorated both sides of the oak door. Their strong, sweet scent was very welcoming. Under the vines, the honey-colored stone of the cottage was the same as used for the colleges, and the roof was made of slate.

Inside, it was almost bare of furniture.

"We just moved here from Zürich, and all of our furniture there was rented. My parents originally went to London to shop for more. We do have a table and chairs, but I am afraid we won't be terribly comfortable unless we go out into the back garden. There are some lovely lounges and chairs made of wicker, left by the previous occupant. I thought we could eat out there. There is a bit of a pond with frogs and rushes. Rather quaint."

Amalia noticed piles of books in almost every room, awaiting bookshelves. Many she recognized from her uncle Lorenz's collection. "Rudi told me your family is socialist. There is a book my uncle wrote. How comforting to see it here."

"Rudi told me how devoted you were to him. It is an honor to meet someone who knew him so well."

"Poor Uncle Lorenz—the Bolsheviks and the Fascists would both disappoint him very much. The Great War would have killed him if his heart hadn't done the job first."

Except for Christian, who preferred to explore the garden and the woods beyond, everyone sat, and Hannah ordered luncheon be served to the family. Though he had never, to her knowledge, been attracted to a female with brains, Rudi seemed very comfortable to watch his mother and his new female friend interchange views on the new generation of drugs that was in the offing. It had been a long time since her days as a nurse, and Amalia was terrifically impressed by Hannah's knowledge of her subject.

"We all owe you quite a debt, my dear. Dr. Zaleski is completely recovered."

"I am so glad. The work I am doing is very rewarding when I see firsthand what it can do."

"Rudi says your family are refugees like we are," Amalia said.

"Yes."

For the first time, Hannah seemed a bit uncomfortable. "My brother was very prominent in the socialist world. He was shot by the Nazis on a streetcar in full daylight."

"You have my condolences, dear," Amalia said to Hannah's bowed head. "I imagine Rudi has told you our story."

"Yes. It is dreadful. You have my sympathies, as well, believe me." Hannah raised her head. "The Man must be stopped." Her eyes were defiant.

Rudi entered the conversation. "I am here to see if I can infiltrate the Nazi sympathizers among the students and professors."

"What will you do then?" asked Hannah.

"Take names. Glean any information I can about them for Churchill. If there is a war, they could become fifth columnists possibly spying for the Reich."

"They may be spying, even now," Hannah said.

"That's possible," Amalia said. "They hate the Jews, and they could be assembling lists of their own."

Hannah rose abruptly from her wicker chair. "Let's take a walk, and I can show you some of my favorite Oxford places."

"What time is our train, Rudi?" Amalia asked.

"We should probably be getting on to the station, unfortunately," her son said.

Rudi went to call a taxi and Hannah walked them to the front door. Putting out her hand, she said, "It was marvelous to meet you."

"And I you," Amalia said. "I will be interested to hear about the progress of your work. If there is another war, it could potentially save hundreds of thousands of lives."

Hannah smiled her very charming smile and gave them a wave as they walked down the street to meet the taxi.

Amalia thought about her son and Hannah as her train drew through the gentle hills of Oxfordshire on the way to Bath. She was completely unlike any woman Rudi had ever shown any interest in. Both pleased and slightly alarmed by this fact, she asked her youngest son, "What do you think of Hannah?"

"I think she can run rings around Rudi intellectually, but she seems to like him."

"Yes. But then, your brother is a very attractive boy. I suppose I should say man."

"Where Hannah is concerned, you should definitely say 'man.'"

&

During the two-and-a-half-day train journey to Berlin, Andrzej took note of several things once they crossed into Germany. There was a lot of action on the railways, particularly in the Rhineland. As they passed through the heavily industrial areas around Saarbrucken, he noted incoming cars loaded with scrap metal in many forms, principally old automobiles. On the eastern-bound tracks, there were new, formidable looking tanks and hundreds of closed railway cars pulled by multiple engines, signifying hefty loads.

All of Europe knew that Germany had set about rearming in 1934 when they reoccupied the Rhineland, but the practical evidence of it was sobering. One thing he did not see, however, was troop movements or supplies heading westward to the Siegfried Line. But just because they were not moving at this moment in time did not mean armies were not already in place.

When Andrzej and Max finally arrived in Berlin, they were met by a car from the Polish embassy and driven to their hotel. An envelope was handed to the doctor, containing an invitation from the Polish Ambassador, Josef Lipsky, for dinner at the embassy that night.

The feel of the streets of Berlin was very odd. Andrzej could not put a name to his impressions. Everything was neat and clean, as usual. There were brown-shirted sentries wearing swastikas on their sleeves patrolling the streets, as there had been the last time he was here. Red banners affixed to every street lantern showed emblazoned black swastikas, but even that was not new. His hotel was near the Tiergarten with its lake and outdoor restaurants. People there seemed to be enjoying themselves.

When he was deposited at his hotel and a very correct doorman removed their luggage from the curb, the driver of the embassy car asked him in Polish, "Your man, is he Jewish?"

Andrzej was startled by the question. Looking at Max, he said, "I really have no idea." The chauffeur looked at him with disdain, saying only, "I will be here at seven o'clock to collect you for dinner."

It was then that Andrzej realized what was striking him as strange. Berlin was putting on a false front. There was a whole race of people who lived in fear here. Instead of being out on the street, they were inside, behind the closed curtains he saw in so many of the flats' windows, though it was mid-afternoon. He remembered all the empty storefronts he had seen, even on some of the main streets. He now noticed a printed sign in front of his hotel: *Keinen Juden hier*. No Jews here.

When they reached their pale green and cream suite, Andrzej sat down as though he were suddenly winded. "Max, if you are Jewish, I never should have brought you here."

"I am not, Herr Doktor."

"I can't help but feel that is a good thing, under the circumstances." He pulled off his shoes. "I am going to run a bath. I'm feeling dirty for some reason."

"That is my job, I believe."

"Come, Max. You are not really my valet. You would be much happier reading a newspaper. Then you could tell us what is going on."

Max left to find a paper and Andrzej took his bath. He wished Amalia were dining with him at the embassy later that night. She could glide through the room on his arm and vocalize all her insights. And maybe later there would be another kiss. That kiss at the train station hadn't been because she was seeking comfort in her grief. That kiss had been for him. A milestone.

Suddenly, much as he had looked forward to it, he wanted to be finished with this business and back in England.

Today's Berlin would be even less to Amalia's liking than it had been when she'd lived here in 1914, during her first marriage. And she had hated it then.

The Polish embassy was pretentiously large, of gray stone and with large Corinthian columns embracing the entry. A butler opened the door to him, but Amabassador Lipsky himself met Andrzej in the marble front hall, grinning from ear to ear as he extended his hand. "It is good to have some friendly company."

Over dinner in the grand hall on a long, gleaming table, the two of them were waited on by a profusion of footmen. Andrzej asked, "Where is the rest of your diplomatic staff?"

"At a party that did not require my presence but could benefit from theirs. I preferred dinner here with you. I understand from August that you are here on a mission of sorts."

"Yes. He wanted it to be unofficial. What is the formal state of affairs between Poland and the German government?"

"They are not exactly taking us into their confidence, but their intent to integrate the Sudeten Gemans into the Reich is fairly well known in the diplomatic community. We have let them know, through back channels, that we consider Czechoslovakia an absurdity—a state artificially created by the Versailles treaty. We have no quarrel with their ambitions in that regard."

Andrzej kept his opinion that this was very unwise to himself. If Poland did not side with the Czechoslovaks, who did they suppose would side with Poland when the time came? They were only alienating future allies—Britain, France, and Russia. And nothing was a more "artificial creation," in Andrzej's opinion, than the so-called Polish Corridor, running right through the province of Eastern Prussia to give Poland access to the seaport city of Danzig.

"Is this thinking of yours generally known?" Andrzej asked while slicing his savory Polish ham.

Lipsky replied, "Only privately at this point. The Foreign Secretary wants to get the point across unofficially that we favor German partition of Czechoslovakia into its indigenous parts. That way, we begin to lay the case for the occupation of Teschen."

"Our occupation of Teschen is not worth a world war," Andrzej said flatly.

"There won't be a war. The British and French won't fight," Lipsky said with a raised eyebrow.

Andrzej was reminded forcibly of why he had left government service. "You seem very sure of that."

"Everyone knows there is no will behind their words."

"You had better hope that is not the case when the Germans decide they want Danzig and the Polish Corridor back."

Lipsky shot him a startled look. "To whom have you been talking?"

Andrzej decided to stop before he betrayed himself. "It is my opinion only."

"Well, if I were you, I would keep it to myself. As it happens, we are invited to a German government function tomorrow night. We alone will represent Poland."

"What is the affair?"

"As far as I can tell, it is largely ceremonial. The Germans frequently put on these demonstrations of the power and will of the Third Reich. Mostly for the benefit of the Russians, I think. All the top generals will be there wearing their campaign ribbons and medals of honor. And, of course, top party members—Goering, Von Ribbentrop, Goebbels."

"Not Hitler?"

"No. He has journeyed down to Obersalzburg to stay in his fortress for the spring."

After drinking Schnapps together near the fire in the large, wood-paneled drawing room, the doctor and Lipsky parted for the evening. Andrzej was glad of it, for he was having a difficult time holding on to his temper. Lipsky and the Polish Foreign Secretary had a blind spot as big as an elephant, it appeared. Could they not see that a display of power for the benefit of the Russians was meant equally for the Poles, Czechs, Romanians, and anyone else who was likely to get in the way of Hitler's ambition?

He wondered if the French and British would be taken in. Probably. From what he understood, the British Ambassador, Neville Henderson, sympathized highly with the German aims to gain more "living room" by wiping its eastern neighbors off the map. Again, Andrzej wished for Amalia's presence. Perhaps an account of what Austria had really endured prior to the *Anschluss* would shake Lipsky's dreamworld.

He went to bed discouraged. There was only one bright spot in his thinking. Undoubtedly, the German General Ludwig Beck would be at the function tomorrow night. Perhaps Andrzej could begin his mission with a friendly invitation to the general to play a game of chess.

{ 19 }

Amalia could understand how the symmetry and neo-classical beauty of Bath could appeal to the German mind. Though she still preferred the lavishly whimsical Baroque style of Vienna, she liked the brightness of Bath. The buildings were a shade of palest yellow with white trim marching up steep streets until they reached a summit where the Royal Crescent of identical flats was built. The roads were uniformly cobbled with matching brick, and the public buildings—the Assembly Rooms and the Pump Room—were charming.

She and Christian stayed at the White Hart while looking for a flat. It was a comfortable hotel with an excellent concierge who spoke German and obtained for them a membership to the Assembly Rooms. They attended a Bach concert the first night they were in residence. Amalia felt more at home that evening than any night since she had arrived in England. Her depression over Rudolf's death and her anxiety for Andrzej's safety retreated somewhat now that she had something of her own to accomplish. During the concert, she observed the crowd. They were almost uniformly middle-aged or older. One man, of a decidedly Teutonic cast—tall and blond—was younger than most and spent a good deal of time looking over the crowd through an old-fashioned monocle. His gaze focused on Amalia more than once.

The following day, the concierge located a German-speaking estate agent who was eager to help them find a flat to rent. He was exceedingly obliging, and soon she and Chris had settled on a furnished flat, taken for the duration of the spring and summer months in the Royal Crescent. Mr. Churchill had certainly been accurate in his estimation. According to the estate agent, there were many Germans holidaying or actually living in Bath. The estate agent even assured them that their neighbor was German, which Amalia and Christian thought to be an excellent start to their careers as spies.

Frau Schratt had moved to Bath temporarily for her health, claiming that the waters had ameliorated her rheumatism. She was a plump woman who wore her white hair in an old-fashioned coronet wound around her head. A black silk dress decorated only with a long string of pearls proclaimed her status as a widow. Amalia strongly suspected that she still wore stays to confine her overly curvaceous body.

"I must take you to the Pump Room as soon as you are settled, Frau Faulhaber," she said the next day when Amalia was settled in her new flat. "Even if you do not take the waters, it is a lovely place to spend the morning. A string quartet performs there, and they serve light refreshments. Most importantly, it is the place to be seen. You will meet all of Bath's best society there. Maybe even a handsome man?"

Amalia was on her way to liking the kindly Frau Schratt very well until she visited her flat that morning to take coffee. There in the overcrowded dwelling, she saw a picture of the Führer hanging prominently over the mantle. Her stomach clenched and she remembered the reason she was in Bath.

"Ah! I see you are looking at my picture of our great Führer. He is doing wonderful things for the Fatherland, nicht wahr?"

Amalia, who was posing as a citizen of Munich, smiled brightly. "Yes. Under the Führer, Germany will become great again."

Frau Schratt gleamed. "You are right!"

"Do you have children, Frau Schratt?" asked Amalia.

"A son, yes. He is serving as a colonel in the Wehrmacht. But he is very secretive, I am afraid. I do not know where he is stationed. Have you children other than Christian?"

Her reply was interesting. So the Wehrmacht's troop movements were secret?

"Yes, I do. My eldest son is studying biochemistry at Oxford. That is why we moved to England. But, I did not like Oxford. Too English. I heard there were many Germans living in Bath, so we came here, Christian and I."

Her hostess placed her cup in her saucer with a brisk motion. "Come, let us not delay. We will go to the Pump Room this morning. I should like you to meet a few of my special friends."

Traveling in one of the old-fashioned pony carts which abounded in the town, they arrived at the famed establishment. Baskets of red, purple, and white petunias hung on hooks on either side of the tall doors. Amalia went over the details of her new persona in her mind.

At that moment, Christian sailed past her on a bicycle but stopped when he saw her.

"Mutti! Good morning!"

"Good morning, Chris. You remember our new neighbor, Frau Schratt?"

"*Guten Morgen*, Frau Schratt! Mutti, I am bound to buy a crew uniform. I met some fellows who row on the Avon. They are one short and asked me to join their Eight."

Amalia was gratified that he had found some young people. And Chris's English was far better than hers.

"Have a good time, then!" she said.

Once they entered the grand Pump Room with its white walls, large sunny windows, and high ceilings, she tried to relax into her role. Frau Schratt headed for a knot of people surrounding a bar which evidently contained the famous water pump. After purchasing a small liqueur glass of water, Frau Schratt began introductions.

Amalia immediately became aware of the tall, blond man she had noticed at the Bach concert. His eyes were light blue and he was looking her over appreciatively. He let his monocle drop, and the hand which went to straighten his tie knot was beautifully manicured. Hitler would have thought him the perfect Aryan. His steady regard made her uneasy.

"My friends, this is my new neighbor, Frau Faulhaber. She is from Munich." Turning to Amalia, she said, "Frau Faulhaber, this is Frau Knebel from Mainz."

Amalia shook the hand of a tall, fiftyish woman with a flat chest, broad hips, and a stern expression. Her gray hair was waved all over her head. "I am pleased to meet you," she said.

Frau Knebel nodded a somewhat cold greeting.

Frau Schratt continued, introducing a fair, blonde woman with bright red lipstick who was assessing Amalia openly. "This is Fraülein Knebel, her daughter."

Ah, she sees me as competition for the Aryan gentleman.

After introducing another matron with winged eyebrows and steel gray hair worn in a ballerina bun on top of her head as Frau Vogel, she finally came to the man. "Meet Herr Rheinhard Boos, from Berlin. He is on holiday in England, but the rest of us are living here for now."

Herr Boos raised the hand she offered to his lips and kissed her knuckles. "It is my pleasure," he said smoothly. "What brings you to Bath?"

"My son is studying at Oxford. As I am a widow, I traveled here to be near him, but I found Oxford too difficult for a woman with no English." She smiled hesitantly, trying to seem vulnerable and impressionable. "My youngest son and I came here where we heard there was a small enclave of people from our country. I thought we would be more comfortable."

"And yet, you do not speak like a Münchener, Frau Faulhaber. I would have said you were an Austrian."

Her mind raced. "How clever you are!" She gave him the benefit of a dazzling smile. "My husband met me on a skiing holiday in Innsbruck. When we were married, of course we went to live on his family estate outside Munich."

I shall have to watch myself with this one. If I am not mistaken, he is a bona fide Nazi.

Amalia quelled the shiver that threatened to betray her.

"Faulhaber . . . Faulhaber, I cannot say that I know the name," he said, narrowing his eyes.

Amalia thought it best to ignore this. "Frau Knebel, what brings you to Bath?"

The question seemed to stymie her. Finally, she replied, "The waters, of course. My daughter is delicate."

Fraülein Knebel rolled her eyes at that. "I am an Anglophile," she said. "My mother is deeply ashamed of the fact."

Frau Vogel said, "I am very pleased to meet you, Frau Faulhaber. I am originally from Hamburg. You will find that there are others from our country here as well, though many of them have not been back to Germany for years."

Did she imagine it, or was this group in the grip of some sort of tension? She said, "For myself, I do not understand why anyone would prefer to live here over Germany. I find the English to be very cold and unsympathetic. A carryover from the Great War, possibly?"

"More likely it is hostility to our Führer," said Frau Vogel. "But he has made Germany a country to be proud of again!"

"Yes, indeed," agreed Amalia.

Herr Boos said, "There is saber-rattling in some quarters, but on the whole, I think England believes Hitler does not want another war. What is your impression, Frau Faulhaber?"

She said with complete truth, "I believe you are right. I think the British government is dedicated to peace."

Fraülein Knebel said, "Herr Boos and I are holding a meeting tonight for the purpose of disabusing people of any ideas they might have that Hitler wants a war. Would you and your son like to attend? It will be held at the White Hart at eight o'clock."

"I should be delighted," Amalia replied. "It sounds a very worthwhile cause." Such a meeting would surely be worth reporting on to Mr. Churchill.

Herr Boos walked across their little circle, extending his arm. "A stroll around the room, perhaps?"

Taking his arm, she said, "Thank you. That would be delightful."

For a while they walked in silence, listening to the string quartet playing Vivaldi. Finally, she said, "This is a very pleasant room."

"Yes," he replied. "Tell me, I am curious: As an Austrian, what do you think of the *Anschluss*?"

Amalia was completely unprepared for the question. Images of Rudolf being riddled with SS bullets flashed into her mind and she clenched her teeth. She could not possibly emit unbridled enthusiasm. "I have been living in Germany for half my life, you must remember."

"Still, you must have an opinion," he insisted, smiling down at her.

"The Austria I lived in before the war was the center of a great empire. After the war, it was reduced to almost nothing. Union with Germany causes me mixed feelings, I must admit."

"Because Germany is now the greater power?" he asked.

She willed her voice to be steady. "More because Austria no longer exists at all. On the other hand, I am not blind to the advantages we now have. Having a strong, charismatic leader cannot be underestimated in today's Europe."

"You are correct. But I did not expect you to be quite so honest about your feelings."

Amalia could feel his subtle approval and was glad she had been able to subdue her true thoughts. Nevertheless, she felt she was on shaky ground. This was much harder than she thought it would be. "Ah! They are playing Bach. Wonderful. My son is a violinist and he does Bach very nicely."

"Pardon me if it is a sore subject, but for how long has your husband been deceased?"

She longed to blurt out, "A month," but instead she bowed her head and murmured, "A little more than a year. I miss him terribly. He was a very good man."

"Forgive me. I can see that it is a painful topic."

"It was very sudden. I still have difficulty believing it." She had no need to simulate emotions in this instance. "May we please change the subject?"

"I am truly sorry for you loss, Frau Faulhaber. Excuse my intrusion on your grief."

She didn't know what to say, so she remained silent. There were more people in the Pump Room, she noted. And the circle of Germans had grown. Could she really keep up this charade? The man strolling next to her struck her as dangerous. He was certainly her enemy.

But then, she had been dealing with her enemies for years.

With Hannah's help, Rudi was able to find several German-language literature classes to audit at Balliol College. These he used as cover to meet other German-speaking students, telling them he intended to enroll during the special summer term as a visitor studying English. At first, he met no one remarkable.

After several days of classes, however, he was invited out to the pub with two young men known to him as Felder and Kuhlmann. Felder was a rather scrawny fellow with closely cut red hair and a habit of biting his nails. Kuhlmann was smoothly handsome with blade-like cheekbones, a cleft chin, and dark brown hair. An improbable pair.

They chose a pub on Broad Street upstairs over a shop. As they entered, Rudi saw a group gathered around the darts board, and booths full to bursting all about the outer walls of the room. The light was dim, as the shades were pulled halfway down and only a few solitary bulbs dangled from the ceiling. Felder and Kuhlmann walked up and leaned on the nickel-plated bar, each ordering a pint of bitters. Rudi ordered the same.

Felder asked him, "Why Oxford, Schoenenburg? Why not Heidelberg?"

Rudi answered. "I have a girl here. Met her in Switzerland. She's studying biochemistry."

Both young men laughed and slapped him on the back.

"What are you two doing here?"

They shrugged. "We're part of Germans for Peace in Europe. We hold meetings with our English counterparts on the Cornmarket each night around eight. We get a decent crowd."

"Sounds interesting. You really think the Führer wants peace with England, then?"

"We think he wants the Sudeten Germans in the Reich, where they belong. And of course he wants Danzig and the Polish Corridor back. Those are our right. But he doesn't want war with England or France," Felder said, his voice positive and sincere. He took a large swig from his tankard.

Kuhlmann contributed, "My father was killed at Verdun in the Great War. Felder's was killed at Ypres. Many of the Englishmen here are in the same situation. We have even met some whose fathers were killed in the same battles as ours." He drained his pint. "We have a bond, of sorts. No one wants another war."

Rudi nodded solemnly, feeling unexpectedly sympathetic. These very young men would most likely be fighting for Hitler before the year was out. "My father fought as well," he said. "Let me buy this round."

As they were drinking their second pints, Rudi said, "Do you think the English and the French will really let Germany take the Sudetenland and the Polish Corridor without a fight?"

Felder said, "That is the big question. That is why we're here. We want to help feed the groundswell movement for peace."

"And you're not attached to the Party?"

"No," Kuhlmann said. "We're just students. There are others like us in France and the Low Countries. We developed our movement while we were at University in Heidelberg."

Rudi felt a tap on his shoulder. Turning, he recognized Hannah's co-worker, Reinquist.

"Hello, Baron. Care to put your skill to the test?" He held up a handful of darts.

"By all means. Do you know Kuhlmann and Felder?"

He nodded curtly at the two men. "We've met."

Rudi's new friends' faces turned hard. They returned Reinquist's nod but said nothing.

What is this? What's happening here?

He didn't understand his unease. Rudi liked his fellow students, and he definitely didn't like the lab assistant. But he couldn't afford likes and dislikes. He was scouting for information. Taking the handful of darts presented him, he said, "Until later," to Kuhlmann and Felder and joined the group around the dartboard.

Rudi was an exceptionally fine dart player. As with anything athletic, he had a natural gift. Reinquist seemed to play with deadly intentions. Sweat broke out on the man's forehead and under his arms. When Rudi won the first game, Reinquist insisted that they play the best of three. Upon Rudi's winning the following game, Reinquist said, "The best of five, and just to make it more interesting, this is for the Jew whore!"

Rudi turned to the man, perplexed. Reinquist's eyes were glassy, his grin a leer.

"Of whom are you speaking?" Rudi asked, keeping his voice low.

"Didn't know Gluck was a Jew, did you? Or a whore!" The lab assistant gloated.

The instant Rudi realized the man was referring to Hannah, he did not even stop to think. Drawing his fist back, he hit Reinquist squarely on his long, thin nose. The man's head snapped back, but he pulled up his fists and went for Rudi's face. Rudi was able to deflect the blow while planting another one on Reinquist's left eye. While he was staggering, Rudi finished him off with an uppercut to the chin which knocked him down. A crowd had grown around them. Reinquist had hit his head hard on the floor and appeared to be out cold.

Rudi looked around him. There was more than one leer in the crowd. Before he lost his temper completely and hit someone else, he gathered his hat from the coatrack, placed it on his head, and left the pub.

Felder and Kuhlmann followed him.

"What was that about?" Kuhlmann asked. "Reinquist is a nasty fellow to get on the wrong side of."

"He insulted my girl. Called her a whore." Rudi couldn't think about the other accusation. Not now. "What do you know about the beggar?"

"Rumor has it he's a Party member," Felder said.

"A Nazi?"

"Right."

Rudi considered this. The man was probably a spy, gathering information from the lab for the Germans. Penicillin would be worth millions during wartime. Rudi had to tell Heatley. But now, he needed to go somewhere to think. Was Hannah really a Jew? Wouldn't she have told him? How could there be any future for them?

He and his new friends went back to the dormitory. Rudi let himself into his spare-looking room. Its walls were bare; his bed had only sheets, a scratchy wool blanket, and a flat pillow. The ancient, scarred desk held his anthology of classic German short fiction for his class, and a bound notebook.

The desk chair was ladder-backed and uncomfortable, so he stretched out on the bed.

Hannah is a Jew.

Anti-Semitism was as much a part of Viennese culture as Apfelstrudel, but he had never understood it. The great twentieth-century minds that had given Vienna much of its music, theater, and scientific thinking were Jewish. His mother's closest friend, Rosa Gruen, was a Jewish nurse she had worked with during the War. He could honestly say that he was not an anti-Semite.

The real problem was that the Catholic Church was the only legitimate church in Austria. Would a marriage between a baron and a Jew even be recognized?

Marriage. Since when had he even begun to think of marriage? He was only eighteen!

Rudi examined his mind and his crazy heart. The truth was, he realized, Hannah was not the type of woman he usually dated. Even though he was not going to marry for years, she was the type of woman one married—intelligent, high-minded. It didn't hurt, of course, that she was entrancing and made his pulse race.

He just couldn't imagine dallying with her and moving on. He had already noted that in many respects, she was as unusual a woman as his mother. Would she, in time, become to him what his mother was to Zaleski? He could imagine it.

But what does she even think of me? She probably sees me as a boy.

Nevertheless, he couldn't put his troubling concerns out of his mind. Perhaps it would be best if he didn't see her for a few days.

Andrzej and Amabassador Lipsky arrived at the elaborate party when it was in full swing. Most of the round tables were filled with champagne-drinking guests. The huge hall was hung with three giant red, white, and black swastika banners at each end. An enormous portrait of Hitler on the wall opposite the double entrance doors greeted them. Andrzej spotted members of the military in their field green and red dress uniforms, wearing gleaming Hessian boots. The party elite were surrounded by sycophants. He wondered at what table he and Lipsky had been placed.

With the usual efficiency of the Germans, there was a waiter inside with a list. Looking up their names, he pointed them to table thirty-seven in the far corner. Andrzej guessed they were probably seated with Lithuanians and Latvians—if they were lucky.

It turned out to be worse. They were seated with the Belgian and Dutch legations. Andrzej talked politely with them about spring in Berlin, the German Opera, and his admiration for the Rijksmuseum in Amsterdam. No one dared to speak what was really on their minds. Would Hitler go into Czechoslovakia or wouldn't he? And if he did, would the Western democracies fight?

During the lengthy four-course dinner—soup, fish, game, and chocolate torte with coffee—Andrzej tried to be unobtrusive about locating his acquaintance, General Beck. He was not at the head table. Von Brauchitsch, the Wehrmacht liaison with Hitler, had that honor. He finally located Beck sitting directly under the Hitler portrait. When the tables began to break up, Andrzej excused himself to the Belgians and Dutch and headed in that direction. He felt a surge of adrenaline. There was a great deal riding on this meeting.

"Herr General Beck!" Andrzej greeted the man with assumed heartiness as he bowed. "Herr Doktor Zaleski, if you remember me."

"Ah, yes, Herr Doktor. I remember you, of course. The chess player." He actually looked pleased to see him. "I am desperately in need of a diversion just now. And chess is the best diversion, don't you agree? It sharpens your mind and relaxes it all at once."

"I do agree. But, of course, it would be of great interest to a military man of your stature. One must plan several moves ahead if one is to win against a talented opponent. What better exercise in strategy?" Andrzej asked.

Beck narrowed his eyes, no doubt wondering if the doctor was about to sound him out on military strategy. He had a very ascetic face—high cheekbones, deeply set eyes. One could immediately perceive his intelligence. Andrzej had found him to be a worthy chess opponent and was certain he was a gifted general. But surely those were new lines on his forehead?

"I was surprised not to see your Führer here tonight," Andrzej continued.

"Ach!" said Beck, jerking up his chin. "He is communing with nature at Obersalzburg. He goes there when the weather thaws."

"Hmm. A nature lover? Maybe he paints there?"

Beck laughed heartily. "No. He has given that up. I think instead he spends his time playing chess with himself. He considers himself a brilliant strategist, you realize."

Andrzej was surprised at such open scorn. Churchill was right. The military did see itself as more significant than its commander-in-chief.

"As I said, I am in need of a diversion," Beck said, as though making a grave announcement. "Say you will join me for an evening of chess soon."

Andrzej gave a slight bow of his head. "I am at your service, Herr General. When and where would you like to meet?"

"Hmm. Today is Monday. I must go down to Karinhall on Saturday for a weekend with the Goerings. What have you to say about Friday night? I can send my driver for you at eight o'clock."

"That would be most enjoyable," Andrzej answered. He gave Beck the name of his hotel, they shook hands, and the doctor walked off, wondering at his easy success. Beck must want to pick his brain about something. Andrzej had detected weariness in the general's voice, and perhaps an unconscious look of vexation at his Führer's portrait.

What was going on with the military?

{ 20 }

Hannah had not seen Rudi in days. She was surprised how much she missed him. In addition to that was the fact that Reinquist was making her job intolerable. He had shown up at work with a black eye, a broken nose, and a surlier attitude than ever before. She caught him looking at her with a hate that actually frightened her.

One day when Dr. Heatley was meeting with other scientists over a case at the Radcliffe Infirmary, the lab assistant approached her while she was looking through her microscope. "Wondering where your sweetheart is?" he asked.

"Not in the least," she replied, keeping her eyes on the slide she was examining.

"The truth is I frightened him off."

Startled, she looked up. His one visible eye sparked with mischief.

"I informed him of your racial inferiority. He didn't take it well."

Hannah bit her lower lip. "Go away," she said. Her voice came out as a harsh whisper.

Laughing, he strolled off to his own research station while her heart pounded. For the rest of the day, she couldn't keep her mind on her work.

She couldn't really blame Rudi for staying away. He had been growing to care for her, and now he must know there was no future between them. Aware of a sharp ache inside, she tried to dismiss the entire relationship, to cut it off at the root. They had never even kissed! What did it matter? She reapplied herself to detailing the results of her experiment. But the ache persisted. The truth was that it mattered to her deeply that he did not think well of her.

Hannah was surprised, therefore, when he met her at work's end that day. He was waiting on the bench outside the laboratory in a fine, misty rain.

"Rudi!" she said. "I thought you'd left Oxford."

"No," he said, his voice low and solemn. "I've been here. Thinking."

He looked so serious and uncertain that she burst out, "So I didn't tell you I was Jewish! We're just friends, Rudi!"

Standing in one motion, he strode over to her, gathered her to him, and kissed her with such disturbing passion, it shocked her. A current zinged clear through her, and Hannah found she was kissing him back.

"Just friends?" he asked when he finally ended the kiss.

"I'm sorry, Rudi," she said, looking down. "I should have said something when you made a point of coming to Oxford the second time. But I was growing fond of you."

"Were you?" he asked.

"You know, of course, there is no good ending to a story between us," she said. He looked more handsome than ever today, his brown eyes deep and soft with desire. Hannah took his hand and stroked it with her thumb. "I wish we lived in a less complicated, less judgmental world."

"I am not anti-Semitic, Hannah. I am not even a good Catholic. I wasn't raised to be."

The smile she gave him was from deep in her heart. "But my parents are very good Jews. Judaism is not something you can put on or take off. Particularly not in this day and age. It is who you are."

At that moment, the door to the lab opened and Reinquist joined them on the stoop. When he saw Rudi, his face contorted in anger. "When you have finished your good-byes, I sincerely hope you are planning on leaving Oxford. You are not welcome here."

Rudi put his arm around Hannah and drew her to his side. "This is a very large university. There is certainly room for both of us."

"Accidents happen," Reinquist returned. "Particularly to Jew-lovers." He moved off and was soon lost to view in the heavy mist.

"It's very wet out here, darling," Rudi said. "Let's find a taxi and go to our pub. The one we went to the other day."

"Rudi, why prolong this?"

"I haven't had my say," he told her.

When they entered the fastness of the good English pub, Hannah felt her spirits lift. It was full, but they found an empty corner to stand where the din dissolved into background noise, giving them an illusion of privacy.

"All right, Rudi," she said. "Let's have it."

"The world is going to go through a period of upheaval shortly. I really, truly believe there is going to be a war. I intend to fight. Whether we have any future together at all is uncertain." Taking her chin in his hand, he tilted her face up, meeting her eyes. "Please, Hannah. Let us at least have today."

Perhaps it was the wine she was drinking, perhaps it was the warm conviviality of the pub, but Hannah felt a weight lift from her breast. "Rudi, I think that . . . I find that I want to give you today."

Standing on her tip-toes, she kissed him briefly on the lips. Electricity arced between them, pulling them closer until she was standing with her head pillowed on his chest, crushed on all sides by the after-work crowd. But for all she sensed, they could have been alone on a meadow. In that moment, Rudi was her world.

&

Amalia didn't know if she was being courted by Herr Reinhard Boos or whether he was suspicious of her for some reason. He strolled with her each morning at the Pump Room and asked her questions about herself. She stuck to the truth as closely as possible, mainly so she could remember her answers and wouldn't trip herself up.

The discussions at The White Hart were unremarkable in the sense that she learned nothing new. There were rarely any people there who were not German, and the discussions principally revolved around Hitler's "reasonable" intentions of gaining the Sudetenland and the return of the Polish Corridor.

After a few days of this, Amalia began to grow bored. She decided to step up her game. On her morning stroll with Herr Boos, she asked, "How long is your holiday to be?"

"I am retired," he said. "I have no matters of business to attend to. I am enjoying the company in Bath, Frau Faulhaber. How is your son at Oxford? It isn't term time at the moment, is it?"

She gave a little laugh. "I actually have no idea. He doesn't write much. He has a girlfriend."

"An English miss?"

"No. She is Swiss. A biochemist, also."

"Will they be married, do you think?"

"Oh," Amalia replied, "I shouldn't think so, with the future so uncertain."

Herr Boos stopped strolling and looked down into her eyes. "You believe there will be a war?"

"Yes. I think there must be. You may think the German demands are reasonable, but the Polish and the Czechs each have a French guarantee to come to their aid if they are attacked by Germany. I believe you conveniently forget that. If the French fight, of course the English will fight. And I do not want a war."

"So you think our Führer is wrong? That he should not pursue his course?"

"I did not say that," Amalia said stoutly. "I just do not think you should discount France and Britain as you do." Deciding she was getting nowhere by playing it safe, she looked up into his light blue eyes. "My first husband was Prussian. He died at Verdun. I do not think there is anything glorious about blood."

Herr Boos narrowed his eyes. "You are very emphatic. Why have you never voiced these thoughts during our discussions at the White Hart?"

"They would not be welcome. They are not welcome to you, if I am not mistaken." Amalia's heart was beating hard. Had she crossed the line?

He put her arm through his and began walking again. "Do you feel the Versailles Treaty was just?"

"Certainly not," she said with perfect truth. "I don't believe anyone feels it was just anymore."

"You puzzle me greatly, Frau Faulhaber."

"Why is that?" she asked.

"I think you are being deliberately provocative today."

"Not at all," Amalia said with a laugh. "I am merely speaking the truth as I see it."

Herr Reinhard Boos had no answer to that, and Amalia hoped she had given him plenty to think about. She couldn't really explain her desire to draw him out. He was certainly not going to own up to being an enemy to Britain if she tangled with him this way.

She told herself that she just wanted her German acquaintances to be realistic. They made everything sound so reasonable. Aside from Herr Boos, she liked them. She wanted them to see they were being led into a dangerous conflagration by a man full of hatred who cared for nothing but his own will, his own glory. Amalia doubted her ability to play at being a Hitler-worshipper for much longer.

She wasn't sleeping well, but it had nothing to do with her mission in Bath. It was then, when she was alone and the room was dark, that her fears and feelings of abandonment crept in. She found herself bargaining with God again.

"I have lost my husband. I was true to him. I loved him as much as I possibly could. I miss his dependability, his sense of honor, his support. I feel like part of me died with him: The

Amalia of Vienna. Now I am in a foreign country where I do not speak the language. My life and the life of my children could be in danger."

Then in a moment, her mind would leap to Andrzej. "Please protect him. Please don't let him be caught. That is the one thing of all others that I could not bear."

Then her mind would sink into a whirl of anxiety which caused her to toss in the bedclothes until light started to show through the curtains. Only then, with the hope of dawn, could she calm herself enough to sleep.

&

General Ludwig Beck lived in a small suburb of Berlin in a modest stone house set on a wooded lot. He met Andrzej at the door himself, holding out his hand, "Ah, Herr Doktor! Welcome again to my home."

"You are very kind to offer me your hospitality."

"Your cousin, Undersecretary Zaleski, he is well?"

"Yes. And your family?"

"They are well, thank you. Staying in the country now, so I am glad of your company."

He led Andrzej back to his comfortable study, where a fire burned and his intricately carved chess set awaited them. The doctor noticed with interest that there was a separate, windowed door to the room that led out into the back garden. As Beck lit a pipe, Andrzej threw a brief glance at the desk, which appeared to be piled high with documents. It crossed his mind to wonder if, in addition to his other talents, Max was adept at picking locks.

He also felt something changed about the room. Something was missing. It wasn't until his third chess move that he realized what was gone. Since his last visit, the portrait of Hitler which had hung above the mantel had been replaced by a nineteenth century battle scene.

That was something worth knowing.

As he was concentrating on his fourth move, the general asked, "Did you fight in the Great War, Herr Doktor? I do not remember that we have ever discussed it."

"I did, Herr General."

"Ah, ja! I remember now! You fought with Britain and France against us. For the future Polish state."

"That is correct."

"Tell me, if you would be so good, what do you think of the French as a fighting force?"

Andrzej made his move and then looked up at his opponent. The general was studying him, intent upon his response, his slender, chiseled face motionless.

"I don't know that I could really give you a meaningful answer based on my own experience in the war. I fought beside the British."

Beck made his move. He said thoughtfully, "Today I believe the French have the strongest army in Europe. Your country has a close relationship with France, does it not?"

Andrzej debated what he should answer as he studied the board. Beck was digging for information.

Surely his sources are better than mine.

"Czechoslovakia, Poland, Yugoslavia—we are all dependent on France to preserve the stability in Central Europe. It is in their best interests to do so, after all."

"Yes . . . you are wise not to trust Russia. But then, Stalin just purged half his army, so perhaps they are not such a threat."

Andrzej knew that both of them were very aware that the real threat was Germany. But perhaps this worry over France indicated that Beck was not entirely confident of the strength of his army?

I must get Max in here with his camera. Beck is Chief of Staff. I'll bet that desk is a treasure trove of information.

Andrzej decided the best strategy was to let Beck win, so at the last minute, he made a calculated bad decision and threw the game. His host, well pleased, brought out a bottle of peppermint Schnapps and they relaxed before the fire.

"Your wife is a Berliner," Beck said.

"Former wife. Yes."

"You have remarried?"

Andrzej shook his head. "No."

"You should remarry. A wife is very important to a man in your position."

"I hope to one day," Andrzej said, allowing his thoughts to linger on Amalia. He had not learned enough from Beck to make this foray into the enemy camp at all worthwhile. He had been caught up with the whole idea as if it were a game. He and Max had left Amalia alone and unprotected. Suddenly, he wanted to toss this entire mission and return to her. What if she overplayed her hand in Bath? What if her true identity caught up with her?

The evening wound down as Beck shared memories of the Great War. Andrzej had difficulty concentrating on the discussion, but he received the impression that Beck missed those days of the Reichswehr and its autonomy. The Wehrmacht's commander-in-chief had only been a corporal in the trenches after all, while Beck had been a staff officer in the conflict. It had to be galling.

Somehow, I've got to find out something concrete. Those documents on the desk are the best option.

{ 21 }

Max smiled broadly at the news that he was to break in to General Beck's study.

"He will probably take all his documents to Wehrmacht Headquarters during the day," Andrzej said. "But he was complaining of a party Goering is giving at Karinhall that he must attend this weekend. It is a house party. He will be gone from Saturday morning until Sunday evening." He smiled as Max jumped up from his chair and began to quickly pace the room. "I think Saturday night would be the ideal time to stage a break-in."

"I will need to buy darkroom supplies and photo paper."

"Do it," said Andrzej.

Saturday evening could not have been better for such a job. It was overcast and drizzling. Max pulled up the collar of his raincoat as he dismissed the cab, which had left him a quarter of a mile from Beck's home. Zaleski had never noticed a manservant, but being in the military, Beck probably had a batman acting as a valet. If so, hopefully he had taken him to Karinhall.

As he neared the house he had surveyed from a cab window that afternoon, he noticed no lights on. Good news. Of course, it was midnight, so any servant might be in bed by now.

Making a broad circle around the house through the thick, fragrant evergreens, he entered the back garden and switched on his torch. Stepping carefully, he walked close to the house and soon identified the windowed door to the study. He extracted the lock picks from his pocket. There was a challenging dead bolt. Shutting off his torch, Max worked by touch until at last the bolt yielded.

He opened the door and stepped into the room. It smelled of pipe smoke. The first thing he did was to draw the heavy velvet drapes, which had been left open. Switching on his torch once again, he stepped to the desk, which was covered with files.

He removed the small camera from his pocket. A file labeled "Memoranda: Von Brauchitsch" was the first thing he saw. Sticking a second, brighter torch between his teeth, he focused on the pages of the file and snapped pictures rapidly.

Another file: "Troop Disposition." He followed the same procedure.

It was then that he heard the footsteps. Someone was proceeding cautiously down the stairs. Cursing inwardly, he snapped one last photograph, switched off the torch, and replaced the files. He fumbled behind the draperies for the doorknob. As he opened the door, he heard a gasp coming from the room behind him.

Max ran.

&

As Rudi walked Hannah home after an evening in the Eagle and Child, he insisted that it was time for her to introduce him to her parents.

"That's not a good idea, Rudi," she said.

He squeezed her about the waist. "You aren't ashamed of me, are you? I'm very respectable, you know."

"It would worry them," she said.

"Because I'm not Jewish?"

"Yes. Let's not make this any harder than it has to be."

Rudi disliked anything that smacked of subterfuge, but he had no choice other than to go along with her wishes in the matter.

"What are you going to do about Reinquist?" he asked.

"What makes you think I can do anything?"

"It's not like you to be passive. I think you should go to Heatley and tell him the man is harassing you. What if he's a Nazi? What if he's stealing the lab's research and sending it back to Germany?"

"I've thought of that, believe it or not. He says he despises Hitler, but then he would say that, wouldn't he?"

The night was dead black and with no lights to guide her, Hannah tripped over something in the road. Rudi caught her before she could fall. With her in his arms, he couldn't resist another kiss. He had never been so ignited by a woman. He was on fire for her. They were encircled by the warmth of their own little world.

From out of the darkness, he suddenly became aware of something hard poking him in the middle of his back. For a moment, his senses, inflamed by Hannah's kiss, failed to identify his danger. When he realized he was being held at gunpoint, he ended the kiss, stiffening and pulling Hannah closer. He looked over his shoulder and saw the sharp features belonging to Reinquist.

"What do you want?" he asked harshly.

"I found out who you are, von Shoenenburg. You and your precious barony are supposed to be dead! There is no place for your kind in the Third Reich." His enemy's voice was full of hatred.

"So you are a Nazi."

"An SS officer, actually," he said. "And you're right. I'm here about the penicillin. But you and your Jew whore aren't going to live long enough to tell anyone."

Rudi felt Hannah's hands fumbling between them. Then there was the ear-splitting blast of a whistle.

The shrill sound made the pistol waver, so Rudi twisted around and chopped Reinquist's wrist hard enough to make the gun fall. They heard running footsteps and saw a light coming from the direction of the pub. The SS officer cursed both of them and ran in the direction of Carfax and the Cornmarket. That thoroughfare still had a crowd, even at this time of night.

Rudi picked up the pistol just as the bobby approached, brandishing a flashlight and night stick.

Hannah broke into a spate of English. When Rudi heard the words "SS," he relinquished the pistol to the bobby.

"He wants us to go to the station and make a full report about the threat to us and the penicillin and everything," Hannah told him.

"All right. You saved our lives with that devilish whistle," Rudi said.

Hannah was shaking. "My father doesn't like how dark the Oxford streets are at night. He gave it to me. But I have no doubt you would have figured a way to turn his pistol against him."

Rudi wasn't so certain. His heart was still pounding wildly from the encounter.

Andrzej saw Max running toward the taxi he had waiting. Jumping out, he opened the door and his friend climbed inside.

"Someone's coming!" he said. "Let's be off!"

As the taxi sped away, Andrzej questioned his friend. "Did you get anything?"

"I hope so. We'll see how the photos come out."

Andrzej paid the driver handsomely, but he doubted that would desuade him from talking if the Gestapo was called in. It would be an easy matter to trace their cab and their destination. As a precaution, they took only a few necessary items from their room and then took a streetcar to a hotel on the other side of the city. Max immediately began to develop the photographs by candlelight in the bathroom tub. Andrzej paced.

He decided that if the photos revealed important information, the best thing to do would be to leave for England with it as soon as possible. It was a serious offense they had committed, and the Gestapo was very good at its job. They had only bought themselves a few hours, if that. The information, whatever it was, wouldn't be worth anything if the robbery landed them in prison.

Max exited the bathroom. "They are drying now. Give them about twenty minutes. I've got the radiator on in there."

"I think we ought to catch the first train east. Perhaps the morning train to Warsaw. We can get off partway and double back by hired car," Andrzej said.

"Good idea. I've got a railway timetable here." Max pulled a guide out of his pocket and began perusing it. "There's a train for Warsaw leaving at five-forty a.m. I say we catch it at the last minute." Pulling out another guide from another pocket, he looked up the streetcar schedule. "The train station is a half hour from here. There is a tram leaving . . ." he consulted his wrist watch, "in an hour. From the intersection outside. That will give us time to see what we have." He indicated the bathroom door.

The photos were priceless.

The first document Andrzej read contained the information that twelve divisions of troops were concentrated on the Czechoslovak border ready for deployment within twelve hours.

He whistled. "This is serious information, Max. Worth our lives. We'd better hop to it immediately. We can read the rest on the way."

&

Amalia awoke late and heavy-eyed to Christian's knock. He entered her room. "Herr Boos has been talking to my friends, asking questions."

Amalia stared at her son. "What kind of questions?"

"He wanted to know where I grew up. He also was asking questions about my father."

"And what did your friends tell him?"

"They're English boys. They just told him they didn't know where I grew up, but that they thought it must have been in Germany because I was just learning English and my native language was German."

"And about your father?"

"They said they only knew that he was dead."

"Good. It sounds as though you've been very circumspect with your friends. Did they think it was strange that he was quizzing them?"

"Yes. They thought it devilishly odd. They asked him why he wanted to know!"

"And what did he say?"

"He said that you couldn't be too careful who your friends were in these times. They could be German spies!"

Amalia was speechless with fury. Walking to her window, she flung back the drapes, letting in the morning sun. "I will have a word or two to say to Herr Boos! Thank you, Christian."

She washed and dressed quickly. It was after eleven. People would be gathering in the Pump Room.

When she sailed out of the house, Amalia was perfectly groomed in her most becoming periwinkle frock. If one looked closely, she supposed one could see traces of her sleepless night, but her powder had been helpful. And anger added color to her cheeks.

She hailed a taxi to carry her to the Pump Room. When she arrived, she took a moment before entering to calm herself. Upon opening the doors, she saw Herr Boos walking about the room with Fraülein Knebel, who was hanging on his every word.

Amalia would have to wait until he had made a circuit of the room.

Joining Frau Schratt, she engaged in meaningless chatter, enquiring about that lady's rheumatism.

"We were worried you were ill this morning, my dear," Frau Schratt said. "Are you certain you won't try the waters? They are very restorative."

"There was nothing wrong with me but a sleepless night. I suffer them from time to time. I am perfectly well, but thank you for your concern."

At that moment, Herr Boos arrived back in their circle.

"I have a matter to take up with you, sir, if you would be so good to walk with me," she said.

He raised an eyebrow but offered his arm. As soon as they were away from the others, she said, "How dare you infer to my son's friends that he is a German spy?"

Herr Boos seemed not at all upset.

"What in the world did you think you had to gain by questioning them about my son? Why would you do that?"

"There were some things that didn't make sense to me about your background. I began to wonder if you were an enemy of the Reich."

Amalia began to shake with anger. "How dare you! This is England, not Germany or Austria!"

He seemed not to hear her. "The name Faulhaber was not familiar to me. I lived some time in Munich and Bavaria. On a hunch, I made some trunk calls to Vienna."

Amalia's heart began to pound and her palms grew sticky inside her gloves. She removed her hand from the crook of Boos's elbow where he was holding it.

Herr Boos continued, "It seems that Faulhaber is a well-known name in the Party there. Is Wolf Faulhaber known to you?"

"No," she said shortly.

"Odd, since he claims to be your brother."

"He has disowned me long since," Amalia said tightly.

"It seems your husband was a long-standing thorn in the side of the Party in Austria."

"And he was murdered for it." Amalia clenched her teeth, knowing she must look murderous herself.

"I was told he had an important piece of information. One that could do damage to the Führer's plans."

"Are you SS?" she asked. "Because before you murder me, too, you should know that that information has been delivered to the proper quarters. Rudolf's mission was carried out. Hitler's true intentions are known."

"I am not SS." His voice was smooth. Almost soothing.

Amalia had a flash of insight and her anger soared. "You are a propagandist. You work for Herr Goebbels! That is what you are doing here in Britain. Spreading around the lies that Hitler only wants peace!"

He continued as though she had not spoken. "I understand that a Gestapo Colonel Dietrich has disappeared."

"Yes. We outwitted him in Switzerland and managed to elude him. He engineered the death of my husband. I do not know where he is now." The lie came easily to her lips.

His mouth pressed into a firm line. "And your lover? The Pole, Andrzej Zaleski, where is he?"

"Ah! Wolf again. Dr. Zaleski is not my lover. My brother has always hated him. He broke up our engagement during the Great War. That is ancient history."

"But Faulhaber said he was traveling with you. Where is he, Baroness?"

"I have no idea. Perhaps you think he is hiding in my flat? That I am carrying on a shameless liaison in front of my son, who has just lost his father?"

"Zaleski, Zaleski . . . I know that name is familiar to me."

Anxiety bored into her stomach like a twisting screw. "I am certain it is a popular Polish name."

"No matter. I have an excellent memory for names. It will come to me. What exactly are you doing in Bath, Baroness? And why the assumed name?"

"I don't speak English and I detest London. And I have gone back to my maiden name because of people like you!"

"People who might recognize the name von Schoenenburg as that iconoclastic Austrian cabinet minister?"

"Yes!"

"Well, I hope you will stay for the simple reason that this Dr. Zaleski is bound to visit you."

"He won't. I doubt he is even in England. Our attachment was over long ago."

Herr Boos raised an eyebrow and looked directly into her eyes. "You are a beautiful woman, Baroness. He will not be able to stay away."

Amalia was growing angrier. Was there no place she was safe? Now that her true identity was known in Bath, what was the point of staying here? One thing she must do for certain: she must inform Anthony of this turn of events. When Andrzej returned, he must not visit her in Bath.

"This stroll has certainly been enlightening, Herr Boos. You will forgive me if I part company with you here."

So saying, she left his side and walked out of the Pump Room, her chin in the air. She scarcely saw the townhouses with their blooming varicolored petunias as she walked up the steep hill to the Royal Crescent.

Now was the time for a cool head. She must think. Boos was bound to remember soon enough that Andrzej's cousin, August Zaleski, was in the foreign mission that had visited Britain. He would place yet another trunk call—this one to Warsaw. Undersecretary Zaleski would tell him that Andrzej was currently in Berlin on a mission for Poland. Now that Boos knew of Andrzej's connection to her and Rudolf, he would not believe that mission to be benign. He suspected Andrzej of Dietrich's murder. It would not be long before he alerted the Gestapo in Berlin to pick up Andrzej for questioning. Amalia grew cold from head to toe. Pacing her small drawing room, she rubbed her arms with her hands.

If only I could alert him somehow!

She went into her morning room and looked out at the Crescent, with its large old oak tree planted in the greensward across the way. Her first instinct was to flee, but if anyone followed her to London, that would be disastrous. If Andrzej should get free, Anthony's would be the place he would go. Boos's people would be watching, waiting to pick him up.

My family and Andrzej are not safe as long as that man is in England.

Walking over to her small desk, she removed stationery from the drawer and began a letter to Anthony. She wrote what had transpired with Boos and her fears for Andrzej, urging him not to tell him where she was.

He may write to me, but I do not think we should see each other if or until this man Boos leaves England.

The decision saddened her. Her anxiety over Andrzej was at fever pitch, and if he returned home, she wanted nothing more than to greet him by laying her head on his chest, holding him in her arms, and savoring his presence and safety.

She wrote another letter, this one to Rudi, explaining the circumstances and begging him to stay in Oxford.

Who knows what crazy plan Boos may put in motion to rid the world of a "traitor's" heir?

As she was sealing up her letter, Christian came in.

"Boos knows who we really are," she told him. "Your Uncle Wolf told him about your father's death and our escape. He knows about Dietrich being missing. But worst of all, he knows Andrzej's name. He says Zaleski seems familiar." Amalia drew a long breath to calm herself, then turned to face the window. "As soon as he remembers August Zaleski is the Undersecretary of the Foreign Office in Warsaw, he will place a call there. August will be co-operative, of course. He will tell him that Andrzej is in Berlin."

Chris finished for her, "Knowing that Dr. Zaleski escaped Austria with us, he won't have much trouble realizing he is not on any sort of Friendship Mission to Berlin."

"The Gestapo may even arrest him," her voice cracked with anguish, "for questioning in the disappearance of Dietrich."

"We must leave immediately, Mother. He could remember the name Zaleski at any moment. We don't want more questions. Forget your clothes. You can buy new ones. I'll call a taxi."

"No, Christian. That was my first instinct. But we would be followed. Herr Boos is trying to frighten us into something that will cause us to damn ourselves. Let us keep all our actions as much in the open as we can. That said, I have some letters for you to post. To Mr. Fotheringill and Rudi—warning them. But I must also write one to Mr. Churchill."

Her son came to stand by her at the window, putting his arm around her waist. "I think we could throw off any follower, Mutti. I really feel that we should go. Boos is dangerous."

She turned to face him. "Please go along with my wishes, dear. If we leave, we will look guilty—as though we have something to hide. When we finally leave Bath, I don't want Herr Boos to think it has anything to do with him."

Christian frowned. "All right. I suppose you are right. What are you going to tell Mr. Churchill?"

"Every detail I can think of about Herr Boos, including the threat to Andrzej. That is my job here, after all. I suspect the horrible man to be a tool of Goebbels, the Minister of Propaganda. But we won't stop there. We are going to try to dig up something on the man that will get him deported. It is the only way our family will be safe."

{ 22 }

On the train to Warsaw, Andrzej and Max read the photos of the Von Brauchitsch Memorandum file. They were astonishing.

In the smoky train compartment with the spring green fields of Prussia whizzing past, Andrzej read General Beck's specific instructions to General von Brauchitsch on military matters that were being "mismanaged" by the Führer. He obviously thought their leader was receiving overly optimistic assurances from the military. Beck, as Wehrmacht Chief of Staff, wanted Hitler to know that if they used a force big enough to overthrow Czechoslovakia, they would not have the soldiers or the materiel available to defend the Western Front. They would fall to the French. Their army was not yet of the strength that the Reichswehr had been in 1914. This was not the time to execute "Case Green."

Andrzej wondered if these things had actually been communicated to Hitler and he had chosen to ignore them. If so, it could only mean that Hitler didn't believe France or Britain would come to the aid of the Czechoslovaks. This information must be taken to Churchill; a stand against Germany at this time was critical. Perhaps this could help persuade the British and French governments of that fact.

Max folded the photographs carefully and Andrzej stowed them under the lining of his hat. At each station, they watched out the window carefully, looking to see if anyone looking to be the Gestapo boarded the train. When the secret police had not joined them by the time they reached Poznan in the Polish Corridor, Max and Andrzej disembarked.

"This information is so astonishing and dangerous that I don't think we should make further attempts to cross Germany," Andrzej said. "I think we should go north to Danzig and buy passage to Britain on the first ship out."

"I agree," said Max. "After reading that material, there is no doubt the Gestapo will be coming for us."

"Maybe we can find a lorry to take us," Andrzej said, walking to the end of the station platform. "I grew up around here, you know. I have an idea. Today is market day."

Ignoring the rank of taxis, the men strode away from the station until they came to the outdoor market a ways away in the town square. It was still early in the morning. Fruits and vegetables lay out under canopies, tempting them with their brilliant colors.

Max bought strawberries, apricots, and some fresh-baked rolls while Andrzej strolled behind the display to speak in Polish to the stocky young lorry driver who was still unloading produce.

"I used to live near here," he said. "In the days when it was German. Now things are better—as they should be. You have a farm near here?"

"Yes. Outside the town. Later in the summer we will have peaches and pears."

"Have you lived here long?" Andrzej asked.

"My family has had this farm for generations. But we have always remained Polish. Even when it wasn't convenient. But now, thanks to Our Lady, our farm has been Polish ever since I was born. I am named for General Pilsudski, our hero in the Great War!"

Andrzej lowered his voice. "I fought with the General on the Western Front. My friend and I are in a spot of bother with the Germans. We need to get to Danzig. Can we pay you to drive us there?"

Max came to stand next to him, handing him a strawberry. "Nothing like a fresh strawberry on an April morning. These are delicious!"

"Your friend is not Polish," the farmer said.

"He is Austrian and as much against the Nazis as I am, I promise you."

"Are you spies?" the man asked, his eyes large.

"Yes. But you must tell no one in case the Germans come looking for us," he said. "We were never here."

"I will take you to Danzig," the young man decided. "As soon as I have unloaded. My sister can watch the stall today."

Andrzej extended his hand and shook the young man's. "It is probably better if you don't know our names."

"I am Jozef," he said. "There is fresh straw in the back of the truck, and I can tie the canopy down."

"That would be best," the doctor said with a smile.

"It will be a long ride," said Jozef. "We will probably not arrive until late in the afternoon."

"Just drive normally. Don't call attention to yourself. It doesn't matter when we get there, just that we do get there."

When the fruit was unloaded, Jozef pulled the canopy over the truck and tied it down, leaving the back flap open.

"We will meet you around the corner out of sight in the alley," Andrzej told him.

While they awaited Josef in the alley, Max took the opportunity to burn all evidence of their true identity. He took their false passports from a canvas holder strapped to his leg and handed Andrzej the document that now identified him as Wladislaw Kochanski.

Soon they were stretched out full length on the straw in the bed of the truck under the secured canopy. It was dark.

Max said, "An ideal time to catch up on our sleep. We don't know what lies ahead."

Andrzej was glad of the time to think. Never had he imagined that his association with Beck would lead to such dividends: the hard evidence of troop movements and Beck's memorandum relating opposition in the ranks of the military. Churchill would jump on these. And the von Brauchitsch memorandum was vital to Britain's foreign policy. If Amalia hadn't insisted, he wouldn't have brought Max, and the yield of this excursion would have been far less.

Amalia. Sighing deeply, he allowed his mind to drift. He hoped she was well occupied in Bath. He doubted there would be much danger if she remained discreet.

He remembered her passionate kiss at the railway station. It had been over twenty years since their last kiss. Time had not dimmed their passion for one another, it seemed. But was that kiss for the Andrzej of the past or the present? Would she ever learn to care for him as someone other than a flippant man waltzing through life in evening clothes in a world no longer relevant?

&

Hannah made their report at the police station.

"I'm just an ordinary bobby," their rescuer told them. "This Nazi thieving research sounds like a matter for the Home Office. I will telephone straightaway, but it will take them awhile to get here." He beat his nightstick into his palm. "You had better give the details and a description over the telephone so they can set up watch points at the airports and seaports. Do you have a safe place to stay for the night?"

Hannah translated for Rudi.

"Not really," answered Rudi. "Reinquist is a Jew hater. I don't feel right about leading him to Hannah's parents if he is keeping us in his sights. He's a violent bully. As for me, I can't promise to keep Hannah safe. I just have an ordinary dorm room. The lock on the door is broken."

Hannah translated the basics of this for the bobby, then said to Rudi, "He's offering us beds in the cells. He doesn't know how comfortable they are, as you can imagine, but we'd have the advantage of having two constables on duty watching over us all night." She went on, "I ought to telephone Dr. Heatley. I wouldn't put it past Reinquist to toss the lab. He has his own key."

When she mentioned this to the constable, he said, "You can telephone him after we make the call to the Home Office. We should do that first. There's a telephone the Super's office." The bobby led the way down the hall.

The call to Mr. Warren at the Home Office took some time. Hannah detailed her history with Reinquist, his fight with Rudi, and the recent incidents and threats. Then at Mr. Warren's request, she gave a description.

"He's very tall with a red face, a recent black eye, and yellow-blond hair."

She was reassured that a watch would be put out for the lab assistant immediately. Warren then spoke to the constable, instructing him to visit the lab and, if there was damage, to have scene-of-the-crime experts go over it. He also requested a sketch be made of Reinquist.

When Hannah telephoned her employer to inform him what had happened and what his traitorous lab assistant intended, Heatley swore and said, "I'll meet you at the lab in ten minutes. Pray he didn't get into the files."

Before they left, Rudi reminded Hannah to put in a call to her parents, who would be worried about her. It was now eleven p.m.

Berating herself for forgetting this important detail, Hannah put in the call. With conscious deliberation, she told them only about the suspected damage to the lab and that she might not be home until morning. Nevertheless, when she hung up, she knew she had worried them. Silently, she cursed Reinquist.

Hannah's employer met them at the door to the lab. His face was gray and pinched and a lock of his wispy hair stood up in the back. "I'm sorry you had to bear the brunt of his nasty temper, Hannah." Before he could put his key into the lock, he noticed that the door was open.

As Dr. Heatley stepped through first, he swore loudly and fluently. The place was a shambles. Test tubes, slides, and petri dishes had been flung about at random. Microscopes were smashed. The doctor's desk had been ransacked, and he confirmed at once that important files had been stolen.

Hannah felt ill as she thought of all Dr. Heatley's careful work destroyed. In a moment, her nausea gave way to anger.

Heatley sank to his desk chair and groaned. "This will set research back a year, at least."

"A year we could have had the healing properties of penicillin," Hannah said, her anger sharpening her voice. "This destruction will cost lives, Dr. Heatley. Not just time."

"You are right, Hannah."

The constable radioed for the scene-of-the-crime experts. Then he said, "I have confidence in the Home Office. They will catch this fellow. I'm telephoning them now to give an update. He'll not get out of Britain."

Hannah walked through the scene aimlessly, with difficulty keeping herself from beginning to straighten the mess. The photographers and SOC crew had to have everything *in situ.*

Rudi put a hand on her shoulder, stopping her. "Hannah, we've had a brutal night. You need to get some sleep. Ask the constable to take us back to the jail."

Hannah did as he requested, but Dr. Heatley asked, "Why should you sleep at the jail?"

She said, "Reinquist threatened both of our lives. Me because I'm Jewish, and Rudi because he is the son of an anti-Nazi leader in Austria who was murdered by the SS."

"What kind of an animal is he?" Dr. Heatley demanded. "It makes me wonder about my German colleague who recommended him! Perhaps he is a Nazi as well!" He ran a hand through his thinning hair. "But if you are worried about being safe, you can stay at my home. It will be more comfortable." Turning to the bobby, he asked, "Constable Brown, can we have someone watching my home for the remainder of the night?"

The policeman agreed.

"We can't do anything here until the scene-of-the-crime crew has finished," Heatley said. "Let's be on our way."

Hannah translated the conversation. Rudi thanked the doctor and the two men shook hands. They left in Heatley's car.

Her employer's home was a modest one. It was quite obvious her boss was a bachelor and didn't spend much time there. The carpet and furniture were serviceable gray, the walls were beige. There were no pictures or ornaments of any kind.

Another constable had followed them in a police car, and Heatley installed him in the front parlor.

"Let me take you two upstairs," he said. "My daughter's room will do for you, Hannah. She's been married and gone since last year. Baron, you shall have the guest room. It overlooks the front walk."

Once she was in bed, Hannah curled into a fetal position and held onto her arms, shaking with belated shock. Tears coursed down her face. Her life had never been threatened before, and though she had been careful not to let anyone see, Reinquist's weapon had frightened her. She had never even seen a gun that close before. It was a shock knowing how far the man would have gone to destroy her, just because she was a Jew.

A long time passed before the shaking lessened. She thanked God for her father's whistle. Her parents would be horrified, but her father's understanding and foresight had saved them to-night.

She came to realize that the former Miss Heatley loved laven-der. Sachets of lavender rested under the pillow and beneath the sheets. The pleasing, calming scent brought her back to a more ordered world where people grew flowers and made them into packets of pleasure, bringing sunshine, hope, and calm into lives that have been disturbed. After a while, she pushed Reinquist and his pistol to the back of her mind by intentionally calling up an image of Rudi to soothe her.

Handsome, wonderful Rudi. I think he would have died protecting me.

Hannah felt warmth spiral through her, chasing away the fear. She was too tired to begin to even think about the future, so she let it go and fell asleep.

&

Amalia made an appearance at the Assembly Rooms that night to hear a Mozart piano concerto. She didn't know how she would be accepted by her former friends now that Herr Boos had discovered her true identity and political leanings. Very likely, she would not learn anything more about this group, but she was anxious to show Herr Boos that he hadn't intimidated her.

Fraülein Knebel greeted her outside the concert room with a smile that was unusually merry. "My dear Frau Faulhaber! Or, pardon me, it is Baroness, isn't it? Von Schoenenburg?"

"Yes, you are right," Amalia said. "I was afraid I wouldn't be welcomed if you knew my true identity."

Herr Boos was not present, she was disappointed to observe. However, Chris had undertaken to find out where he lived.

Frau Schratt smiled timidly. "I have never known a baroness. To think, you are my neighbor!"

Had Herr Boos not revealed her anti-Nazi orientation?

"You are very kind," she murmured. "Shall we go in? I am very fond of this concerto."

"Mozart was an Austrian, wasn't he?" Frau Schratt said. "Yes, let us go in."

Frau Knebel and Frau Vogel had nothing to say to her, both looking at her with distended nostrils and raised brows. Amalia followed in Frau Schratt's kindly wake, taking a seat in the front of the concert hall.

The notes of the concerto merely formed a background for her racing thoughts. How much had Herr Boos told these women? With their political sympathies, she had expected a harsher reception. She had been prepared to cross swords with Herr Boos tonight. Had he spoken to Warsaw? Did the Gestapo even now have Andrzej in custody? A fine sheen of perspiration broke out on her brow at the thought. She twisted her leather gloves in her lap until they were totally out of shape. Would Herr Boos even tell her if they did? Somehow she thought he would relish the idea. At that, her stomach heaved. How long could she sit here? Were these women in league with Boos?

Coffee and cake were served after the concert, and Frau Schratt continued at her elbow, but the other ladies kept their distance. It appeared that she was going to be of no use as a covert observer now that they knew her identity.

"I am sorry to have deceived you, Frau Schratt," Amalia said.

The woman replied in a low voice, "It is your own business. You have been a good neighbor."

Amalia felt she had been reprieved. She made inquiries about Colonel Schratt, and agreed with her that he was a very satisfactory son. Resisting the temptation to express motherly pride about her own sons, she made polite conversation until Christian arrived to escort her home.

As they rode up the hill in the pony cart, Amalia asked, "Any luck on ferreting out Herr Boos's address?"

"It turned out to be very easy. My first inquiry was of that surprisingly helpful concierge at The White Hart. It turns out that Boos keeps a suite of rooms there."

"Did the concierge happen to let fall where the man was this evening?"

"Just that he was in. It was a bit awkward. The fellow seemed to think I was there to call on Boos. He told me that the man had left word that he was on no account to be disturbed."

"Hmm," Amalia murmured. "Interesting."

Again that night, sleep did not come easily.

If Andrzej is caught and executed by the Gestapo because of Wolf's hateful words, I know I could not bear it.

Throwing back the blankets, she rose from her bed and paced through all the rooms, seeing nothing but the figure of Andrzej against a wall, jerking as the shots from the firing squad hit his body. The image was so brutal, she vomited. Then, weak and shaking, she tried taking a bath, in the hopes it would calm her. It failed, but she sat in the bathwater until it cooled, staring at the dark.

Thinking back to the time Eberhard had been killed at Verdun, she clearly remembered the blackness that had almost taken her own life. After six weeks of denial, she had gone into a twilight world, locked in her bedroom, sleepless, staring into a void.

Fighting her way out of the darkness had been the hardest thing she had ever done. She could not afford to go there again.

And that had been Eberhard, not Andrzej.

She thought of Rudolf then. Why was she handling his death so much better than she had dealt with Eberhard's? The marriage to Eberhard had been fraught with problems and regrets.

She surely had regrets where Rudolf was concerned, and his death had been equally tragic, but at least the character of their life together had been better. He had understood that she loved him, hadn't he?

A sad memory surfaced: gladiolas. After Andrzej had resurfaced in her life during her marriage, he had once sent her a sheaf of the flowers. A note had accompanied them saying that they reminded him of her—brave and beautiful. They had been sent with all his love.

She had not known of the gift until after Rudolf had found them. He had read the note, which she had found crumpled on the floor. They had never spoken of the incident, but she had been very angry with Andrzej.

He had rescued Rudolf, saving his life, during the Putsch. After witnessing her joyful reunion with her husband, Andrzej had vanished. Amalia had not seen him again until he had materialized in Salzburg to help her escape the Gestapo five years later.

During that five years, Amalia had been truly wedded to Rudolf. She had chosen him and had lived happily with that choice. Had Rudolf understood that?

Thinking back, she honestly thought he did. Even so, according to Andrzej, when Rudolf had spoken about his death, he had requested Andrzej care for her and his sons. Clearly, he had supposed that Andrzej was the love of her life.

Now, in the midst of her grieving, she had to admit that if Andrzej were killed, that would be a blow from which she would take the rest of her life to recover. They had never explored the promise of their love. They had never had a life together. She could no longer deny that she loved him and longed for that life.

{ 23 }

Andrzej and Max arrived in Danzig at nightfall, well rested and on alert. Andrzej paid Jozef for his gasoline, but the man refused payment for his help.

"You are the enemy of my enemy. That is enough. Best of luck to you."

Prowling the docks, Andrzej and Max surveyed the huge ships at anchor. Their black hulls sat at various depths in the water according to the amount of cargo they currently held. Taller than most buildings, they flew the flags of many of the seafaring countries in Europe. A stiff, salty breeze blew off the Baltic, welcome after their hours confined in the back of a farm truck.

Andrzej was happy to be in Danzig again. It was now officially an "open city" under the rule of both Germany and Poland. Last time he had been here, he was only a boy of twelve, and the city had been a German port. After living a rural life, the excitement of his surroundings and seeing the enormous ships from all the great countries of Europe had nearly convinced him to run away to sea. There was no great future awaiting him as the second son of a second son in an aristocratic family.

However, his love of medicine finally won out, and the chance came for him to study in the foremost medical school in the world—The University of Vienna. It was while studying there that he had met Amalia.

Splitting up, Max and Andrzej went to find a likely ship to carry them to Southampton in England. Andrzej walked up the steep gangplanks of a number of ships and talked to the pursers. He managed to find both a Polish ship and a Danish ship with space for passengers that were sailing that evening.

"What do you think?" he asked Max when they reunited in a low-beamed bar full of sailors drinking German beer, laughing, and talking in a cacophony of languages.

"It is a problem that they both stop in Copenhagen. But I think the Danish ship is perhaps the least risky."

"It seems hard to believe that we've gotten clean away," Andrzej said.

"Don't underestimate the Germans. We're not out of here yet, and we have a three day voyage ahead of us."

They went to book their passage and were shown small, neat quarters with passable bunks and two portholes. Andrzej took the photographed documents out of his hat and placed them under his mattress before leaving their new accommodations to buy fresh linen and dinner.

He and Max dined on fresh Baltic Sea flounder at a café near the docks. Like the bar, it was informal, loud, and full of sailors, but the food was outstanding. He was swept with an unwelcome wave of melancholy.

In a low voice, he said to Max, "My poor country. If France and England don't stand up to Hitler over Czechoslovakia, she's next. Our mission must succeed. Churchill must convince his government to take a stand against Germany. According to Beck, they are expecting it."

At that moment, two unmistakable German military types entered the restaurant and looked around. They were not in uniform, but their hard, suspicious eyes branded them as police. Andrzej and Max exchanged a glance and busied themselves with their flounder and fried potatoes. Luckily, they didn't stand out too badly in shirtsleeves and the black caps they had just bought.

The men approached several diners toward the front of the restaurant and subjected them to a search, resulting in loud complaints. The tall, bearded manager came out of his office somewhere in the rear. He protested in Polish, "You have no right to come into my restaurant and search my customers! Who are you?"

The taller of the two pulled out papers. Thrusting them at the Pole, he said in German, "Polizei! We are looking for dangerous men who have stolen important documents."

The manager threw up his hands, submitting them to a loud, emotional spate of Polish, declaring that he could not understand them. Several husky sailors got to their feet and joined him. They began pushing the Germans toward the door, insulting them loudly. Soon a brawl ensued. Tables and chairs were knocked over.

Max signaled to Andrzej and in the confusion, they managed to slip out the door.

"Don't hurry. Don't call attention to yourself," Max said.

They reached the Danish ship and boarded. "We embark in less than an hour," Andrzej said, checking his pocket watch. "I say we get the documents and find someplace to hide them on the ship."

At length, they chose a lifeboat on the opposite side of the ship. Using sticking plaster from the ever-helpful Max's pocket-sized first aid kit, they taped them to the bottom of a bench.

Just as they returned to their cabin, there was a loud knock. Max opened the door. Two different policemen shouldered their way in and without a word began to tear the cabin apart.

"What are you doing?" Max protested.

"Who are you?" Andrzej pushed one of the men on the shoulder.

"Polizei!" a stout, grim-faced man pronounced. "Papers!" He held out his hand.

Max and Andrzej handed him their false passports. After examining them, the German threw them to the floor. They slit the mattress and pillows without ceremony. When they did not find anything, they commanded, "Undress!"

"I will not!" pronounced Max.

The tallest policeman pulled an ugly pistol. "I will not ask you again! Undress!"

Andrzej slipped off his shoes, thanking the heavens they had been in the restaurant and received warning. Their clothing and their persons were meticulously searched. When nothing was found, the two policemen left abruptly.

Andrzej sank onto his gutted mattress. He and Max merely looked at each other. Never had he been so glad to have the man as a friend. Clearly, word about their actual identities was out. Andrzej prayed their false passports would hold out until he could get home to Amalia.

&

Rudi and Hannah took a break from sweeping up glass in the lab. He could tell that Hannah was so angry over the destruction that she was close to exploding.

"It will be awhile before the lab is up and running again," he said. "I think it would be a good idea for you to come up to London with me until we hear that Reinquist has been caught."

To his surprise, she said, "That is a good idea, Rudi. I don't want him going near my parents, and I don't like to continue to stay at Dr. Heatley's."

He grinned at her. "I'm only asking, of course, since you are such a handy translator."

She frowned. "You really do need to make an effort to learn English if you are going to stay in this country, Rudi."

"I'd avoid it if I could, but I can't think of another place to go."

"Face it," she gave him a half-grin, the first he'd been able to coax from her, "you're going to have to exert yourself."

Dr. Heatley came out of his office and spoke to Hannah. She answered him and then translated for Rudi. "He's going to write to several of his colleagues about beginning a joint effort on the penicillin project. There are several who are interested, and their sending Reinquist makes him think that the Nazis are intent on war, if they're already looking ahead to healing the wounded." She refastened a strand of hair that had come out of its pins. "I told him we are going to London until Reinquist is located."

"Good," Rudi replied.

Hannah went home to tell her parents she was going to London for a few days to stay with friends and to pack her bag. They traveled up to London by train and took a taxi to Fotheringill House.

They didn't arrive at their destination until that evening. Rudi had telephoned his host to ask permission to bring Hannah, telling him what had occurred. Fotheringill had expressed concern and had extended a formal invitation to Hannah to stay as long as she liked.

Rudi introduced her to their host in the drawing room before dinner, regaling him with the story of the Nazi lab assistant.

"He sounds like a nasty bit of goods," said Fotheringill. "I hope they were able to stop him before he got out of the country." He poured her a small glass of sherry. "I am sorry that you should have experienced such events in England, Miss Gluck, when you had every right to think you would be safe."

Hannah replied, "He wasn't English. And the fellow from the Home Office was very polite this morning."

"Any word from my mother or Dr. Zaleski?" Rudi asked as they walked into the dimly lit dining room. With Hannah on his arm, he felt like an old-fashioned cavalier escorting his lady. She was dressed in a simple black dress, not an evening gown, but he felt her warm allure just the same.

"I received a letter from your mother today. She ran into a bit of bother. Another Nazi, this one in Bath—apparently the country is crawling with them—did some checking on her. The blighter talked to your uncle in Vienna and found out about her past. Also connected her to Zaleski. I'm not sure of the details, but she feels his mission is in danger."

"And what about my mother? Is she in danger?"

"Not at this point. She just doesn't want any of us to visit her there, especially Zaleski. The man knows about you, too, Rudi. She said she was going to write. You probably left before her letter reached you."

"Didn't Christian expose pro-Nazis in the Home Office?" Rudi asked suddenly.

"What are you worried about?" asked Fotheringill.

"As Hannah said, they are responsible for pulling Reinquist in. What if these fellows 'intentionally fail' at their job?"

"There is a fellow there that I can depend on. Maybe I ought to give him a call and see how the search is shaping up."

It was with difficulty that Rudi remained in his seat and did not pace the room.

&

After her sleepless night, Amalia made an appearance in the Pump Room the following morning, arriving with Frau Schratt. Herr Boos was there, speaking to Fraülein Knebel among his group of ladies.

"My dear, with your blonde hair and blue eyes, you are the perfect Aryan woman. Your children will be blessed growing up in the Third Reich."

As Amalia and Frau Schratt had at that moment joined them, Fraülein Knebel eyed them, saying, "I don't know, Herr Boos. You seem to prefer auburn hair these days."

The man lowered his brow in annoyance. "I intend to marry a German woman," he said, pointedly ignoring Amalia. "Will you walk with me, Fraülein Knebel?"

Amalia hid a smile when that woman replied, "But I am an Anglophile, Herr Boos. I intend to live in England."

"Why?" he asked. "You would desert the Fatherland?"

"I favor England," she said. Turning to Amalia, she said, "Which do you prefer, Baroness? Germany or England?"

"I prefer the English political climate," Amalia said.

"Hah!" said Frau Vogel. "You do not approve of our Führer?"

Coldly and deliberately Amalia said, "He had my husband killed, Frau Vogel. At the time of the *Anschluss*."

"But the Austrian aristocracy was in favor of the *Anschluss*! Why was he killed?" Frau Knebel asked, her heavy brows knit.

"My husband was not a Nazi. He was a cabinet minister to Chancellor von Schuschnigg."

"Oh!" cried Fraülein Knebel. She paused for a moment, taking this in. "And he was killed for it? How utterly foul!"

Rheinhard Boos's mouth thinned and his jaw hardened. "Baron von Schoenenburg was a danger to the Reich!"

Her heart pounding at the confrontation, she stared into Herr Boos's eyes with the hatred she felt for Hitler himself. "He was trying to get to Switzerland," Amalia said. "Why didn't they just let him go?"

"You know why!" Boos exploded.

"Yes, I do," she said quietly. "He knew what Hitler is really up to. And it is not peace."

At that moment, while everyone was staring at Amalia, a well-groomed young man approached the Nazi and said something in a low voice that she could not catch. She discerned that it was said in well-bred English, however.

Herr Boos made them a sharp bow. "I am called away. Entschultigen Sie mir, bitte."

Fraülein Knebel immediately pressed her. "What did you mean, Baroness? What did your husband know?"

Amalia hesitated. Then she decided it was up to her to spread counter-propaganda when she could. "Hitler does not intend to stop with the so-called modest claims on the Sudetenland and the Polish Corridor. If he is not stopped, he will keep going until he has all Europe under his domination."

"Even Britian?" the young woman asked.

"Even Britain," Amalia said. "Does anyone know who that man was who interrupted Herr Boos?"

"He is part of his group," the Fraülein told her.

"Group?" Amalia asked.

"After our peace meetings at the White Hart, he has a number of young men—British—who meet with him in his suite. We are not invited to those meetings."

"Hmm," said Amalia. "Interesting." She faced the three older women. "I cannot tell you how much it means that you stood with me today."

"Was it the SS who shot your husband?" Frau Schratt asked.

"Yes. Four of them ambushed us on a mountainside when we were trying to escape."

Her neighbor puffed out her considerable bosom like a pouter pigeon. "My son and I do not approve of the SS. Time will show that the Wehrmacht holds the true power in Germany, not the bullies of the SS."

Frau Vogel said, "My husband was in the Reichswehr in the Great War. He was killed on the Marne. I wonder what he would think of Hitler. I am not so certain." Her winged eyebrows slanted down toward her nose.

Fraülein Knebel put her arm through her mother's. "We are good Germans, but we are not rascists. My grandmother was Jewish. In Hitler's eyes, that makes me a Jew. But don't reveal that to Rheinhard, please. I thought he was different. Until today when he told me I was a perfect Aryan. If he only knew!"

"You can be certain the man will learn nothing from me," Amalia said.

"Nor me," said Frau Schratt.

"I know how to keep my own counsel," added Frau Vogel.

Amalia smiled at each of the women. "I never thought to find such friends here."

She had a lot to think about. Primarily those secret meetings at The White Hart. What was Herr Boos up to? Perhaps this was the information she needed to get him deported.

"I must write some letters," she told the women. "I hope to make the afternoon post. Please excuse me, and thank you again."

Dear Mr. Churchill:

The Nazi I wrote about yesterday, Rheinhard Boos, is known to be holding secret meetings with young Englishmen at night in his suite at the White Hart. I suggest you have someone investigate. Each day, he reveals more dangerous aspects to his character. I must say, I have a strong feeling that it would be in Britain's best interests (and certainly my own), if you could manage to get the man deported.

Is there any chance this can be done independently of the Home Office? With Christian's revelations regarding the pro-Nazis in that part of the government, I wouldn't like to tip them off that we know anything about Herr Boos, if he turns out to be someone nefarious.

Sincerely,

Baroness Amalia von Schoenenburg

{ 24 }

Andrzej lay awake in his small quarters the night they left Danzig behind. Next stop, Copenhagen. The police search had left him twisted up too tightly inside for sleep. He had checked the photos of the documents twice to make certain they were safe.

How had the Nazis known who they were looking for? Had Beck put things together, or was there some leak from England?

He wished there was some way of getting in touch with Amalia or Fotheringill. He hadn't felt this uneasy since he tried to sleep in the trenches back in 1919 with the Germans only a few kilometers away.

When dawn began to streak the sky outside his portal, Andrzej washed and dressed. Stepping out of his cabin onto the deck, he felt his spirits revive in the brisk sea air. He walked around the deck several times before entering the dining room.

After a breakfast of ham, bread, and coffee, he was feeling restored. He checked the lifeboat and found Max there.

"The documents are still secure. I put on some fresh sticking plaster," Max said. "How did you sleep?"

"I didn't," Andrzej answered. "I probably won't until we've left Copenhagen."

"We dock there at 1500 hours," Max said. "After I've had breakfast, I'll teach you to play poker."

As the ship drew into the dock, Andrzej was standing at the bow, examining the crowd that awaited boarding. The Germans had no official presence in Denmark, so if they came aboard, he imagined they would be disguised as passengers.

While the passengers boarded, Andrzej and Max stayed out of sight in their cabin.

"It just occurred to me that this might not be like Danzig," Andrzej said. "They may come aboard and stay aboard until Southampton."

"I have thought of that," said Max.

"We had better cease our visits to the shrine."

"I think that is advisable. I believe we also should monitor all speech, even in the cabin."

"I understand," said Andrzej.

&

Hannah put a call through to Dr. Heatley the evening of the day she arrived in London.

"I was calling to see if there was any news about Mr. Reinquist," she said.

"No one has told me anything," her employer said. "Are you all right? Have you had any problems in London?"

"No. I am tucked up nice and safe. Don't you worry about me."

As soon as she put down the telephone, it rang. Without thinking, she picked it up. "Hello? Fotheringill House."

"Robert Warren for Mr. Fotheringill, please."

Hannah called Mr. Fotheringill to the telephone and rejoined Rudi in the drawing room. It was cold and raining outside. She was beginning to destest the English weather. Though the fireplace was large, Fotheringill House seemed to have no central heating and except in the immediate vicinity of the fireplace, the room was cold and dank.

Rudi was pacing, a frown on his face. "Did Dr. Heatley have anything to say about Reinquist?" he asked.

"No," Hannah said. "He hasn't heard anything from the Home Office."

Rudi came to seat himself next to her on the sofa. "How are you doing? I imagine you are tired."

"I am a bit. Aren't you? We didn't get much sleep last night."

"Feel free to go up now and have a nap if you like. We can have your dinner sent up later."

She put her fingers to his forehead, trying to smooth out the lines of concern there. "You don't need to worry about me."

Rudi looked into her eyes as he brought a hand up to caress her cheek. He felt some of the worry slide off his back at her words. "You are a very special woman, Hannah. Not many people could go through an experience like you did last night and still be functional the next day. And you've spent most of the day cleaning up the lab."

"I'm no delicate flower," she said. "But I appreciate your concern." Leaning down, he kissed her. It was a long, urgent caress. The current between them made Hannah's toes curl.

"You are absolutely splendid," he said.

Her heart lifted, but before she could reply in kind, the door opened and Fotheringill returned.

"My friend is going to check to see who is handling the Reinquist manhunt and what progress they've made. He's going to call back with a status report."

Rudi frowned. He said, "With all due respect to the Home Office, surely they should have caught the man by now. If he is still in England. He's had plenty of time to escape."

Fotheringill looked rueful.

"I thought Churchill was able to take care of those traitors in the Home Office. Perhaps he wasn't believed. Possibly they thought he was on a witch hunt," he said.

They were interrupted by Stinson, who announced that Fotheringill was wanted on the telephone.

Their host excused himself.

"Is it possible Churchill didn't take Christian's list seriously and didn't act on it?" Hannah asked.

"Maybe," Rudi said. "Or as Fotheringill said, perhaps he wasn't believed."

Their friend came back into the room. Throwing himself into a chair, he pinched the bridge of his nose and shook his head. "No one was ready or willing to risk offending government officials on the say-so of a sixteen-year-old boy. The men are still at their jobs and have been taken into confidence in the matter of Reinquist."

Rudi sighed. "So Reinquist most likely got away."

"I think we can assume so. Warren thinks it a probability. He's going to check and see if the alert even went out."

Hannah remarked, "Proving someone didn't do something is not as easy as proving they did."

"True," said Fotheringill. "If Reinquist has gotten away cleanly, I am sorry for it. Tell me about the research he stole."

"I may have been a bit dire about how serious that was," Hannah said. "The fact is most of what Dr. Heatley has done so far is to eliminate possibilities of ways to produce and package penicillin for use." She bit her lower lip in thought, then proceeded. "We have learned more about its curative powers, as well. That research will help the Germans to avoid our mistakes, but little more. And I'm more certain than Dr. Heatley is about his ability to document those mistakes from memory. He really is a brilliant man."

"Well," said Rudi, "if that's the case, then I'm glad Reinquist is gone. He threatened you, Hannah. I seriously think the man was crazed."

"No more than any other Nazi, unfortunately. You remember how they treated the Jews in Vienna."

"You are Jewish?" Fotheringill said, raising an eyebrow.

"Yes," Hannah said, lifting her chin slightly.

"Can it be that our Mr. Reinquist was a bit captivated by you? And that his attraction went against his Aryan sensibilities? You are a very beautiful woman, Miss Gluck."

"Thank you, Mr. Fotheringill, but I doubt that Reinquist harbors any tender feelings for me at all. The man actually intended to kill Rudi and me."

"Hannah's whistle saved the day," Rudi said, putting his arm around her. She relaxed against it, more than slightly disturbed by Fotheringill's suggestion. "We were rescued by what you English call a bobby."

"Well, I am glad for that, but more sorry than I can say that he appears to have gotten away."

&

That evening, Amalia arrived at the White Hart with Christian, presumably to dine. A chalkboard in the entry notified interested patrons that the "German/British Peace Initiative Meeting" would not be held that evening. Amalia and Christian dined on breaded cod, new potatoes, and the inevitable mushy peas. She was getting very tired of English food.

They ate quietly, not wishing to draw any attention to their German-speaking status. Herr Boos did not eat in the dining room.

She had half a mind to investigate Herr Boos's meeting herself, but knew that the task must be left up to official government types who could see to his deportation. She would only forwarn Boos, and her word would not be worth much with His Majesty's Government. However, she did intend to find out what she could in a more clandestine way.

After dinner, Christian sat out in front of the Inn, on an inconspicuous bench in the evening shadows. Amalia sat in a deep corner of the lobby, knitting. From there, she could see comings and goings. She counted a total of a dozen young Englishmen taking the stairs. Surely most of these people were headed for Boos's meeting. The number was alarming. They stopped arriving after nine o'clock. Gathering her knitting, she collected her son and they took a taxi home, where she wrote another letter to Mr. Churchill. What was Herr Boos doing with twelve young Englishmen?

{ 25 }

Andrzej and Max decided to pose among their fellow passengers as businessmen, selling tractors, several models of which were supposedly on board in the hull. There were other Danish businessmen on board selling a myriad of equipment.

Andrzej could not detect any Gestapo agents that first day out of Copenhagen, but he was certain they were there. Their cabin was searched during the noon meal. When he was on deck the first afternoon, he could feel the presence of watchers; they made the little hairs on the back of his head stand up. He and Max dared not go near the concealed papers.

After dinner, they met some of their new Danish friends for cards in their cabin. As they smoked and drank Danish beer, Andrzej hid his anxiety, making certain he did not step out of character. Max, an actor by trade, was the life of the party, telling wholly fictitious stories about his women "in every port." He had their new friends roaring with laughter.

Toward the end of the evening, one of the Danes announced, "Someone searched my cabin today. Does anyone know what that was about?"

A chorus rose among the businessman, claiming their cabins had been searched as well. Max added his voice to the others.

Andrzej felt a wave of relief. They weren't being singled out.

An unusually swarthy Dane felt the same way. "That's actually comforting," he said. "I'm a Jew. I thought I was being harassed because of that."

"Probably some member of the crew looking for money. Did anyone have anything stolen?"

No one had. The Jewish Dane was delegated to report the incident to the captain.

With some trepidation, Andrzej and Max set out for their own cabin at one a.m., not sure what awaited them. Andrzej decided then that if an attack came at all, it would be the next day when the ship docked at Southampton and they had disembarked with the papers. In a very low voice, he and Max made their plan.

In the morning, they remained in the dining room, spending time with the Danes again, playing cards and drinking.This time, Max told stories of a widowed mother with a checkered past. Andrzej began to wish he had seen his friend in his glory days on the stage before the fall of the Empire.

When time came for disembarkation, Andrzej went to the Danish ship's purser's office. Hoping for the best, he explained to the big, bald-headed man, "You have a couple of Gestapo agents on board who are after some papers we are carrying to England." Passing over fifty Deutschmarks, he continued, "If you will allow us to reboard tonight, we will retrieve them from their hiding place and spend the night on the ship."

"Ah. This is who has been searching the cabins, then! You need not bribe me, Mr. Kochanski. I am no lover of Germans. Especially not Gestapo. Good luck. I hope they do not kill you." The man slapped him on the back and handed back his Deutschmarks.

"I hope not, too," Andrzej said. Returning to his cabin, he met Max and they prepared to disembark.

When he and Max walked out onto the busy dock, they were glad there were so many people around. Andrzej estimated there were something close to forty ships at anchor. Their colorful flags were bright in the dizzying sunlight. Walking the pier between the huge hulls, they headed for The King's Arms, supposedly to await the unloading of their tractor models.

The pub was crowded to the rafters with sailors, some of them their Danish friends. Max put in an order at the bar and they stood in a corner, drinking their bitters. Andrzej would be very glad when he was no longer forced to consume so much beer. He preferred wine or Schnapps.

A bar fight broke out somehow during the late afternoon. Andrzej was unable to determine how it began, but before long, the chaos was complete. Furniture was broken over people's heads, glasses of beer went flying through the air, and before long, Andrzej saw Max struck over the head by a fierce stanger with a dismantled chair leg. He went after the man with his fists and managed to disarm him, but another man joined the fight, knocking Andrzej out with an upper cut.

When he regained consciousness, he saw that Max was still unconscious. The pain in his own jaw was staggering, but he managed to get to his feet to examine his friend. He lay on the dirty floor of the pub, and Andrzej saw that it had been cleared, except for a few others who shared Max's condition.

He felt Max's head where he had seen the chair leg come down. He found a large, bloody bump. Andrzej cursed. He had absolutely no doubt that his loyal friend's condition was the doing of Gestapo thugs. Feeling for his pulse, he noted with relief that it was still strong.

Willi, one of their Danish friends walked over to him. "Hans is in the same condition."

"They must get to the hospital," said Andrzej. "We need a couple of ambulances."

"They're on their way. This was not a random fight. Whoever started it was looking for something. Check your pockets and his."

Both their billfolds were missing, but they still had their passports. Fortunately, Andrzej had anticipated some sort of search and had hidden his pound notes in his shoes. They had enough money to get back to London at least. If Max recovered. He would never forgive himself if the man lapsed into a coma.

Those papers had better be worth it. Damned Gestapo.

To his relief, he heard claxon sirens coming toward the pub. Moments later, both the police and emergency personnel entered the pub, which looked like it had been visited by a typhoon.

He stood. "Officers, I will be happy to speak with you after we get my friend to the hospital."

By the time Max came out of x-ray, he was conscious. The attending physician declared that he had a serious concussion and must be watched for the next twenty-four hours lest he slip into a coma. As Andrzej knew, the most pressing need was to stop the intracranial bleeding. The doctor proposed packing Max's head in ice, but keeping the rest of his body warm. Since he was reluctant to reveal that he was a doctor at this point, Andrzej was relieved that the correct treatment was going to be administered.

Andrzej managed to speak to Max out of earshot of the doctors. "Don't worry, you're going to be fine. Your pulse is still strong, which contraindicates any serious bleeding. I'm sorry as hell that this happened."

"How are you feeling?" his friend asked.

"I got away with a knockout punch to the jaw. The police want to speak to you. I think we should deny all knowledge of what the scuffle was about. Of course, it is significant that we and the Danes bore the brunt of the attacks. We were both searched, but only our billfolds were taken."

"You must get to the ship," Max said as the doctor drew near. "Go now."

Andrzej gave Max's shoulder an encouraging pat and left the emergency room. He moved through the dark of night back to the Danish ship and climbed aboard. To his relief, he found the documents, which were somewhat damp from the sea air. He tucked them inside his cap. Finding the purser, he explained that they would not be spending the night on board after all.

He walked back over the docks until he came to the bustling police station, where he had promised to give a statement. There he found Willi, head in his hands, waiting to give his statement.

"Have you any idea who did this, my friend?" the Dane asked.

"No," he lied. "How is Hans?"

"I'm afraid he may not make it. He was hit twice. How is your friend?"

Hans was the Jewish Dane. Andrzej's stomach clenched in anger. "He has a concussion, but he's conscious. They want to watch him for twenty-four hours."

Willi shook his head. "Bad business. Do you think it has anything to do with what happened on the ship? No one I've talked to saw what started the fight in the pub."

"No idea, " Andrzej said.

After giving his statement to the police, Andrzej asked if there was a telephone he could use to call London. He was shown into a small, bleak office at the rear of the station. All impatience, he dialed Fotheringill's number. He had to be circumspect, but he needed to reassure Amalia as soon as possible.

When he had his friend on the line, he said, "We're in Southampton. The mission was a success, but Max is in the hospital with a rather nasty concussion."

"Congratulations on making it out. We've been worried. I'll tell you more when I see you, but it seems the Gestapo may have had a tip coming from this end. What's the word on Max?"

"He was injured in a bar fight. Intentional, certainly. But the evidence we gathered is secure."

"Do you want me to come down there?"

"There is nothing to be done. Can Amalia be reached? I'd like her to know that I've returned." His heart thudded with the prospect of speaking to her at last.

"She has no telephone. I will send her a telegram immediately. She will most likely be followed, so you can't reunite here. She will have to go to a hotel. There is a Nazi in Bath who is trying to make trouble. He knows about her connection to you, so we will have to arrange a secure meeting somehow. Have you reported to Churchill?"

His heart gave a nasty jolt. "Is she in danger?"

"I don't think so. She's the means to finding you, so I don't think they'll injure her."

"How the devil did they find out about Amalia's connection to me?" Andrzej ran a hand anxiously over his scalp.

"There has been an unfortunate incident with her brother. Don't connect yourself to Amalia in any way."

"Faulhaber! I might have known. How on earth did he become involved?"

"Amalia thought using her maiden name would deflect suspicion from her, since Wolf is a well-known Nazi. She didn't count on this particular Nazi becoming curious about her. I'm not clear how it happened, but he ended by speaking to Wolf in Vienna. He found out about the baron and Colonel Dietrich. He was also told that Amalia escaped with you, her lover. We suspect that you are now wanted for questioning in the matter of Dietrich's disappearance. Also, the devil recognized your name and most likely got in touch with your cousin in Warsaw, which would have tipped them off to your presence in Germany. This whole thing has been a nightmare for Amalia, as you can imagine. She will be very glad to learn that you are safely returned."

As Andrzej grasped the story, he cursed. "That explains a lot of things. Thanks for the warning. But please take care of Amalia. There is no way she could have anticipated this. Why is she still in Bath?"

"She is determined to gather evidence against the man. Enough to get him deported. She is in touch with Churchill."

Andrzej closed his eyes and sighed. He felt utterly helpless. "All right. I admit, there is not much to be done when Amalia has her mind set on something. Could you go to Bath yourself . . ."

"I have thought of it, but if I become involved, I will be put under the microscope and you will have no place to return to. I can only guess how you must be feeling, Zaleski. My only advice is to focus on the job. Make your report to Churchill."

In his anxiety, he had all but forgotten his mission. "I will wait until I see how Max does before getting in touch with him. We may be here a couple of days."

"Right. Update me on Max as soon as you know anthing."

"Of course. I'm off to the hospital now. In that telegram . . . send Amalia my love."

"I will. Good luck."

As he made his way to the hospital, Andrzej's stomach churned. He could not even think what tortures Amalia must be going through, thinking she had betrayed him. Being prevented from going to her went against every instinct he had. His head began to ache with a fury.

He found Max in a ward with several of the Danes, including the unfortunate Hans, who was still unconscious.

"He's in a coma," Max told him.

"How are you?" asked Andrzej. His friend looked pale as parchment.

"I should be fine, like you said. I'm feeling more lucid, if a bit cold."

Andrzej was relieved. "I recovered the documents," he said.

"That's the important thing." Max gave a little grin and clapped Andrzej on the arm.

"I hope so. I hope they're worth what has happened." He reported his telephone conversation with Fotheringill. "I don't know yet what that worm, Faulhaber, has done, but it seems we were luckier than we knew."

His friend sighed. "And the baroness? Were you able to speak to her?"

"She is without a telephone. Fotheringill will telegraph her. She will know we are here shortly. But he says she is most likely being watched, supposedly to the end that she will meet up with me."

Max groaned. "Someone should have rid the world of Faulhaber years ago. He has never forgiven you for amputating his leg, even if you did save his life."

Ɛ

Amalia was dressed in her nightgown when the knock came at the door. Terror leapt in her breast. Who could it be?

Quickly, she realized that if it was someone who meant her harm, they wouldn't knock. She called to Christian to answer for her.

A few moments later, he came to her room and handed her a telegram. Her alarm returned. She tore open the flimsy paper.

"A HAS RETURNED SAFELY STOP AT SOUTHAMPTON STOP SENDS LOVE STOP MAX INJURED STOP WHEN YOU RETURN TO LONDON GO TO PETERMAN'S HOTEL STOP ANTHONY"

Amalia sank where she stood. Andrzej was safe! He had returned. She hugged the telegram to herself as tears of relief sped down her cheeks.

"What is it, Mutti? Bad news?" Chris asked, kneeling next to her and encircling her with his arm.

"Andrzej has arrived in England safely!" She handed Christian the telegram.

"It says here Max is injured. It must have been a close thing," he said.

Amalia took the telegram back and reread it. "Yes, poor man. I hope he is going to be all right." She looked at her son. "They must have encountered danger of some kind. I don't know where Southampton is. Oh, Christian, I am so glad he is all right. I'm so glad he has returned. I was so certain he wouldn't . . . So certain the things Wolf said . . . Oh! I don't even want to think about it. It didn't happen. He came back safely!"

Chris helped her to her feet and enveloped her in a hug. "I am so glad for you, Mutti. I didn't want you to lose him right after losing Father."

Amalia didn't know what to do with herself. "I want to go to the hospital in Southampton by the first train, but of course I can't. It would lead Herr Boos straight to Andrzej."

"Are we going back to London?" Chris asked.

Amalia thought for a few moments. "We need to see this matter through here in Bath first. I want to see Herr Boos deported. There will be no safety for our family otherwise. I expect to hear from Mr. Churchill tomorrow."

"For safety's sake, you'd better burn that telegram," Chris said. "The flat might be searched."

As they watched it burn in the grate, Amalia felt the depression and pain of the last weeks slowly dissolve. "You go to bed, Christian. I am going to stay here by the fire for awhile, until I am ready to sleep."

After she stared into the blaze for some time, peace descended upon her wild spirits, calming her. She didn't know what lay ahead. But for once, that didn't matter. She was happy in the moment.

An odd feeling began to steal over her. She slowly became aware of the fact that she was not alone. Somewhere nearby, she could feel the comforting presence of Rudolf. After a few moments, she gained the impression that he was rejoicing with her. Could that be possible?

There was only one answer: Rudolf truly loved her. He wanted her happiness. He had rescued her from desperate straits when she felt as though Andrzej had broken faith with her. He had done everything he could to make her happy. And now, his feelings were uncomplicated. He was dead. He could no longer level out the wild twists of fortune her life was bound to take in these next years of European turmoil. But he knew that Andrzej could.

Rudolf knew about that place in her soul where Andrzej had always lived, and he didn't begrudge it—because he knew it had been there even before he had met her. He knew she gave him all the wifely devotion of which she was capable.

But now he is gone. And he doesn't want me to be alone.

She would continue to mourn her loss. It would continue to visit her with unexpected moments of shock and misery. But the guilt was gone. She knew as surely as though she could see her husband next to her that he was offering her his blessing.

These were not ordinary times. Her relationship with Andrzej had never been a garden variety love. The two circumstances combined to create an inevitable pairing; she and Andrzej belonged together. For whatever time they had in the uncertainty of the future.

Eventually, the dialogue with Rudolf faded away and, completely worn out by her sleeplessness the night before, Amalia went to her bed and slept deeply. When she awakened early, her good news filtered through her mind with the morning light. Dressing hurriedly, she told herself she must get a hold of herself. It was important that she appear her normal self at the Pump Room.

However, as it happened, she didn't go to the Pump Room. Another telegram arrived for her.

"SENDING INVESTIGATOR TO BATH TODAY STOP GOOD WORK STOP RETURN TO LONDON SOONEST STOP C STOP"

It took her a moment to realize that the telegram was from Mr. Churchill, translated into German. Her heart bounded. He had taken her news seriously. Amalia knew they were going to find what nefarious scheme Herr Boos was up to with his twelve young Englishmen.

After relating the news to Christian, she began packing her suitcases at once. He burned that telegram, as well.

{ 26 }

Anthony brought Rudi and Hannah up to date on Zaleski's return and Max's injury at breakfast.

Rudi felt relieved for Zaleski, but concerned for Max. "Is the doctor going to keep us informed of how he goes on?"

"I asked him to. Meanwhile, I think the two of you should hold yourselves ready to speak to Churchill about the burglary at the lab. If Reinquist was operating under orders, it speaks in its own way of Germany's intention to fight a war where penicillin would be a huge asset. Churchill needs to know how the Home Office bungled the capture of Reinquist, as well. I will speak to him today to set up a meeting."

Rudi and Hannah agreed. After Fotheringill had departed, Rudi said, "The darkness of this old place is getting me down. It's not raining for once. Let's take a walk in the park."

Hyde Park appeared in its glory that morning—green and inviting with swans on the Serpentine and myriad flowers blooming in a riot of color along its banks.

"Do you miss Vienna?" Rudi inquired.

"Not as much as I imagine you do. For the last five years, it's been a difficult place for Jews. We lived in a shadow there. And I like England better than Switzerland. There is so much vitality at Oxford. It's a wonderful place for a scientist." Slipping her arm through his, she said, "You will find your place here, Rudi."

"They must have some classes at Oxford for foreign students to learn English. I prefer Oxford to London."

"I haven't seen much of London as yet, but I tend to agree with you. Won't your mother need you, though?"

"Not now that Zaleski is back. I imagine they will marry someday."

"And how do you feel about that?"

Rudi sighed. "It doesn't bother me as it once would have. But it feels strange, nonetheless."

"You are seeing your mother in a new light, aren't you?"

"Yes. She has had an amazing life—much of it full of pain. She is completely estranged from her family. She has lost two husbands. In addition to that, she was a political hostess, a nurse, and a scholar. Who knows what she will do next?"

"She has raised two excellent sons, as well," Hannah said. She stopped Rudi and, standing on tiptoe, she kissed his cheek.

Turning toward her, he took both her hands in his. "You are cut from the same cloth, Hannah. You are a formidable woman yourself."

She laughed. "You can keep up with me just fine. Every girl needs a hero. You are mine."

Her words brought hope to his heart, and he grinned.

Ɛ

Max's condition was stable, the doctor informed Andrzej that morning. He had spent the night catnapping in an uncomfortable chair at his friend's bedside.

"How soon before he can travel?" he asked. "We have a rather important appointment in London."

"If he continues to improve, I would consider releasing him tomorrow morning," the doctor replied.

Max was restless. He was no longer packed in ice, but lying in bed clearly went against the grain.

When the doctor went on to the next patient, Andrzej said in a low voice, "I will call Churchill now and set up a meeting for tomorrow afternoon. You stay put."

Andrzej found a fairly prosperous hotel a few blocks from the docks. Entering the Sir Francis Drake, he inquired and ascertained that there was a private telephone available in each of the hotel rooms. He checked in and went upstairs. The room was sumptuous and nautical in theme. He looked with longing at the navy blue quilt that covered the large bed. Perhaps he could manage a short nap after his phone call.

Churchill's secretary was evidently expecting his call. She put him straight through.

"Zaleski!" The man greeted him with a bombastic voice. "I spoke to Fotheringill this morning. It seems you must have had the devil's own luck to get out of Germany with your hide attached."

"My man Hoffman is laid up with a concussion, however. I'm afraid he won't be released from the hospital until tomorrow morning. Can we arrange a meeting for the afternoon?"

"I'll take a suite at the Savoy. Security reasons. I'll bring my secretary. Shall we say three o'clock?"

"If there is any reason we can't get there by then, I will telephone," Andrzej said. "Have you heard anything from the baroness?"

"Yes. We have an operation going on in Bath this very day. She should be on her way back to London. The baroness is a first class ferret."

Andrzej's heart lifted for the first time since they had docked in England. His mental vision began to clear, like a sky after a violent thunderstorm. Amalia was safe.

At the conclusion of the call, Andrzej yielded to the enticement of the big bed. He slept deeply.

&

Peterman's Hotel appeared to have been decorated during the Belle Epoque before the Great War, and therefore had a bit of Vienna in its soul.

How insightful of Anthony. He knew I would feel at home here.

After checking in, Amalia ascended gratefully to her room. The Art Nouveau intricacy in the design of the white wrought iron bed, vanity, and fixtures of her room went well with the Gustav Klimt posters. The room was painted sea green, furnished with a sofa and fluffy eiderdown quilt the color of begonias. Pillows in multiple shades of green were strewn on the furniture. Amalia felt immediately welcomed.

She telephoned Anthony at the Foreign Office. "We are settled at Peterman's. Any word from Mr. Churchill?"

"I am glad to hear you are safe, my dear. Yes, we are all to meet at the Savoy tomorrow at three o'clock. He is taking a suite there."

"And Andrzej? Is he in London yet?"

"Max won't be released from the hospital until tomorrow. He is holding his own. They will travel up by train."

"That is wonderful news. Thank you for arranging this hotel for me, Anthony. It is perfect."

"I thought you might prefer it to my dark old place."

When Amalia hung up, her spirits were high. She related the news to Christian, and then said, "Darling, I feel a shopping spree coming on. Can you find something to keep you out of trouble?"

"I'm coming with you," he said. "You are feeling safe, but you need to remember you are probably being followed still."

His words quelled Amalia's high spirits. There was still the matter of Herr Boos to be dealt with.

{ 27 }

When Amalia entered the suite at the Savoy, Mr. Churchill was already there, ensconced in a capacious armchair, smoking a cigar and dictating to his secretary, who sat at a small desk to his right.

"Ah! Baroness!" He stood and took the hand she offered, bringing it to his lips so he could plant a kiss on her gloved knuckles. "As you see, you are the first to arrive. But I have excellent news that will not wait! Sit down. This is your son? The spy?"

His secretary surprised Amalia by translating his words. Evidently that was to be her role in the meeting.

Amalia introduced Christian, anxious to hear the news. "The investigation of Herr Boos? It was fruitful?"

"Oh my, yes. We sent a young man from the MI5, our Secret Service, that Fotheringill was certain he could trust. He managed a meeting with Boos in the Pump Room, hinted at his admiration for the Führer and was invited to the meeting in Boos's rooms that evening."

Churchill paused to smile, looking like a cat who caught the canary. "He was training his group of young men for specific purposes. They were to perform acts of espionage by infiltrating the government beauracracy. Schoolboy friendships provide unquestioned entrés, you know." He waved his cigar through the air as this was translated. "Furthermore, when war breaks out, they were being instructed how to perform sabotage on airfields, railways, communications, and a number of other targets."

Amalia put a hand to her lips, her eyes round. "How diabolical!"

"Thanks to you, my dear, your Herr Boos is now in custody. He is being questioned. His cadre of followers are also being held."

"What will happen?" Amalia asked.

"The followers will be tried and sentenced. Boos will most certainly be imprisoned as an enemy of the state."

Amalia felt tears spring to her eyes. "I can't thank you enough," she said haltingly. "My family, Dr. Zaleski, they are safe!"

"Yes, my dear."

It was all Amalia could do to keep from embracing the man. At that moment, the door opened and Anthony entered with Rudi and Hannah.

She rose and went to her son and his friend, embracing each of them, unable to contain her exuberance. "I didn't know you were to be here as well!"

Rudi said, "We had some excitement in Oxford, too."

Amalia introduced them to Mr. Churchill. Hannah, who appeared to be fluent in English, took over the translating. It was she who told a chilling story, the particulars of which Hannah translated for Amalia afterward. Her lab had been destroyed and valuable information about the penicillin research stolen by an SS officer masquerading as a lab assistant. Even more disturbing was her information that the Home Office had failed to prevent the man's escape from England. Apparently, Anthony had determined that the search had never even been instigated.

"It is clear my warnings to the Home Office about the Nazi-sympathizers in their midst went completely disregarded," Churchill said, pacing the room in his fury, his cigar ash flying to the carpet. "I shall certainly have something to say to the Home Secretary about this!" He bowed his head toward Hannah. "Thank you for bringing this to my attention."

Amalia checked the watch pinned to her new ivory linen suit. It was four p.m. Where was Andrzej?

&

Andrzej was burning with impatience to see not only Churchill, but more importantly, Amalia, however Max's release was delayed by hours. Then they had to wait for the next train to London, having narrowly missed the last one.

He also worried that he might be rushing his friend to take the journey before he was ready.

"Max, are you certain you are improved? No double vision?"

"No, that's gone. I have a headache, but I imagine that is not going to leave for awhile. It is more important to get the documents to Churchill before the Gestapo figure out how to get to us here."

"Thanks to your forethought, they don't know our aliases."

It was four-thirty by the time the train pulled into the station. When they disembarked, Andrzej ran to hail the first cab in the rank.

When they arrived at the Savoy, the desk clerk looked at them doubtfully and Andrzej had a moment's regret at his shabby appearance.

"Call Mr. Churchill's suite and tell him Dr. Zaleski and Mr. Hoffman are here as requested," he instructed with impatience.

As they ascended in the elevator, Andrzej's heartbeat sped up accordingly. It seemed months since he had seen Amalia.

When the door to the suite was opened, it was she who stood on the other side, stunning in an ivory suit and a little hat with a peek-a-boo veil. For a single moment, they stood there hesitating. The next moment, she threw herself into his arms. He clasped her to him with crushing strength, not caring who was looking on. For days, he had wondered if he would ever hold her slender, beloved frame in his arms again.

"Darling, you look terrible," she said.

"And you look fabulous," he murmured in her ear.

"I'm so glad you're safe. Did Anthony tell you what Wolf did? I was certain he had betrayed you to the Gestapo."

He imagined he could see new lines on her face put there by worry for him.

"Never mind, darling. Thanks to Max's careful planning and a good deal of luck, we managed to elude them."

Mr. Churchill pounded his walking stick on the ground. "Hear, hear! I say, we'll throw your engagement party at Chartwell!"

After Andrzej had translated the words for Amalia, she withdrew from his arms, still smiling, and said. "You are a bit previous, Mr. Churchill."

She extended her hand to Max. "I understand you were injured. Are you going to be all right?"

Andrzej's cohort grinned. "I'm hard-headed, as you know, Baroness. It's good to see you."

They entered the room, and Andrzej saw that they had been taking tea. Suddenly, he was ravenous. Helping himself to a a macaroon, he ate it summarily.

At Churchill's expectant look, he pulled the now-battered sheaf of photos out of his inside pocket and walked over to the man. "Sir, I think you'll find these of great interest. There are troops on the Czechoslovak border. The numbers are there. There is a memo from General Beck, the Wehrmacht Chief of Staff, to General von Brauchitsch, telling of Beck's reservations about the proposed invasion. Our friend and colleague, Max Hoffman, took the photos at great risk to himself."

Churchill nodded at Max, "Well done!" He seized the documents with the eagerness of a young boy, extracted his half-glasses from his pocket, and began to read. Andrzej translated his words for Amalia.

"Tell me the whole story! How did you get them?" she asked.

He sat beside Amalia on the gold tapestry sofa, unable to answer her, he was so distracted. She loved him. He knew it. For years, he had dreamed of winning her back, but now her radiant face told of love beyond what he had ever hoped for. His tired body came alive as he felt her nearness and her smile. She would never know how near he had been to capture. He yearned more than ever to make her his.

With that thought, he instinctively glanced at her sons.

Christian said, "Yes! Tell us everything."

Rudi introduced an enchanting brunette sitting next to him. "Doctor Zaleski, this is Miss Hannah Gluck. Do tell us about this coup of yours."

"First, I must thank Miss Gluck. I do believe I owe you my life."

"It was Rudi who had the idea, Herr Doktor."

"But you had the magical drug."

Churchill looked up from his reading. "This is damned fine work, Zaleski. Damned fine. Must get these troop numbers to Chamberlain. Can't read the memo, of course. But Miss Vaughn can translate it for me." He turned to Amalia. "All of you are in some degree of danger because of the work you have done for my country. You must go down to Chartwell immediately while I get those blackguards in the Home Office taken care of. It is the least I can do, and Mrs. Churchill will be delighted."

Andrzej translated for Amalia and said, "I think it is a wise option for the time being, darling. The Gestapo is not going to give up looking for me. As you know, they hold grudges."

"We have much to tell you about what has gone on in your absence, as well," she said.

Hannah said, "I don't think I am in any danger since Reinquist is undoubtedly out of the country. I should return home to my parents."

"Reinquist?" Andrzej queried.

"All part of the story, darling," Amalia said.

Everyone stood as Churchill rose and shrugged on his overcoat. He shook hands vigorously with them all. "You have each done splendidly. I will see you at Chartwell. You will all be quite safe under my roof, I promise you." He turned to Andrzej last. "I will be forever in your debt, sir. Anything you or yours might need, you have only to ask."

&

Rudi accompanied Hannah to the train station in the taxi, keeping his misgivings to himself. The truth was this parting after spending days a couple of days constantly in her company was difficult for him.

"You have talked to Dr. Heatley?"

"Yes. He is anxious for me to get back. While he is waiting for the new equipment to be shipped, he wants us to try to write down as much as we can remember about the experiments we conducted. It will be an onerous job."

Casually putting his arm across the back of the seat so that it just touched her shoulders, he said, "I don't envy you."

"What will you do?" she asked.

"All this business with Churchill has made me realize I must learn to speak English quickly. How did you learn to speak so well?"

"I took classes at the University of Vienna. I knew it would be important for my career for me to be able to read and speak English. With all the foreign students attending Oxford, I am certain they have some English classes especially geared for them. I can look into it, if you like."

"That would be good of you," Rudi said, feeling suddenly hopeful. "I do feel time is of the essence right now."

They were silent for a few moments, watching London slide by outside the taxi windows. For once, it wasn't raining.

"What did you think of Churchill?" Hannah asked.

"He wasn't at all what I expected," Rudi said.

"He resembles a gleeful child in some respects," she said.

"Exactly. I hope he will have some luck with the Home Office, however. I worry about my mother's and Zaleski's safety."

"I imagine they will be safe enough at Chartwell."

"They can't stay there forever."

"Doctor Zaleski is rather like a swashbuckler out of a novel, I think," Hannah said. "Was your father like that, as well?"

"Not nearly so dashing," Rudi said. "I can't see him undertaking a commission like that one."

"It will be odd having him for a stepfather, I should think."

Rudi faced away from her, looking at the station as they pulled in.

"My mother deserves some happiness."

He paid the driver and they exited the taxi. Checking the outgoing trains, Rudi began guiding Hannah to the correct platform.

"You will let me know about the classes? You can reach me at Chartwell."

For an answer, Hannah stood on her toes and kissed him with surprising enthusiasm. "Of course. Oxford will be lonely without you. I am anxious for your return."

Rudi grinned, and some of the ache in his heart eased.

{ 28 }

Chartwell was very British looking, Andrzej thought. An imposing red brick edifice, it sat on a piece of high ground in the midst of a small wood, with an extensive garden and park. Most of all, however, it gave the impression of safety and security. After having heard Amalia's and Rudi's stories, he was very glad of the sanctuary.

Putting his arm around Amalia's shoulders, he said, "Home, darling, at least for the next bit."

The hired limousine pulled into the graveled drive and an elegant woman emerged from the house to greet them. "That'll be Mrs. Churchill, I think. Splendid woman, from what Fotheringill tells me."

The statesman's wife greeted the four of them in German. That she spoke Amalia's language was a wonderful surprise.

After introductions were made, Mrs. Churchill said, "Winston just called, and there's a panic on. The information your brought has hit His Majesty's Government with a fury, Dr. Zaleski."

"Good," said Andrzej. "That was the effect it was meant to have."

"It is wonderfully kind of you to have us, Mrs. Churchill," Amalia said.

"It was the least I could do, seeing what all of you have done for my husband. He doesn't think things through sometimes. I don't think it occurred to him that you would be in danger here in England."

She led them into her beautiful home. The rooms were large and light, with plenty of sunshine coming in through the windows. It was a nice change from the dreariness of Anthony's home. After they were settled in their rooms, their hostess told them that tea would be served in the garden in an hour and they were welcome to explore indoors or out, whatever they preferred.

Rudi and Chris opted to stroll the grounds. Amalia and Andrzej explored the lovely library, walled completely with books, except for a painting set right in the middle of the bookshelves.

"Amalia, we should talk," Andrzej said.

She said, "Yes. It is past time. Let's sit down. I do love this room. Don't you?"

"It's very nice." After they sat, Andrzej took possession of her hands. "Darling, I am sorry to have put you through so much worry. Especially when you just lost Rudolf."

"You were doing something important, Andrzej. Crucial, actually. And I realized some things while you were away."

"What things?" he asked, stroking her cheek with the knuckles of one hand.

&

Amalia tried to sort her jumbled thoughts as he caressed her cheek. "You know that I married two men for the wrong reasons." The admission was a hard one to make, but they both knew it to be true.

"Yes. And it was my infernal pride that kept us apart."

"Not entirely. It's my tragic flaw as well." She brought his hand to her lips and held it there for a moment. Her eyes traced the features of the face she had loved so long. "I loved you when I married each of those men, but I did everything I could to put that love aside during my marriages. I gave everything I had to make them a success."

He pulled her into his arms then and kissed the top of her head. "That is one of the things I love about you. Your strength and determination to do what is right."

Looking up into his face again, she saw that he was studying her with softness in his eyes. "I don't regret my marriage to Rudolf. And something rather strange happened the other night. I'm afraid I don't know how to describe it."

"Try, darling."

"It was very late and I was very tired." She twisted her fingers together. "Suddenly, I felt Rudolf's presence. It was very calming." Licking her lips, she continued. "This will sound strange, but he let me know that we had his blessing. That you and I belonged together."

"We do. And I don't find it the least bit odd that Rudolf would want you to know that."

"I love you, Andrzej. But my marriage to Rudolf lasted nineteen years. It is part of me. Part of who I am. Sometimes, I miss him dreadfully. My grieving is not finished."

"You wouldn't be the woman I love if that were not the case. I am not trying to rush you, Amalia."

"But while you were gone, I realized that I don't want to go forward into a new war without you. Am I making any sense?"

"Yes, darling. I understand. You want a future for us, but you still need room to grieve."

She drew a deep breath. "Kiss me, Andrzej. Just kiss me."

As he gathered her to him, she felt again the oneness she had missed for so many years. His embrace was familiar, even after all the time that had elapsed. His kiss was gentle at first, then escalated in sweetness and passion, stirring fires inside her she thought long dead. Andrzej was her present, her future, and her past.

He said softly. "We are finally on the same plane of understanding. But it has taken me years to earn your complete love, Amalia. I wasn't worthy of it before. I think I always put myself first. There are so many things that I would have done differently if I could go back in time."

"Don't," she said, putting her fingers on his lips. "We are going to go forward. We're not going to look back anymore. We are together now."

"But your sons . . ."

"They have come to admire you greatly. They will adjust. They still need a little time, I think."

Andrzej embraced her heartily. She had longed for the wholeness of this moment her entire adult life. All her worries and concerns dropped away at the feel of his lips, his entire being mastering her soul. Amalia felt cherished.

"Would you mind an engagement?" he asked.

"Let's celebrate it here in this beautiful room. Mr. Churchill is counting on it, after all."

"Then we shall."

{ 29 }

Rudi watched his mother glowing with quiet happiness, the center of attention at her engagement party.

"She looks stunning," Hannah said, taking glass of champagne from a waiter with a tray. "That gold gown suits her marvelously. You look very handsome in your tuxedo, as well."

"Thank you," Rudi said and smiled. "Of course, you are the most stunning woman here. Thank you for making the effort to come. It means a lot to me." He watched his mother for a moment. She was finally recovering the animation her voice had lost at his father's death. "She is in her element, meeting all these cronies of Churchill. That's Lord Anthony Eden speaking to her now. He's the former Foreign Secretary. Resigned because of differences with Chamberlain."

"He must speak German. Your mother is impressing him, I can tell."

"Her English is coming along. She has a tutor and spends hours at it each day." He turned toward Hannah again. He had missed her during the month they had spent at Chartwell. "I'm looking forward to coming up to Oxford next week."

"I will be very glad to have you back," she said softly. "I've missed you."

Rudi's heart softened and he wished they were alone so he might kiss her. "Care to take a stroll around the garden?"

"When is the wedding to be?" Hannah asked, moving toward the French doors that opened onto the outside.

"They are talking about a Christmas wedding. I know my mother doesn't want to rush things because of Christian and me."

"And how do you feel about it? Honestly."

"I'm still mourning my father in many ways. I hope by Christmas, I will be ready to see her with another husband. I know she still grieves, too. I caught her crying just the other day. It was her wedding anniversary."

Outdoors now, they walked through a lane of tall white hollyhocks, scents of a high summer English garden wafting gently on a light breeze.

"This is a beautiful spot," said Hannah. "I've never spent much time in the country."

"Someday I will take you to our family's estate. It is a magical place."

Hannah sighed. "I wonder how long it will be before Hitler is defeated."

"We are only beginning, darling. There is a long road ahead. Shall you travel it with me?"

They were now out of sight of the house. Hannah turned toward him and put her hands on the lapels of his tuxedo. "I shall, Rudi."

He pulled her into a long, satisfying kiss.

Epilogue

Andrzej, Amalia, Rudi, and Christian climbed the stairs and seated themselves in the Gallery of the House of Commons. Prime Minister Chamberlain had recently just returned from Munich to jubilant crowds hailing his slogan "Peace in Our Time." In spite of all of Andrzej's intelligence and all of Churchill's efforts to the contrary, Chamberlain had just signed an agreement with Hitler, giving him the freedom to march into Czechoslovakia and take back the Sudetenland with no interference from England or France. Today, Churchill was to give his speech in response to that action.

Churchill stood and surveyed the noisy house, tiered up the sides of the hall. The Speaker recognized him, and he began speaking without notes, his grave tones silencing the room.

"All is over. Silent, mournful, abandoned, a broken Czechoslovakia recedes into darkness . . . I find unendurable the sense of our country falling into the power, into the orbit and influ-

ence of Nazi Germany, and of our existence becoming dependent upon their goodwill or pleasure. It is to prevent that that I have tried my best to urge the maintenance of every bulwark of defense—first, the timely creation of an air force superior to anything within striking distance of our shores; secondly, the gathering together of the collective strength of many nations; and thirdly, the making of alliances and military conventions, all within the Covenant, in order to gather together forces at any rate to restrain the onward movement of this power. It has all been in vain. Every position has been successively undermined and abandoned on specious and plausible excuses.

"I do not grudge our loyal, brave people, who were ready to do their duty no matter what the cost, who never flinched under the strain of last week, the natural, spontaneous outburst of joy and relief when they learned that the hard ordeal would no longer be required of them at the moment; but they should know the truth. They should know that there has been gross neglect and deficiency in our defenses; they should know that we have sustained a defeat without a war, the consequences of which will travel far with us along our road; they should know that we have passed an awful milestone in our history, when the whole equilibrium of Europe has been deranged, and that the terrible words have for the time having been pronounced against the Western Democracies: 'Thou art weighed in the balance and found wanting.' And do not suppose that this is the end. This is only the beginning of the reckoning. This is only the first sip, the first foretaste of a bitter cup which will be proffered to us year by year unless, by a supreme recovery of our

moral health and martial vigor, we arise again and take our stand for freedom as in the olden time."

The speech was greeted with a mixture of applause on the opposite side of the house and boos from Churchill's own conservative party.

"Hitler will not stop with the Sudetenland," said Andrzej with bitterness. "He will take all of Czechoslovakia. And Poland is next."

Amalia covered his hand with hers. "This government and country are still blind. I agree that it is a huge disappointment. But we know Britain and France will have to fight Hitler eventually." She turned to face him. "We will all continue to do what is necessary. Remember, we have promised Rudolf we would take him home."

The End

Historical Notes

A writer of historical fiction must learn to take the tiniest of bare facts and build a story around them. *Exile* is a work of fiction, however, it is based on fact.

Readers will no doubt question the number of active Nazis and Nazi sympathizers in Britain before the war during the Hitler years. I would refer you to the book *The Churchill Factor: How One Man Made History,* by Boris Johnson. This word documents the pre-war sympathy of Britain for Hitler, based on the dictator's success in dealing with what the upper classes thought to be the more immediate threat: Bolshevism. Even as France was falling, Lord Halifax was in favor of making peace with Hitler.

As for Amalia and Andrzej's association with Churchill, that of course is fictional but is based on the account given by Churchill himself in his book *The Gathering Storm.* In the chapter, "Locust Years," he talks about the many people who came to visit him from Germany who gave him a true account of what was happening in that country. *In Search of Churchill,* by Martin Gilbert, Churchill's biographer, documents cases where people in sympathy with Churchill forwarded his cause abroad and gives the names of many people who gathered information for him.

Concerning the materials photographed by Max in General Beck's study, such materials truly existed. An interesting fact that I gained from William Shirer's book, *The Rise and the Fall of the Third Reich,* was that no one has ever determined how England and France learned about the German troop movements by the Czechoslovak border. Andrzej's espionage gives a possible explanation! The intelligence in the other item that was photographed could certainly have been gained by Churchill in another ways, as he had a massive, though informal, intelligence gathering service. He was fond of giving people missions to accomplish.

August Zaleski, who became the Polish Foreign Secretary in 1939, was indeed a real person. This is a case of pure serendipity. I named my character, Andrzej, back in the 1970's before I had this information. It came from a recently published book, *The Eagle Unbowed: Poland and the Poles in the Second World War,* by Halik Kochanski, which tells the tragic and largely unknown history of the Poles during this period.

Another book that was of great help to me was *The Diplomats: 1919-1939, Vol 2, The Thirties,* edited by Gordon A. Craig and Felix Gilbert. This source gave detailed evidence of the relationship between Lord Halifax, Neville Chamberlain, and the German Foreign Minister, Neville Henderson.

The information on penicillin and sulfa drugs was gleaned from articles on the Internet. Dr. Norman Heatley was an actual scientist at the Sir William Dunn School of Pathology at Oxford, and eventually was part of the team that worked on penicillin trials in the years after 1939.

Following is a sample chapter from G.G. Vandagriff's best-selling historical romance, *Lord Grenville's Choice*:

Alexander Lambeth, Fifth Earl of Grenville, opened the door to the nursery on the second floor of his townhome.

"Hello, Papa!" His son scrambled off his nanny's lap and ran across the wooden floor to greet him, throwing his arms around Alexander's legs and hugging his knees. "I found a birdies' nest today."

"What a clever boy you are." Alex hoisted his son in the air, lowering him slowly until their noses touched. "Did it have eggs in it?"

Jack wiggled in his arms. "Throw me in the air, Papa!"

"Not until you tell me about the nest!"

"It had blue eggs."

"Did you steal it?"

"No. Nanny would not let me. She said it belonged to the mama bird and that inside the eggs were her babies."

"Well done." Alex threw Jack in the air and caught him. "Once! Twice! Thrice!"

His son giggled uproariously before Alex set him down. At that moment, Felicity came through the nursery doorway. He could smell her vanilla scent as she moved up behind him.

"Mama!" Jack ran on his sturdy four-year-old legs to embrace his mother, who immediately knelt down to his height.

"We are having strawberries for tea tomorrow. Shall you come?" Jack asked her.

"Of course I shall. I would not miss it for anything."

In spite of her caramel-colored satin evening dress, she picked up the youngster until she cradled him in her arms. Felicity began kissing him under his chin, behind his ears, and finally asked him *sotto voce*, "Jack-Jack, do you know how much I love you?"

"More than all the stars in the sky!" he said.

He giggled again, and Alex's heart warmed as it did every time he saw his wife's unrestrained affection for their son. Her chignon of golden hair began to loosen precariously and her honey-colored eyes were bright with mischief as she tickled him.

It was all quite unfashionable. But if Felicity had her way, she would be in the nursery all the day long. He wondered, as he so often did, how such a loving mother could be such a difficult wife.

All too soon, Nanny Owens said, "Now, now, your ladyship, you are getting Lord Jack far too excited before bedtime. He will never go to sleep." She shooed them both out of their son's rooms.

As the doors closed behind them, Alex was feeling the glow of fatherhood when Felicity said, her voice strained, "I need to speak to you, Alex. Now, if you please."

With a small sigh, he said, "Come, then. We will speak in my library." He led the way down the three flights of stairs.

When they reached his very masculine room, lined with his well-read philosophy tomes and volumes of modern poetry, he stooped to light the fire.

"Shall I ring for some wine?" he asked, pouring himself a short whiskey.

"No, thank you," Felicity said, sitting gracefully in a straight-backed chair before his desk. "This will not take long."

He was relieved to hear it. Seating himself behind his desk, he raised his drink.

"Alex, I thought you ought to know that your Elizabeth's husband died suddenly this afternoon. It seems he had a defective heart. He collapsed at the Norwich card party. A physician was called, but nothing could be done." She looked him in the eye. "The love of your life is now a wealthy widow." Her words were as much of a challenge as though she had dashed his face with a glove.

Stunned, Alex could only look at his wife. Her head was held high, her golden hair wrapped around it like an aureole, her eyes not quite steady.

Then her words hit him, and his heart leapt in his breast. There had been a time when Elizabeth, with her white-blonde hair and sea green eyes, was all he thought of morning, noon, and night.

He swallowed his whiskey in one burning gulp. "How do you know about Elizabeth?"

"Alex, the last thing I want to appear is a jealous wife. I know that is not seemly. But do you really think I do not know who my rival has always been? The woman who has always owned your heart?"

Her words jolted him. He supposed all of society knew of his love for Elizabeth, and his wife was not a stupid woman. She had known from the start that theirs was not a love match. They had been paired by their fathers after Elizabeth had become Countess of Beaton. Felicity knew she was not his choice. A gremlin of guilt entered his breast, but he banished it. She was not the first woman in history to make a dynastic marriage; she knew the rules.

"What do you expect me to do? Run off with her to the Continent? There is a war on, Felicity."

"Please do not laugh at me." She lowered her head and pleated the satin of her gown. "I know I am meant to look the other way."

He stood. "You are being melodramatic. Elizabeth chose another. Our infatuation ended long ago. Now, if you please, I am off to the club."

Felicity raised her chin. "I will order Easter lilies for her tomorrow. From both of us." She rose and preceded him out of the room.

Alex chose to walk to the club, his stride measured and confident. Even his closest friend would not be able to discern that his mind was in an uproar. As he strolled out into the brisk night, he thought, not for the first time, how different life would have been if he and Elizabeth had been able to marry. She was a polar star in his life. She would have been tractable, elegant, a companion, not only in his bed, but in the rest of his life as well. Alex had always thought of her as his natural mate. But they had married elsewhere, and both had chosen to honor their vows. How would things change now that she was a widow?

As thoughts of Felicity intruded, he tried to push them aside. It was true she had surprised him by being an eager and passionate lover. She still was. The only time he felt like he was not disappointing her was in the bedroom. But she wanted from him what he could not give—his whole heart. As Felicity appeared to have guessed, Elizabeth still held a large piece of it, and he supposed she always would.

What now? What lies in the future for Elizabeth and me? Can we at least be companions?

Taking out his pocket watch, he could scarcely make out by the pea-sized glow of the street lantern that it was now just on nine o'clock. Elizabeth would not be gracing society tonight or any night soon. She was in mourning. He would pay a call of condolence tomorrow.

Once he was settled in his favorite armchair at Brooks,' pretending to read the latest edition of *Punch*, his friend Sir Charles Winton approached. "Grenville! Well met!"

Alex stood and greeted his friend with a hearty handshake. "Winton! Did you buy those chestnuts after all?"

His friend was a natural born rider, holder of many records among racing gentlemen. Lean, with a handsome face given to generous smiles, he was still unmarried but greatly sought after. As a matter of fact, Alex now remembered, he had frequently been seen about town with Felicity before Alex had become betrothed to her.

After discussing his new chestnuts, Winton asked after her now. "How is Lady Grenville? Still mad about that boy of yours?"

"I know it is highly unfashionable to say so, but he is the light of our lives. You need to busy yourself about finding a wife and producing an heir yourself, Winton."

His friend gave one of his hearty laughs and instead busied himself lighting a cigar. "I hear Lady Beaton will be available in a year's time." He looked at Grenville, one eyebrow cocked.

Alex shifted uncomfortably on his feet at the mention of Elizabeth. "Sit down, Winton. Brandy?"

When his friend agreed, he changed the subject from women to the news of the day, casting *Punch* aside. "The country is in more danger from within than from Napoleon, I think," Alex said. "With this assassination of the Prime Minister, are we to go the way of France, do you think?"

"Anytime a PM can be shot on the floor of the House by a mere commoner with a grievance, I think we must worry. Poor Perceval. He left twelve children, you know."

Alex sighed, "Yes, Felicity and I called on his widow a couple of days ago. Though Perceval was a Tory, we were friends. The woman is wretchedly downcast."

"Who do you suppose will be the new PM? Liverpool?"

"Undoubtedly. We Whigs have fallen out of favor with the Regent."

"Yes, and I do not know how long we are to endure this cursed war," his friend said fractiously, tipping his ash onto the carpet.

They fell to discussing the recent defeats on the Peninsula. Alex's younger brother, John, for whom his son was named, was fighting, his well-being a constant source of worry.

They came to no conclusions but grew more mellow with further discussion and the consumption of brandy. By the time Alex returned home, the night was far advanced.

His wife was not waiting up for him, reading by candlelight in their bed as was usually the case. She must be in her own room. Annoyed, he wondered if her unavailability had anything to do with Elizabeth.

Elizabeth, Countess of Beaton, looked stunningly regal in black as she received her calls of condolence. There were so many callers that she stood in the drawing room at the head of a veritable receiving line.

Alex thought she looked not one bit older than eighteen instead of the still relatively young age of twenty-four. Her father, Lord Whitby, stood by her, and he knew that the man would not be at all pleased to see him.

When he approached the love of his life, he noticed that she trembled and wondered if the cause was grief, exhaustion, or possibly the stern presence of Whitby. He could not flatter himself that it was because of his own appearance. Elizabeth had always been fragile, had always been in awe of her father.

He took her small black-gloved hand in his. "Lady Grenville and I extend to you our sincerest condolences," Alex said quietly. "If there is anything either of us can do for you in your time of grief, you have only to ask."

Those sea green eyes seemed to look a question at him. He wondered what it was. Through the glove, her hand was icy. She said, "Thank you for coming, my lord. I hope Lady Grenville is well?"

"Very well, indeed."

Whitby was looking daggers at him, and he felt the press of other callers behind him. Alex held Elizabeth's hand just an instant more and then took his leave. He carried her image in his mind all the way home, where he ensconced himself in the library to attempt to read his post and the *Times*.

Her image fled as he noticed there was a letter from his brother, John. Moving quickly, he sliced it open.

Dearest Brother,

By the time you receive this, no doubt I will be right as rain, but this is just to inform you that although I have so far survived the continuing carnage of Salamanca, I have sustained a wound in my upper arm. There is hardly anyone I know who has not received a wound of some sort. It is a bloody battle, though Field Marshal Wellesley continues to be a brilliant leader. I think we will eventually be victorious. We fight alongside the Portuguese, but our losses are heavier.

Hope my namesake is well and thriving. I expect his marching will have improved when I return for my autumn leave.

Give my love also to Felicity and thank her warmly for the new socks and blister salve she sent. She is ever thoughtful.

Yours,

John

For John to mention his wound at all, it must be significant. Greatly alarmed, Alex sprang to his feet and began to pace, pinching the bridge of his nose.

Which arm was hit? Was it a flesh wound, or did it contain a ball? Was it inflamed? Was there a danger of amputation?

He might not know the answers to his questions for weeks. He should never have bought the commission for his brother. Guilt had plagued him ever since. But John had wanted a pair of colors ever since he was a boy. He had played with his painted lead soldiers on the nursery floor, and their father had always shared details about the battles being fought against Napoleon's armies. John's chief worry had always been that the war would end before he could take part.

One of the first things Alex had done, once he had received Felicity's sizable dowry, was to purchase a commission for his brother. He remembered thinking that at least one of them should have what he wanted.

Sitting behind his desk once more, he dipped his quill, pulled out a sheet of vellum, and began to write.

My dear brother,

Your letter was welcome, but pray tell me frankly how you do. You are a hero in our little family, though you may not see yourself that way. I must confess I am anxious about your wound and wish I could be certain that it was getting the proper attention. I am following the details of your battle as they appear in the newspaper and am glad to know of your confidence in the Field Marshall.

Please write as soon as you are able.

Your devoted brother,

G.

Sealing and franking the letter, he knew of one thing only that would lessen his anxiety—spending a few minutes with his son and heir before he had to go out again. Alex read rapidly through the remainder of his post, finding nothing of significance. He made a stack of letters to attend to, another stack of invitations for Felicity to respond to, and a third stack that he must answer himself. After removing his jacket, he went quickly up the stairs to the nursery, where he found Nanny Owen reading a book to Jack.

"What ho, me hearty!" Alex exclaimed. "What is this you are reading?"

"It is a book about springtime, Papa. About little birdies hatching, and lambs and colts being born. It even has some kittens. May I have a kitten, Papa?"

"There are kittens in the stables, as a matter of fact. I am certain Mama will take you to look at them if you ask her."

John clapped and then extended his arms. Alex hoisted him onto his shoulders and obediently played the role of horse for several minutes, allowing his son to clutch at his black hair for a mane. Never mind that it had been carefully styled.

"Faster, you slow old horsey!" Jack chivvied him.

"Mind your manners or I shall buck you off onto the ground!"

When the ride was over, Alex sat his son in the window seat and looked into his golden-skinned features. He looked very much like Felicity now that the baby chubbiness was disappearing. His cheekbones were high, his little chin pointed under a small mouth shaped in a perfect bow. Jack's eyes were particularly large and honey-golden.

"You are a handsome rascal," Alex said.

"Nanny says I look like Mama. Mama's not handsome. She's beautiful."

He pinched Jack's cheek. Was Felicity beautiful? Not a classic beauty like Elizabeth, but attractive enough in her own way. Her features certainly became Jack. Who would have thought this engaging scamp could have such a hold on his heart?

"Well, son, you are none too bad to look at, let us say that." He stood. "And now, I must away. I have business to attend."

The boy's face suddenly became thoughtful. "Are you coming with us to Grandpapa's?"

Startled, he said, "I did not know you were going."

John nodded. "We are. Even Nanny Owen is coming."

Alex frowned while something shifted in his chest. Why would his household be decamping to his father-in-law's? "I must speak to Mama about this. Then I will tell you."

When he left the nursery, Alex tried without success to find his wife. Norse, the butler, informed him that she had gone out the night before and had not yet returned.

Why had no one informed him? Before he could think, he asked, "Where was she going, Norse?"

"I believe to Lord Morecombe's house, my lord. A footman in his lordship's livery came for her at ten o'clock. She left almost straightaway. Her ladyship was most agitated."

What was this mystery? Between seeing Elizabeth and getting his brother's news, he was not ready to face anything else today. In fact, it was precisely times like these when he needed his wife. Glancing at his watch, he saw that he must leave at once for Perceval's funeral at Westminster Abbey.

Stepping out into the street, he signaled a hackney coach. When his head cooled, he realized what he should have seen in the beginning. Perhaps Felicity's father was ill. Yes, that was it, most likely. His mood softened. He would go to her later. She was terribly fond of her remaining parent.

Realizing suddenly he had come out in his shirtsleeves, he redirected the coach back to his townhouse. Undoubtedly, he should see to his "horsey mane" as well.

Really, it was turning into a very disconcerting day.

About the Author

G.G. Vandagriff has been a scholar of 20th Century Central European History for many years. She received her bachelor's degree in International Relations with a concentration in Central Europe from Stanford University. Desiring more in-depth study, she completed a rigorous Master's Degree program at George Washington University in the same subject.

In 2009, Vandagriff published the award-winning *The Last Waltz: A Novel of Love and War*, drawing on her studies while living in Austria and studying the politics and history of that country with Austrian professors. In that novel she introduced the characters of Amalia, Andrzej, and Rudolf, taking them through the Great War and beyond to the *Anschluss* of Austria by Germany. *Exile* marks the beginning of a series of books that will take these characters (and some new additions) through the Second World War.

The author of twenty books, Vandagriff writes in many different genres. You can become acquainted with her mysteries, romances, and women's fiction at her website http://ggvandagriff.com.

She has lived all over the country, but she and her husband David now live on the bench of the Wasatch mountain range in Utah. They are the parents of three children and grandparents of five delightful grandchildren.

Made in the USA
Las Vegas, NV
22 April 2022

47830002R00184